HITCHCOCK TUNES YOU
IN TO TERROR

. . . with Saki's eerie tale of the evil that lurks
in the hearts of children

. . . with William Sansom's irresistible invitation to an infernal embrace and the kiss of
death

. . . with M. R. James' horror-ridden explora-
tion of the darkest depths of the supernatural

. . . with Philip MacDonald's gruesome chiller
about a mind-blowing last laugh after a perfect crime.

Whatever page you turn to in this superlative
collection, you can be sure of a clear picture
of vivid viciousness—and the only interrup-
tions will be the trembling of your hand.

**ALFRED HITCHCOCK PRESENTS
12 STORIES THEY WOULDN'T
LET ME DO ON TV**
(and you'll easily see why)

ALFRED HITCHCOCK

presents

12 STORIES THEY WOULDN'T LET ME DO ON TV

A DELL BOOK

Published by
DELL PUBLISHING CO., INC.
1 Dag Hammarskjold Plaza
New York, N.Y. 10017

ISBN: 0-440-13645-8

Reprinted by arrangement with
Simon & Schuster, Inc.,
New York, N.Y.

Printed in the United States of America
Previous Dell Edition #D231
New Dell Edition
First printing—April 1978

Contents

Preface

Good evening, ladies and gentlemen, this is Alfred Hitchcock speaking.

Being what is probably one of the most obtrusive producers on television has spoiled me. I cannot conceive of giving people stories without adding my own comments. The publishers of this book, being far wiser than my television sponsors, have limited my interference to this short preface.

First of all I should make it absolutely clear to you that these stories will not be interspersed with long-playing commercials. You may enjoy them while facing in any direction in any room in the house. Or outside, if you like. Furthermore, you may read them at any time, and if you take longer than half an hour for one of them you will not be penalized. Of course, this information is for those of you with poor memories and good television sets who may have forgotten some of the freedom allowed a reader.

An anthology of stories, like a soufflé, reflects the taste of the person who selects and mixes the ingredients. It matters a great deal, for example, whether onions or garlic are used and when the arsenic is added. I doubt that you will find much garlic or onions in this volume, but I am certain that you will find more than a little arsenic. I only hope that, like me, you have developed a taste for it.

This particular selection of tales is primarily aimed at those of you who find television fare too bland. You may not care for some of these stories because you think them too *shocking, macabre or grotesque, but I am confident that you will not find any of them bland or dull.*

The reason why some of these stories cannot be produced on the home screen will be obvious on reading. After all, actors are only human. (Debatable but true.) And this quality is a severe limitation for anyone attempting to produce Edward Lucas White's "Lukundoo," William Hope Hodgson's "The Voice in the Night."

These and several other eerie tales of the supernatural make up a part of the book, but the chief staple is that ever popular crime—murder. However, you will look in vain for a story of an underworld killing—homicide as practiced by hoodlums. I have nothing against gangsters, you understand. Some very delightful murders have been committed by professional criminals. By and large, however, the more interesting work in this field is done by amateurs. Highly gifted amateurs, but still amateurs. They are people who perform their work with dignity, good taste and originality, leavened with a sense of the grotesque. Furthermore, they do not bore you afterward by telling you how they got the way they are. Here is polite and wholesome mayhem as practiced by civilized people and I think it makes good reading.

I was Johnny-come-lately to television, and some persons have claimed that I was waiting for the screens to become wide enough to accommodate me (an allegation which I stoutly deny). However, I have become quite fond of the medium, and I trust that this book will not be interpreted as a criticism but merely an admission that there are a number of taboos and that there are some stories to which TV cannot do justice. As for my dear sponsor: he is really a rather tolerant fellow, and on the program when I bite the hand that feeds me I really have my tongue firmly in my cheek. I am sure this is the neatest trick of the week, and if you want to see how it is done you are welcome to tune in any Sunday evening.

But now I had better fade away while you select the first story to read.

Good night and good hunting.

ALFRED HITCHCOCK

Being a Murderer Myself

by ARTHUR WILLIAMS

Being a murderer myself, I was very interested in the statement recently made by a well-known reviewer of murder stories that "the best and most stimulating detective stories being written today are those that stress the puzzle of 'why' at least co-equally with 'who' and 'how.' "

It is gratifying to see, even if it is only in the field of fiction, that the character of a murderer is at last being considered worthy of more detailed analysis. In the past too much importance has been attached to discovering the identity of a murderer and the means of apprehending him. On the other hand, I do not consider wasted the time spent on the puzzle of "how," since after all, the method adopted is an indication of the type of man employing it; furthermore, it often decides whether the killer is to become famous, as a failure—or unknown, as a success.

I would also like to mention that we murderers do not *always* make a mistake. That fallacy has arisen because only those murderers who *have* made mistakes ever come to the notice of the police. On the whole, we are very efficient, and taking the number of known cases only, it is evident that we have got away with many murders, in spite of the very large organizations directed against us.

But the most common misconception held by most people is that a murderer is different from the ordinary man. Too often he is described in exaggerated terms such as "an insane monster" or "a cold-blooded brute." Such melodramatic ideas are far from the truth. Actually, a murderer is quite normal, merely possessing greater courage to act on the universal conviction that the true golden rule is "Every man for himself."

It is for this reason, therefore—to provide authentic data for the detective-story writer—that I have decided to make public my experience of murder. I have been fortunate in being so clever that I am able to relate this experience without fear of unpleasant consequences.

I felt no animosity toward Susan Braithwaite, personally, when I killed her, though some might consider that I had reason to hate her. I had been very fond of her once and would have married her if she had not been so stupid as to choose Stanley Braithwaite for a husband. Still, as I consider myself a civilized man of the world, I had felt that if she wanted to marry money-bags, that was her own funeral.

I suppose it was the feminine in her which had attracted me, that was in turn more attracted to the obvious maleness of Braithwaite—a great lout of a fellow, but with the right sort of brains to make his way in the world. He had inherited a little money, and being a city man he was able to make the best use of it. He had made a fair income by dealing on the Stock Exchange, not by the haphazard methods of a gambler, but with the unspectacular method of the investor. It was typical of him that during the record boom on the Johannesburg Stock Exchange, brought about by the discovery of gold in the Orange Free State, he continued his phlegmatic way of taking a profit as soon as a deal showed any, in spite of the fever of optimism that raged on the Exchange. He was thus able to build up and consolidate a small fortune, and when the inevitable recession came, his funds were mostly liquid. Then, instead of being affected by the pervading depression, he quietly bought shares which had dropped to next to nothing and so almost doubled his already swollen fortune when the equally inevitable recovery took place. An infuriating man!

When I introduced him to Susan, she became greatly attracted by his masterful manner and the success which it spelled. In fact, she was carried away to such an extent that she flew to Europe with him—thus terminating our engagement.

I had hoped never to see her again.

Eighteen months later, on answering a knock at the back door of my house, I found Susan on the step, suitcase in hand. When she had comfortably settled herself on the Chesterfield couch in my study, she told me her story. I was not surprised at what she revealed. I could well imagine that Braithwaite's self-assured dominant maleness, which she had preferred to my modest intellectual qualities, would develop into a complacent egoism, ruling with efficient tyranny. When she could bear his insensitiveness no longer, she had walked out on him and had come to me, for she felt that I would help her for old times' sake.

She did not notice, however, that I was not enthusiastic at the prospect of helping her. Actually, I was highly displeased. After she had jilted me, I had worked her out of my system, at the same time making extensive improvements on my poultry farm. I had made the whole farm self-supporting, and with labor-saving devices and processes was able to run the whole place singlehanded, for I liked fowls and preferred to do all the work among them myself.

But with Susan there it would have been difficult to continue in the same satisfying way. I knew I would have to entertain her, which meant that I would have had to shelve some of the less important, yet essential work. My routine would probably have got interfered with, and the three thousand chickens, which were at the most awkward age, might have caught cold or contracted some other ailment they are susceptible to.

Unfortunately, I could not think of any valid-sounding excuse for refusing to help her. Also, she had timed her arrival well: she would have had to stay the night at least, for there was no place in the village where she could have found accommodation and there were no trains back to Johannesburg till the following morning. I knew that once the ice had been broken by letting her stay the night, it would have been even more difficult to send her away the next day. After all, I had once been very fond of her and during the delirium of that time I had told her that no matter what ultimately happened between us, if she was ever in trouble she was to count on my help; and as I pride myself on being a man of my word, I could not bear to think of her telling our common friends that in an emergency I proved to be a broken reed.

All this passed through my mind while she chattered away about the cruel things her husband had done to her; but under the pretense of listening I followed the trend of my own thoughts till I became annoyed at the calm way she took my sympathy for granted. From the bits of her conversation I did listen to, I guessed in what manner she wished me to help her, and my annoyance mounted.

I saw my little bit of money being spent on lawyers; my comfortable and satisfying life being disturbed; my future peace being threatened by complicated emotions; in short, the whole of my nicely settled life being completely upset. I became so enraged that I thought, "Really, I could wring her neck!"

The actual strangling was more difficult than one would have thought. But the inability to face her, which had led me to go round the back of the couch to get my hands round her throat, turned out to be an advantage. For by crouching behind the back of the couch I was able to press her neck and head firmly against it, and so, by hanging on like grim death, avoid my hands becoming dislodged by her violent kicking, hitting, and threshing for air. Also, when she went limp, I was in a comfortable enough position not to need to relax till I was sure she was dead.

Her face—dark blue with grotesquely protruding tongue—was rather shocking when contrasted with the pretty animated expression it had had a few minutes before; and her once glossy hair seemed to have lost its blue tints and had become a lifeless-looking black. Otherwise, the sight of Susan's body did not affect me much.

After making sure that Susan was dead, I pushed her tongue back into her mouth and proceeded to dispose of the body in the manner I had been stimulated to devise when reading of the difficulties other murderers had experienced in this respect. I started the process that night, for though there was no urgency, as it would be days or even weeks before there would be any serious inquiry as to Susan's whereabouts, I was keen on putting my idea to the test. The following morning I was up early as usual and busy at my farm routine.

One afternoon, about three weeks later, Sergeant Theron of the local police turned up at my place and wanted to know if I knew anything about a Mrs. Braithwaite.

Sergeant John Theron on duty was a different man from the off-duty Johnny Theron who occasionally, when suitably warmed, entertained us in the back yard of Wiggins' pub by giving a demonstration of Wild West six-shooting. He was a crack shot and crouching slightly, he would fire two guns from the hip with amazing accuracy, at the same time looking from side to side with melodramatic belligerency; then after each salvo he would spit on the muzzles of the revolvers to "cool" them, giving a thigh-slappingly funny impression of a cowboy hero surrounded by dastardly villains.

But Sergeant John Theron of the South African Police was an alert and intelligent policeman who took his work seriously, and I knew by the way his question was worded that he was sure I *did* know something about Mrs. Braithwaite.

I guessed that she had been reported missing and had been traced to my farm. I decided, therefore, to take Theron into my confidence. I told him briefly all about my association with Susan in the past, winding up by telling him that she had been to see me one evening about three weeks before, but that she had left again the same night.

He naturally wanted further particulars and also wanted to know why I had not come forward and reported to the police that I had seen her at a time later than that which the newspaper appeal had stated was the last time she had been seen. I explained that I never read newspapers, but even if I had read the appeal for information, I would not have reported her visit as she had been running away from her husband.

I went on to tell him that she had wanted me to help her, but that I had refused; that we had quarreled till she had finally got into such a rage that she had walked out of the house leaving her hat, gloves, and suitcase behind. In reply to his questions I said that I did not know where she had gone, or how she intended to manage without her suitcase, or whether she had had a handbag with her or not.

After exhausting the subject of Susan's visit, Theron asked to see her suitcase. I gave it to him. He found it unlocked and opened it. On top was a brown handbag, which on being turned out was found to contain some money, a pair of earrings, a pearl necklace, a diamond ring, the usual feminine requirements, and a few loose keys, one of which fitted the suitcase. After carefully examining the rest of the suitcase's contents, Theron then asked me what Mrs. Braithwaite had been wearing that night.

That question had come sooner than I had expected, but I gave him the previously thought-out answer which was a genuine-sounding yet worthlessly vague description of the clothes I had carefully packed, together with the handbag, in the suitcase three weeks before. I had opened the case with one of the keys I had found in the handbag. I had had to leave the suitcase unlocked as I did not want the problem of disposing of the key. Incidentally, I had done the packing of the clothes, shoes, etc., while wearing gloves. I had no intention of leaving fingerprints inside the case and so making the traditional mistake.

Theron listened closely to the description, then pulled out the one dress in the suitcase which had obviously been worn, and asked me if that was the dress Mrs. Braithwaite had worn that evening. Of course, I replied that it was not, but I know that if that dress had already been described by anyone who had seen Susan going to my farm, that description would be more or less the same as the one I had given.

After asking a few more unimportant questions, Sergeant Theron left, taking the suitcase, and the hat and gloves with him.

The police did not visit me again for a few days. I went to the village for a drink on the evening of the week that Johnny Theron usually spent at the pub, but he did not put in an appearance that night.

But I knew that it would only be a matter of time before I saw him again, for Susan's trail definitely ended at my place, and the police would concentrate there until they had reason to look elsewhere. When Theron eventually came again, about a week later, he was accompanied by Constable Barry, a prematurely bald young man who had wooed and won the village belle, Renée Otto, by so maneuvering his courting that she never saw him without his helmet on—so the story went in the village, anyway. In charge of both Theron and Barry, however, was a man from the C.I.D. Headquarters in Johannesburg. This time the only words Sergeant Theron spoke throughout the morning were, "Mr. Williams, this is Inspector Ben Liebenberg."

I acknowledged the introduction and asked the Inspector what I could do for him. He was a tall, handsome man, more like an actor than a detective. Afterward I learned that he was a very good mixer—of drinks. His hobby was inventing new recipes for cocktails and other mixed drinks. I was told this, and about his variation of a Green Mamba, which is as deadly as the snake, by Theron later, when he was able to have a drink with me again.

Inspector Liebenberg professed himself sorry to trouble me, but would I mind if he had a look around? Mrs. Braithwaite had definitely been seen coming to my place, and had equally definitely not been seen anywhere else; so he would like to satisfy himself that she was not hiding somewhere on my farm.

I assured him that I understood and that it would be a pleasure to show him over the farm.

As we examined the homestead, I explained to them that I liked to be independent of any outside assistance, so had made my house and farm as self-contained as possible. I showed them the coal bin in the kitchen, built like a small room and filled at the top from the outside, having a little square outlet flush with the floor, next to the coal-burning stove. Below the kitchen there was a concrete underground tank for storing rain water. It had a hand pump attached, and pipes were laid from it to the bathroom. The rest of my domestic water supply came from a large gravity tank on the roof, filled by a wind pump from a borehole.

I started the tour outside by taking them to the three-hundred-feet-long, subdivided, intensive-type poultry house where, judging by the sound, the thousands of Leghorn hens were riveting their eggs together. I showed the policemen the incubator room and the brooder house, which I also used for experimental batches of chickens or fowls.

I then took them to the large corrugated-iron barn which housed my machinery—a tractor, a threshing machine, a hammermill, and various smaller machines such as lucerne cutters, etc.; also my general farm equipment such as plows, harrows, steam drying tank, planters, cultivators, etc., and my stocks of food. For round the sides of the barn were rows of large storage tanks, variously containing whole and crushed maize, maize meal, meat meal, peanut meal, bone meal, lucerne meal, and the various other poultry and animal feed requirements I used for making up the different balanced rations.

I could see their eyes measuring the tanks, and the jotting down of copious mental notes.

In the open air again, I pointed out my cultivated lands—the lucerne fields green, owing to the water from the dam, but the maize and other lands a yellowy brown. In the distance we could just make out the few cows, oxen, and horses grazing on the uncultivated part of my farm.

When they had seen the whole farm, Inspector Liebenberg thanked me for my trouble and departed—rather depressed, I thought. I would have liked to suggest that perhaps twenty maids with twenty mops . . . but decided that it was unwise to trade on my security too much.

A week passed without event, though I began to get irritated by being under continuous surveillance. Even Constable Barry had altered his beat so that he was able to pass my gate which, though a fair distance from the homestead, enabled him to have a clear view across the lawns to the house and garage.

I decided to make a move and bring matters to a climax. My best plan, of course, was to make Crippen's mistake, and run away.

I therefore made preparations, and early one morning I departed in my car at high speed. I drove fast for about five miles, then abruptly slowed down, headed the car into the veld and hid it as much as possible in a bushy bit, well away from the road.

I walked the rest of the way to the underground caves not far from the famous Blyvooruitzicht gold mine. These caves, though extensive, are not beautiful and do not attract many visitors. I had decided that the police would have already searched them thoroughly, so the chances were that I would be undisturbed. I had brought a Coleman lamp, a camp Primus, and ample provisions, and soon settled comfortably in one of the smaller caverns.

I knew the fowls on the farm would be all right for a few days, as their food troughs held enough for about three days, and the water troughs with their ball valves would remain full. The eggs would accumulate in the batteries of nests and ultimately make a mess, but one cannot have murder without breaking eggs. The other animals would not starve and there was plenty of water lying about the place. The chickens were then old enough to do without artificial heat for warmth, only requiring a small economical glow from the lamps to collect them in groups at night.

So, with my mind at peace, I was able to relax and enjoy the two detective books which I had brought with me. The stories were very good, though I noticed, with satisfaction, that the various detectives required considerable assistance from their authors.

On the morning of the third day I imagined that things should be about ripe for me to put in an appearance again.

As luck would have it, it was Sergeant Theron who met me first when I stepped out of the car in front of my house. The human face is not designed to express amazement, excitement, satisfaction, curiosity, wonder, relief, official reserve, friendliness, and regret all at once, but Theron's did its best.

When he recovered he demanded to know where I

had been. I told him that I had gone to the caves to see if Mrs. Braithwaite had not perhaps gone there and got lost and died there, and that I had become lost myself and had found my way out only that morning. He snapped his fingers in exasperation and I guessed that he had spread his net far and wide, but had not thought of looking for me so close at hand.

While he was thinking what he ought to do next, I looked around to get details of the impression of an upturned ant heap which I had received when I drove up.

I had expected to see signs of activity but nothing like what I saw then. Evidently the police had decided to use more than twenty maids, for the place was in a turmoil.

There were men everywhere—on the roof of the house, round the house, half under the house; there were men walking about with heads bent examining the ground, men digging at various places, men around the dam, round the borehole, in the fields, and on the lands. I could not see into the barn, but it must have been full of men, for outside the main double doors a collection of agricultural hardware was scattered like the throwback of a burrowing terrier.

But the most joyous sight was the long hen house. The hens had, very unwisely, all been chased outside so that the concrete floor inside could be examined. To lay the floor bare a six-inch layer of manured straw had first to be removed. This considerable task had already been mostly achieved, for the straw lay in large mounds outside, in front of the entrance doors.

Along the outside of the poultry house there were men trying to uncover the foundations, for whoever was in charge of the searching meant to leave no stone unturned. I write "trying" advisedly, for the diggers were being considerably hampered by the thousands of hens who had no place to go, but who were trying, with henlike persistence, to go back where they belonged. Hens are very conservative—besides, they had eggs to lay. There was a precarious and continually changing line of them along the narrow ledge between the mesh wire front of the house and the edge of the low front wall on which the wire front rested. And this was one of the walls the foundations of which the men were hoping to examine.

They were almost smothered in hens. When it wasn't hens, it was dust and dirt. A Leghorn is a very highly strung bird, and jumpy at the best of times. With Leghorns you have to keep up a continual chatter, or be forever silent. While I was watching, one of the men digging had to reply to a call from a distant policeman. His sudden shouted answer resulted in the thousands of hens leaping into the air as one bird, with, literally, a roaring of wings. The men became lost to view in a cloud consisting of a mixture of fine particles of manure, straw, earth, spilled food, and down.

I was not able to see more, for by then Theron had decided that I had better come along with him to the police station to answer some questions. At the station I was left in charge of Constable Hurndal, who received my nod of recognition rigidly. After a short delay Theron started questioning me, trying hard to give the impression that he did not attach much importance to my answers.

I was halfway through my third cigarette when a constable burst into the room and shouted, "We've found the body!"

I jumped up, and exclaimed, "How exciting! Where?"—a remark thoroughly in bad taste considering that I had known Mrs. Braithwaite well, but one that could not be interpreted as coming from a guilty and apprehensive mind. I turned to Theron who had been watching me closely and saw doubt in his eyes.

Not that it mattered whether I betrayed guilt or not. I was perfectly safe and could never give myself away no matter what trick they tried. But if I had shown any signs of a guilty conscience, Theron would have known definitely that I was a murderer. This I wanted to avoid, or there would not have been much future pleasure in visiting the pub. I did not mind his official suspicion, but his private certainty would have been different.

Theron continued the farce and also asked the constable where the body had been found. The latter went on, with less enthusiasm, to describe vaguely some spot in the uncultivated land. They both looked at me with a last hope that I might indicate they were getting warm. I said, "Fancy, I wouldn't have thought that was a good place to bury a body. This means that she was murdered, doesn't it?"

Of course they never found Susan's body on my farm, or anywhere else. Nor any trace of it. They examined the stove for any signs of human ash, they swept the chimney for the same purpose. They dug up the drains to see if I had possibly dissolved the body in a bath of chemicals. In short, they looked everywhere and tried every box of tricks possessed by the Johannesburg C.I.D. All to no avail.

Finally, they had to give up, baffled, and no matter how much they suspected that Susan had been murdered, they had no proof. In spite of a most thorough search of my farm, no body was found, and this fact plus no obvious motive on my part resulted in the cloud of suspicion hanging over my head gradually becoming dispersed.

That Christmas, to show that there was no ill feeling, I sent Sergeant Theron a brace of cockerels.

The months passed in uninterrupted peace. My content was marred only by the news that Sergeant Theron was leaving to join the Rhodesian Police.

We gave him a fine farewell party, Bill Wiggins providing the drinks, while I contributed the poultry. Poor Johnny was not able to give us a last demonstration of six-shooting that night, for when we went out into the yard the fresh air had a bad effect on him, and it took him all his time to stay relatively upright, hanging on to the swaying washing lines.

The building of a new brooder house began to occupy all my thoughts. But doing it by myself took all my time, with the result that I could not keep my house clean and tidy. So after much indecision, I engaged a housekeeper—a blonde, tall, but giving the impression of childlike plumpness. She is most efficient, yet her warm smile suggests that she could be very kind and affectionate.

It is because she runs the house so well that I now have time in the evening to write this record of my experience with homicide.

I am looking forward to having an interesting time should I get this published. I am particularly curious about Theron's reaction should he read this and so learn the make-up and constitution of those plump chickens he so enjoyed.

I suppose he will be disgusted, though he need not be. After all, how was he to know that those chickens had been feeding on the body of Susan Braithwaite?

I do not mean by crudely pecking at it. On the contrary, the fowls ate Susan in well-balanced rations. Every bit of her body had been through the hammermill, to be ground into fine bone meal and meat meal. A separate process made blood meal.

These processes entailed no difficulty as I had learned how to do it from an article in the *Farmers' Magazine*, and had been doing it with animal carcasses long before. And as far as the hammermill process is concerned, human bodies, not requiring to be skinned and having smaller bones, are much easier to manage.

I had only to take extra care that every single piece of the body was powdered. The teeth I had to put through the milling process a couple of times till they became indistinguishable from the rest of the bone meal. The hair I burned on the head, making a sort of charcoal.

After I had processed the body, I wiped everything that it had touched with handfuls of green lucerne, which in turn was ground fine. Animal carcasses were then put through the mill, followed by heaps of lucerne and bags of maize, so that all traces of human cells were completely removed from the machine.

The meat meal, bone meal, and blood meal were made into a ration with other foodstuffs and were fed to my experimental batch of chicks—and what fine chickens they grew into, as Theron can testify. As a matter of fact, I have established quite a reputation for fine pullets and cockerels, and other poultry farmers have pestered me for the recipe of my balanced ration.

This will surely be brought to the attention of Inspector Liebenberg, who now, knowing where to look, may try to find some proof that there was once a human body on my farm. But I am certain he will not succeed. It would be no use slaughtering fowls wholesale, in an attempt to find the ones that have partaken of Susan—with the object of testing them for any traces of human cells in their make-up. I have seen to it that every fowl that shared that human ration has itself been consumed by other humans.

As people do not eat the bones of fowls, I made a point of selling, or giving, the dressed fowls only on condition that I was allowed to collect the bones afterward. My explanation of this was that I was short of bone meal. These bones then went through the mill with other bones. A nice example of *ad infinitum*. Also, there are a large number of anonymous people who, in a remoter degree, took part in this deplorable cannibalism. I mean those who ate the eggs that were laid by the hens.

Then Inspector Liebenberg will no doubt think of the manure. I wouldn't bother if I were he. Every bit of it has been spread over my uncultivated land and thoroughly plowed in. Alas for the Inspector, the plucked feathers, heads, legs, feet, and innards of the dressed fowls sold or given away, after being burned or steam dried, also did not escape a hammering from the relentless mill.

I hope the good Inspector is not driven to trying to make this story of mine have the value of a legal confession. It would be a great pity if an ardent student of detective fiction, desirous of seeing a story of his own published, should be arrested because he invented a feasible explanation to account for the disappearance of a woman he happened to know.

I suppose I must also expect a certain amount of unpleasantness if this is read in our village. Some narrow-minded people will no doubt look upon me with horror and others will fear me. Since the main result of such attitudes will be that I shall no longer be pestered by casual callers, I shall be only too pleased.

A new development has occurred. My housekeeper, Ann Lissen, may turn out to be a disappointment after all. She is evidently falling, or has already fallen, in love with me and is becoming tiresome. Her solicitude on my behalf is overwhelming and I now seem to have no privacy left, for she is always fussing about doing things to add to my comfort.

I would not like to hurt her feelings by telling her to stop doing what she does out of the kindness of her heart. And as she has no technical qualifications, it would be a shame to send her away to battle for a job again.

I have suggested to her that she should go out more, especially in the evenings, but she said it was dull going about alone. She has no friends, or even relations.

Poor thing! She has no one to miss her, and I am most eager to rear especially good stock next season, fed with rich and well-balanced rations. The President of the National Poultry Society has expressed a desire to see my farm and the fine pullets and cockerels for which I am now so justly famous.

Lukundoo

by EDWARD LUCAS WHITE

"It stands to reason," said Twombly, "that a man must accept the evidence of his own eyes, and when eyes and ears agree, there can be no doubt. He has to believe what he has both seen and heard."

"Not always," put in Singleton, softly.

Every man turned toward Singleton. Twombly was standing on the hearth rug, his back to the grate, his legs spread out, with his habitual air of dominating the room. Singleton, as usual, was as much as possible effaced in a corner. But when Singleton spoke he said something. We faced him in that flattering spontaneity of expectant silence which invites utterance.

"I was thinking," he said, after an interval, "of something I both saw and heard in Africa."

Now, if there was one thing we had found impossible it had been to elicit from Singleton anything definite about his African experiences. As with the Alpinist in the story, who could tell only that he went up and came down, the sum of Singleton's revelations had been that he went there and came away. His words now riveted our attention at once. Twombly faded from the hearth rug, but not one of us could ever

From *Lukundoo and Other Stories*, published by George H. Doran Company, copyright 1927.

recall having seen him go. The room readjusted itself, focused on Singleton, and there was some hasty and furtive lighting of fresh cigars. Singleton lit one also, but it went out immediately, and he never relit it.

I

We were in the Great Forest, exploring for Pygmies. Van Rieten had a theory that the dwarfs found by Stanley and others were a mere cross-breed between ordinary Negroes and the real Pygmies. He hoped to discover a race of men three feet tall at most, or shorter. We had found no trace of any such beings.

Natives were few, game scarce; food, except game, there was none; and the deepest, dankest, drippingest forest all about. We were the only novelty in the country, no native we met had even seen a white man before, most had never heard of white men. All of a sudden, late one afternoon, there came into our camp an Englishman, and pretty well used up he was, too. We had heard no rumor of him; he had not only heard of us but had made an amazing five-day march to reach us. His guide and two bearers were nearly as done up as he. Even though he was in tatters and had five days' beard on, you could see he was naturally dapper and neat and the sort of man to shave daily. He was small, but wiry. His face was the sort of British face from which emotion has been so carefully banished that a foreigner is apt to think the wearer of the face incapable of any sort of feeling; the kind of face which, if it has any expression at all, expresses principally the resolution to go through the world decorously, without intruding upon or annoying anyone.

His name was Etcham. He introduced himself modestly, and ate with us so deliberately that we should never have suspected, if our bearers had not had it from his bearers, that he had had but three meals in the five days, and those small. After we had lit up he told us why he had come.

"My chief is ve'y seedy," he said between puffs. "He is bound to go out if he keeps this way. I thought perhaps . . ."

He spoke quietly in a soft, even tone, but I could see little beads of sweat oozing out on his upper lip under his stubby mustache, and there was a tingle of repressed emotion in his tone, a veiled eagerness in his eye, a palpitating inward solicitude in his demeanor that moved me at once. Van Rieten had no sentiment in him; if he was moved he did not show it. But he listened. I was surprised at that. He was just the man to refuse at once. But he listened to Etcham's halting, diffident hints. He even asked questions.

"Who is your chief?"

"Stone," Etcham lisped.

That electrified both of us.

"Ralph Stone?" we ejaculated together.

Etcham nodded.

For some minutes Van Rieten and I were silent. Van Rieten had never seen him, but I had been a classmate of Stone's, and Van Rieten and I had discussed him over many a campfire. We had heard of him two years before, south of Luebo in the Balunda country, which had been ringing with his theatrical strife against a Balunda witch doctor, ending in the sorcerer's complete discomfiture and the abasement of his tribe before Stone. They had even broken the fetish-man's whistle and given Stone the pieces. It had been like the triumph of Elijah over the prophets of Baal, only more real to the Balunda.

We had thought of Stone as far off, if still in Africa at all, and here he turned up ahead of us and probably forestalling our quest.

II

Etcham's naming of Stone brought back to us all his tantalizing story, his fascinating parents, their tragic death; the brilliance of his college days; the dazzle of his millions; the promise of his young manhood; his wide notoriety, so nearly real fame; his romantic elopement with the meteoric authoress whose sudden cascade of fiction had made her so great a name so young, whose beauty and charm were so much heralded; the frightful scandal of the breach-of-promise suit that followed; his bride's devotion through it all; their sudden quarrel after it was all over; their divorce; the too much advertised announcement of his approaching marriage to the plaintiff in the breach-of-promise suit; his precipitate remarriage to his divorced bride; their second quarrel and second divorce; his departure from his native land; his advent in the Dark Continent. The sense of all this rushed over me and I believe Van Rieten felt it, too, as he sat silent.

Then he asked, "Where is Werner?"

"Dead," said Etcham. "He died before I joined Stone."

"You were not with Stone above Luebo?"

"No," said Etcham, "I joined him at Stanley Falls."

"Who is with him?" Van Rieten asked.

"Only his Zanzibar servants and the bearers," Etcham replied.

"What sort of bearers?" Van Rieten demanded.

"Mang-Battu men," Etcham responded simply.

Now that impressed both Van Rieten and myself greatly. It bore out Stone's reputation as a notable leader of men. For up to that time no one had been able to use Mang-Battu as bearers outside of their own country, or to hold them for long or difficult expeditions.

"Were you long among the Mang-Battu?" was Van Rieten's next question.

"Some weeks," said Etcham. "Stone was interested in them and made up a fair-sized vocabulary of their words and phrases. He had a theory that they are an offshoot of the Balunda and he found much confirmation in their customs."

"What do you live on?" Van Rieten inquired.

"Game, mostly," Etcham lisped.

"How long has Stone been laid up?" Van Rieten next asked.

"More than a month," Etcham answered.

"And you have been hunting for the camp?" Van Rieten exclaimed.

Etcham's face, burnt and flayed as it was, showed a flush.

"I missed some easy shots," he admitted ruefully. "I've not felt ve'y fit myself."

"What's the matter with your chief?" Van Rieten inquired.

"Something like carbuncles," Etcham replied.

"He ought to get over a carbuncle or two," Van Rieten declared.

"They are not carbuncles," Etcham explained. "Nor one or two. He has had dozens, sometimes five at once. If they had been carbuncles he would have been dead long ago. But in some ways they are not so bad, though in others they are worse."

"How do you mean?" Van Rieten queried.

"Well," Etcham hesitated, "they do not seem to inflame so deep nor so wide as carbuncles, nor to be so painful, nor to cause so much fever. But then they seem to be part of a disease that affects his mind. He let me help him dress the first, but the others he has hidden most carefully, from me and from the men. He keeps to his tent when they puff up, and will not let me change the dressings or be with him at all."

"Have you plenty of dressings?" Van Rieten asked.

"We have some," said Etcham doubtfully. "But he won't use them; he washes out the dressings and uses them over and over."

"How is he treating the swellings?" Van Rieten enquired.

"He slices them off clear down to flesh level, with his razor."

"What?" Van Rieten shouted.

Etcham made no answer but looked him steadily in the eyes.

"I beg pardon," Van Rieten hastened to say. "You startled me. They can't be carbuncles. He'd have been dead long ago."

"I thought I had said they are not carbuncles," Etcham lisped.

"But the man must be crazy!" Van Rieten exclaimed.

"Just so," said Etcham. "He is beyond my advice or control."

"How many has he treated that way?" Van Rieten demanded.

"Two, to my knowledge," Etcham said.

"Two?" Van Rieten queried.

Etcham flushed again.

"I saw him," he confessed, "through a crack in the hut. I felt impelled to keep a watch on him, as if he was not responsible."

"I should think not," Van Rieten agreed. "And you saw him do that twice?"

"I conjecture," said Etcham, "that he did the like with all the rest."

"How many has he had?" Van Rieten asked.

"Dozens," Etcham lisped.

"Does he eat?" Van Rieten inquired.

"Like a wolf," said Etcham. "More than any two bearers."

"Can he walk?" Van Rieten asked.

"He crawls a bit, groaning," said Etcham simply.

"Little fever, you say," Van Rieten ruminated.

"Enough and too much," Etcham declared.

"Has he been delirious?" Van Rieten asked.

"Only twice," Etcham replied; "once when the first swelling broke, and once later. He would not let anyone come near him then. But we could hear him talking, talking steadily, and it scared the natives."

"Was he talking their patter in delirium?" Van Rieten demanded.

"No," said Etcham, "but he was talking some similar lingo. Hamed Burghash said he was talking Balunda. I know too little Balunda. I do not learn languages readily. Stone learned more Mang-Battu in a week than I could have learned in a year. But I seemed to hear words like Mang-Battu words. Anyhow the Mang-Battu bearers were scared."

"Scared?" Van Rieten repeated, questioningly.

"So were the Zanzibar men, even Hamed Burghash, and so was I," said Etcham, "only for a different reason. He talked in two voices."

"In two voices," Van Rieten reflected.

"Yes," said Etcham, more excitedly than he had yet spoken. "In two voices, like a conversation. One was his own, one a small, thin, bleaty voice like nothing I ever heard. I seemed to make out, among the sounds the deep voice made, something like Mang-Battu words I knew, as *nedru, metababa,* and *nedo,* their terms for 'head,' 'shoulder,' 'thigh,' and perhaps *kudra* and *nekere* ('speak' and 'whistle'); and among the noises of the shrill voice *matomipa, angunzi,* and *kamomami* ('kill,' 'death,' and 'hate'). Hamed Burghash said he also heard those words. He knew Mang-Battu far better than I."

"What did the bearers say?" Van Rieten asked.

"They said, *'Lukundoo, Lukundoo!'*" Etcham replied. "I did not know that word; Hamed Burghash said it was Mang-Battu for 'leopard.'"

"It's Mang-Battu for 'witchcraft,'" said Van Rieten.

"I don't wonder they thought so," said Etcham. "It was enough to make one believe in sorcery to listen to those two voices."

"One voice answering the other?" Van Rieten asked perfunctorily.

Etcham's face went gray under his tan.

"Sometimes both at once," he answered huskily.

"Both at once!" Van Rieten ejaculated.

"It sounded that way to the men, too," said Etcham. "And that was not all."

He stopped and looked helplessly at us for a moment.

"Could a man talk and whistle at the same time?" he asked.

"How do you mean?" Van Rieten queried.

"We could hear Stone talking away, his big, deep-chested baritone rumbling along, and through it all we could hear a high, shrill whistle, the oddest, wheezy sound. You know, no matter how shrilly a grown man may whistle, the note has a different quality from the whistle of a boy or a woman or a little girl. They sound more treble, somehow. Well, if you can imagine the smallest girl who could whistle keeping it up tunelessly right along, that whistle was like that, only even more piercing, and it sounded right through Stone's bass tones."

"And you didn't go to him?" Van Rieten cried.

"He is not given to threats," Etcham disclaimed. "But he had threatened, not volubly, nor like a sick man, but quietly and firmly, that if any man of us (he lumped me in with the men), came near him while he was in his trouble, that man should die. And it was not so much his words as his manner. It was like a monarch commanding respected privacy for a death-bed. One simply could not transgress."

"I see," said Van Rieten shortly.

"He's ve'y seedy," Etcham repeated helplessly. "I thought perhaps . . ."

His absorbing affection for Stone, his real love for him, shone out through his envelope of conventional training. Worship of Stone was plainly his master passion.

Like many competent men, Van Rieten had a streak of hard selfishness in him. It came to the surface then. He said we carried our lives in our hands from day to day just as genuinely as Stone; that he did not forget the ties of blood and calling between any two explorers, but that there was no sense in imperiling one party for a very problematical benefit to a man probably beyond any help; that it was enough of a task to hunt for one party; that if two were united, providing food would be more than doubly difficult; that the risk of starvation was too great. Deflecting our march seven full days' journey (he complimented Etcham on his marching powers) might ruin our expedition entirely.

III

Van Rieten had logic on his side and he had a way with him. Etcham sat there apologetic and deferential, like a fourth-form schoolboy before a head master. Van Rieten wound up.

"I am after Pygmies, at the risk of my life. After Pygmies I go."

"Perhaps, then, these will interest you," said Etcham, very quietly.

He took two objects out of the sidepocket of his blouse, and handed them to Van Rieten. They were round, bigger than big plums, and smaller than small peaches, about the right size to enclose in an average hand. They were black, and at first I did not see what they were.

"Pygmies!" Van Rieten exclaimed. "Pygmies, indeed! Why, they wouldn't be two feet high! Do you mean to claim that these are adult heads?"

"I claim nothing," Etcham answered evenly. "You can see for yourself."

Van Rieten passed one of the heads to me. The sun was just setting and I examined it closely. A dried head it was, perfectly preserved, and the flesh as hard as Argentine jerked beef. A bit of a vertebra stuck out where the muscles of the vanished neck had shriveled into folds. The puny chin was sharp on a projecting jaw, the minute teeth white and even between the retracted lips, the tiny nose was flat, the little forehead retreating, there were inconsiderable clumps of stunted wool on the Lilliputian cranium. There was nothing babyish, childish or youthful about the head, rather it was mature to senility.

"Where did these come from?" Van Rieten inquired.

"I do not know," Etcham replied precisely. "I found them among Stone's effects while rummaging for medicines or drugs or anything that could help me to help him. I do not know where he got them. But I'll swear he did not have them when we entered this district."

"Are you sure?" Van Rieten queried, his eyes big and fixed on Etcham's.

"Ve'y sure," lisped Etcham.

"But how could he have come by them without your knowledge?" Van Rieten demurred.

"Sometimes we were apart ten days at a time hunting," said Etcham. "Stone is not a talking man. He gave me no account of his doings and Hamed Burghash keeps a still tongue and a tight hold on the men."

"You have examined these heads?" Van Rieten asked.

"Minutely," said Etcham.

Van Rieten took out his notebook. He was a methodical chap. He tore out a leaf, folded it and divided it equally into three pieces. He gave one to me and one to Etcham.

"Just for a test of my impressions," he said, "I want each of us to write separately just what he is most reminded of by these heads. Then I want to compare the writings."

I handed Etcham a pencil and he wrote. Then he handed the pencil back to me and I wrote.

"Read the three," said Van Rieten, handing me his piece.

Van Rieten had written, "An old Balunda witch doctor."

Etcham had written, "An old Mang-Battu fetishman."

I had written, "An old Katongo magician."

"There!" Van Rieten exclaimed. "Look at that!

There is nothing Wagabi or Batwa or Wambuttu or Wabotu about these heads. Nor anything Pygmy either."

"I thought as much," said Etcham.

"And you say he did not have them before?"

"To a certainty he did not," Etcham asserted.

"It is worth following up," said Van Rieten. "I'll go with you. And first of all, I'll do my best to save Stone."

He put out his hand and Etcham clasped it silently. He was grateful all over.

IV

Nothing but Etcham's fever of solicitude could have taken him in five days over the track. It took him eight days to retrace with full knowledge of it and our party to help. We could not have done it in seven, and Etcham urged us on, in a repressed fury of anxiety, no mere fever of duty to his chief, but a real ardor of devotion, a glow of personal adoration for Stone which blazed under his dry conventional exterior and showed in spite of him.

We found Stone well cared for. Etcham had seen to a good, high thorn *zareeba* round the camp, the huts were well built and thatched and Stone's was as good as their resources would permit. Hamed Burghash was not named after two Seyyids for nothing. He had in him the making of a sultan. He had kept the Mang-Battu together, not a man had slipped off, and he had kept them in order. Also he was a deft nurse and a faithful servant.

The two other Zanzibaris had done some creditable hunting. Though all were hungry, the camp was far from starvation.

Stone was on a canvas cot and there was a sort of collapsible camp-stool-table, like a Turkish tabouret, by the cot. It had a water-bottle and some vials on it and Stone's watch, also his razor in its case.

Stone was clean and not emaciated, but he was far gone; not unconscious, but in a daze; past commanding or resisting anyone. He did not seem to see us enter or to know we were there. I should have recognized him anywhere. His boyish dash and grace had vanished utterly, of course. But his head was even more leonine; his hair was still abundant, yellow and wavy; the close, crisped blond beard he had grown during his illness did not alter him. He was big and big-chested yet. His eyes were dull and he mumbled and babbled mere meaningless syllables, not words.

Etcham helped Van Rieten to uncover him and look him over. He was in good muscle for a man so long bedridden. There were no scars on him except about his knees, shoulders and chest. On each knee and above it he had a full score of roundish cicatrices, and a dozen or more on each shoulder, all in front. Two or three were open wounds and four or five barely healed. He had no fresh swellings, except two, one on each side, on his pectoral muscles, the one on the left being higher up and farther out than the other. They did not look like boils or carbuncles, but as if something blunt and hard were being pushed up through the fairly healthy flesh and skin, not much inflamed.

"I should not lance those," said Van Rieten, and Etcham assented.

They made Stone as comfortable as they could, and just before sunset we looked in at him again. He was lying on his back, and his chest showed big and massive yet, but he lay as if in a stupor. We left Etcham with him and went into the next hut, which Etcham had resigned to us. The jungle noises were no different there than anywhere else for months past, and I was soon fast asleep.

V

Sometime in the pitch dark I found myself awake and listening. I could hear two voices, one Stone's, the other sibilant and wheezy. I knew Stone's voice after all the years that had passed since I heard it last. The other was like nothing I remembered. It had less volume than the wail of a newborn baby, yet there was an insistent carrying power to it, like the shrilling of an insect. As I listened I heard Van Rieten breathing near me in the dark, then he heard me and realized that I was listening, too. Like Etcham I knew little Balunda, but I could make out a word or two. The voices alternated with intervals of silence between.

Then suddenly both sounded at once and fast. Stone's baritone basso, full as if he were in perfect health, and that incredibly stridulous falsetto, both jabbering at once like the voices of two people quarreling and trying to talk each other down.

"I can't stand this," said Van Rieten. "Let's have a look at him."

He had one of those cylindrical electric night candles. He fumbled about for it, touched the button and beckoned me to come with him. Outside of the hut he motioned me to stand still, and instinctively turned off the light, as if seeing made listening difficult.

Except for a faint glow from the embers of the bearers' fire we were in complete darkness, little starlight struggled through the trees, the river made but a faint murmur. We could hear the two voices together and then suddenly the creaking voice changed into a razor-edged, slicing whistle, indescribably cutting, continuing right through Stone's grumbling torrent of croaking words.

"Good God!" exclaimed Van Rieten.

Abruptly he turned on the light.

We found Etcham utterly asleep, exhausted by his long anxiety and the exertions of his phenomenal march and relaxed completely now that the load was in a sense shifted from his shoulders to Van Rieten's. Even the light on his face did not wake him.

The whistle had ceased and the two voices now sounded together. Both came from Stone's cot, where the concentrated white ray showed him lying just as we had left him, except that he had tossed his arms above his head and had torn the coverings and bandages from his chest.

The swelling on his right breast had broken. Van Rieten aimed the center line of the light at it and we saw it plainly. From his flesh, grown out of it, there protruded a head, such a head as the dried specimens Etcham had shown us, as if it were a miniature of the head of a Balunda fetish-man. It was black, shining black as the blackest African skin; it rolled the whites of its wicked, wee eyes and showed its microscopic teeth between lips repulsively Negroid in their red fullness, even in so diminutive a face. It had crisp, fuzzy wool on its minikin skull, it turned malignantly from side to side and chittered incessantly in that inconceivable falsetto. Stone babbled brokenly against its patter.

Van Rieten turned from Stone and waked Etcham, with some difficulty. When he was awake and saw it all, Etcham stared and said not one word.

"You saw him slice off two swellings?" Van Rieten asked.

Etcham nodded, chokingly.

"Did he bleed much?" Van Rieten demanded.

"Ve'y little," Etcham replied.

"You hold his arms," said Van Rieten to Etcham.

He took up Stone's razor and handed me the light. Stone showed no sign of seeing the light or of knowing we were there. But the little head mewled and screeched at us.

Van Rieten's hand was steady, and the sweep of the razor even and true. Stone bled amazingly little and Van Rieten dressed the wound as if it had been a bruise or scrape.

Stone had stopped talking the instant the excrescent head was severed. Van Rieten did all that could be done for Stone and then fairly grabbed the light from me. Snatching up a gun he scanned the ground by the cot and brought the butt down once and twice, viciously.

We went back to our hut, but I doubt if I slept.

VI

Next day, near noon, in broad daylight, we heard the two voices from Stone's hut. We found Etcham dropped asleep by his charge. The swelling on the left had broken, and just such another head was there miauling and spluttering. Etcham woke up and the three of us stood there and glared. Stone interjected hoarse vocables into the tinkling gurgle of the portent's utterance.

Van Rieten stepped forward, took up Stone's razor and knelt down by the cot. The atomy of a head squealed a wheezy snarl at him.

Then suddenly Stone spoke English.

"Who are you with my razor?"

Van Rieten started back and stood up.

Stone's eyes were clear now and bright, they roved about the hut.

"The end," he said; "I recognize the end. I seem to see Etcham, as if in life. But Singleton! Ah, Singleton! Ghosts of my boyhood come to watch me pass! And you, strange specter with the black beard and my razor! Aroint ye all!"

"I'm no ghost, Stone," I managed to say. "I'm alive. So are Etcham and Van Rieten. We are here to help you."

"Van Rieten!" he exclaimed. "My work passes on to a better man. Luck go with you, Van Rieten."

Van Rieten went nearer to him.

"Just hold still a moment, old man," he said soothingly. "It will be only one twinge."

"I've held still for many such twinges," Stone answered quite distinctly. "Let me be. Let me die in my own way. The hydra was nothing to this. You can cut off ten, a hundred, a thousand heads, but the curse you can not cut off, or take off. What's soaked into the bone won't come out of the flesh, any more than what's bred there. Don't hack me any more. Promise!"

His voice had all the old commanding tone of his boyhood and it swayed Van Rieten as it always had swayed everybody.

"I promise," said Van Rieten.

Almost as he said the word Stone's eyes filmed again.

Then we three sat about Stone and watched that hideous, gibbering prodigy grow up out of Stone's flesh, till two horrid, spindling little black arms disengaged themselves. The infinitesimal nails were perfect to the barely perceptible moon at the quick, the pink spot on the palm was horridly natural. These arms gesticulated and the right plucked toward Stone's blond beard.

"I can't stand this," Van Rieten exclaimed and took up the razor again.

Instantly Stone's eyes opened, hard and glittering.

"Van Rieten break his word?" he enunciated slowly. "Never!"

"But we must help you," Van Rieten gasped.

"I am past all help and all hurting," said Stone. "This is my hour. This curse is not put on me; it grew out of me, like this horror here. Even now I go."

His eyes closed and we stood helpless, the adherent figure spouting shrill sentences.

In a moment Stone spoke again.

"You speak all tongues?" he asked quickly. And the emergent minikin replied in sudden English, "Yea, verily, all that you speak," putting out its microscopic tongue, writhing its lips and wagging its head from side to side. We could see the thready ribs on its exiguous flanks heave as if the thing breathed.

"Has she forgiven me?" Stone asked in a muffled strangle.

"Not while the moss hangs from the cypresses," the head squeaked. "Not while the stars shine on Lake Pontchartrain will she forgive."

And then Stone, all with one motion, wrenched himself over on his side. The next instant he was dead.

When Singleton's voice ceased the room was hushed for a space. We could hear each other breathing. Twombly, the tactless, broke the silence.

"I presume," he said, "you cut off the little minikin and brought it home in alcohol."

Singleton turned on him a stern countenance.

"We buried Stone," he said, "unmutilated as he died."

"But," said the unconscionable Twombly, "the whole thing is incredible."

Singleton stiffened.

"I did not expect you to believe it," he said; "I began by saying that although I heard and saw it, when I look back on it I cannot credit it myself."

A Woman Seldom Found

by WILLIAM SANSOM

Once a young man was on a visit to Rome.

It was his first visit; he came from the country but he was neither on the one hand so young nor on the other so simple as to imagine that a great and beautiful capi-

From *A Contest of Ladies* by William Sansom. Reprinted by permission of the author, Reynal & Company, Inc., New York, and the Hogarth Press, London.

tal should hold out finer promises than anywhere else. He already knew that life was largely illusion, that though wonderful things could happen, nevertheless as many disappointments came in compensation: and he knew, too, that life could offer a quality even worse —the probability that nothing would happen at all. This was always more possible in a great city intent on its own business.

Thinking in this way, he stood on the Spanish steps and surveyed the momentous panorama stretched before him. He listened to the swelling hum of the evening traffic and watched as the lights went up against Rome's golden dusk. Shining automobiles slunk past the fountains and turned urgently into the bright Via Condotti, neon-red signs stabbed the shadows with invitation; the yellow windows of buses were packed with faces intent on going somewhere—everyone in the city seemed intent on the evening's purpose. He alone had nothing to do.

He felt himself the only person alone of everyone in the city. But searching for adventure never brought it —rather kept it away. Such a mood promised nothing. So the young man turned back up the steps, passed the lovely church, and went on up the cobbled hill toward his hotel. Wine bars and food shops jostled with growing movement in those narrow streets. But out on the broad pavements of the Vittorio Veneto, under the trees mounting to the Borghese Gardens, the high world of Rome would be filling the most elegant cafés in Europe to enjoy with apéritifs the twilight. That would be the loneliest of all! So the young man kept to the quieter, older streets on his solitary errand home.

In one such street, a pavementless alley between old yellow houses, a street that in Rome might suddenly blossom into a secret piazza of fountain and baroque church, a grave secluded treasure-place—he noticed that he was alone but for the single figure of a woman walking down the hill toward him.

As she drew nearer, he saw that she was dressed with

taste, that in her carriage was a soft Latin fire, that she walked for respect. Her face was veiled, but it was impossible to imagine that she would not be beautiful. Isolated thus with her, passing so near to her, and she symbolizing the adventure of which the evening was so empty—a greater melancholy gripped him. He felt wretched as the gutter, small, sunk, pitiful. So that he rounded his shoulders and lowered his eyes—but not before casting one furtive glance into hers.

He was so shocked at what he saw that he paused, he stared, shocked, into her face. He had made no mistake. She was smiling. Also—she too had hesitated. He thought instantly: "Whore?" But no—it was not that kind of smile, though as well it was not without affection. And then amazingly she spoke.

"I—I know I shouldn't ask you . . . but it is such a beautiful evening—and perhaps you are alone, as alone as I am. . . ."

She was very beautiful. He could not speak. But a growing elation gave him the power to smile. So that she continued, still hesitant, in no sense soliciting.

"I thought . . . perhaps . . . we could take a walk, an apéritif. . . ."

At last the young man achieved himself.

"Nothing, *nothing* would please me more. And the Veneto is only a minute up there."

She smiled again.

"My home is just here. . . ."

They walked in silence a few paces down the street, to a turning the young man had already passed. This she indicated. They walked to where the first humble houses ended in a kind of recess. In the recess was set the wall of a garden, and behind it stood a large and elegant mansion. The woman, about whose face shone a curious pale glitter—something fused of the transparent pallor of fine skin, of gray but brilliant eyes, of dark eyebrows and hair of lucent black—inserted her key in the garden gate.

They were greeted by a servant in velvet livery. In a

large and exquisite salon, under chandeliers of fine glass and before a moist green courtyard where water played, they were served with a frothy wine. They talked. The wine—iced in the warm Roman night—filled them with an inner warmth of exhilaration. But from time to time the young man looked at her curiously.

With her glances, with many subtle inflections of teeth and eyes she was inducing an intimacy that suggested much. He felt he must be careful. At length he thought the best thing might be to thank her—somehow thus to root out whatever obligation might be in store. But here she interrupted him, first with a smile, then with a look of some sadness. She begged him to spare himself any perturbation; she knew it was strange, that in such a situation he might suspect some second purpose; but the simple truth remained that she was lonely and—this with a certain deference—something perhaps in him, perhaps in that moment of dusk in the street, had proved to her inescapably attractive. She had not been able to help herself.

The possibility of a perfect encounter—a dream that years of disillusion will never quite kill—decided him. His elation rose beyond control. He believed her. And thereafter the perfections compounded. At her invitation they dined. Servants brought food of great delicacy; shellfish, fat bird flesh, soft fruits. And afterward they sat on a sofa near the courtyard, where it was cool. Liqueurs were brought. The servants retired. A hush fell upon the house. They embraced.

A little later, with no word, she took his arm and led him from the room. How deep a silence had fallen between them! The young man's heart beat fearfully—it might be heard, he felt, echoing in the hall whose marble they now crossed, sensed through his arm to hers. But such excitement rose now from certainty. Certainty that at such a moment, on such a charmed evening—nothing could go wrong. There was no need to speak. Together they mounted the great staircase.

In her bedroom, to the picture of her framed by the bed curtains and dimly naked in a silken shift, he poured out his love; a love that was to be eternal, to be always perfect, as fabulous as this their exquisite meeting.

Softly she spoke the return of his love. Nothing would ever go amiss, nothing would ever come between them. And very gently she drew back the bedclothes for him.

But suddenly, at the moment when at last he lay beside her, when his lips were almost upon hers—he hesitated.

Something was wrong. A flaw could be sensed. He listened, felt—and then saw the fault was his. Shaded, soft-shaded lights by the bed—but he had been so careless as to leave on the bright electric chandelier in the center of the ceiling. He remembered the switch was by the door. For a fraction, then, he hesitated. She raised her eyelids—saw his glance at the chandelier, understood.

Her eyes glittered. She murmured, "My beloved, don't worry—don't move. . . ."

And she reached out her hand. Her hand grew larger, her arm grew longer and longer, it stretched out through the bedcurtains, across the long carpet, huge and overshadowing the whole of the long room, until at last its giant fingers were at the door. With a terminal click, she switched out the light.

The Perfectionist

by MARGARET ST. CLAIR

I had nightmares about it for several years afterward
—the kind where something is on your heels, and you
make desperate efforts, each more futile than the last,
to escape it—and always felt bad about them when I
woke up. I never could decide whether I was justified
in having bad dreams at all.

It began when I went to live with Aunt Muriel in
1933. I hadn't had a job for six months when I got the
letter of invitation from her, and I hadn't eaten much
at all for two weeks.

Aunt Muriel wasn't exactly my aunt, to begin with.
She was a sort of great-aunt, once removed, on my
mother's side, and I hadn't seen her since I was a beady-
eyed kid in knee breeches.

The invitation might have surprised me—though she
explained in the letter that she was an old woman,
getting lonely, and felt the need of some kindred face
near her—only I was too hungry to wonder.

There was a money order in the letter, and a ticket
to Downie, where she lived. After I paid the back room
rent with the money order and got myself a meal with

double portions of everything, I had two dollars and thirteen cents left. I caught the afternoon train to Downie, and a little before noon the next day I was walking up the steps to Aunt Muriel's house.

Aunt Muriel herself met me at the door. She seemed glad to see me. She wrinkled up her mouth in a smile of welcome.

"So *good* of you to come, Charles!" she said. "I really can't thank you enough! So very *good* of you!" She ran to italics.

I was beginning to warm up to the old girl. She didn't look any older to me than she had fifteen years before. She'd been held together by whalebone and net collars then, and she still was. I put the more flattering portion of this idea into words.

"Oh, Charles," she chirped, "you *flatterer!*" She gave me another smile and then led me into the hall.

I followed her up the stairs to my room on the second floor front. It had a high ceiling and a tall four-poster bed which should have had curtains around it to cut off the draft. After she left, I put my imitation leather suitcase in the big closet and went into the bath next door to clean up.

Lunch was laid on the dining-room table when I came down, and a maid, who looked a good deal older than Aunt Muriel, was fluttering in and out with more dishes. With my aunt's encouragement, I ate enough to keep me comatose all afternoon, and then sat back with a cigarette and listened to her talk.

She began by doing a good deal of commiserating with herself on the subject of her age and loneliness, and a good deal of self-congratulation because she was going to have a young kinsman around from now on.

It developed that I was expected to make myself useful in small ways like walking the dog—an unpleasant Pomeranian named Teddy—and taking letters to the mailbox. This was perfectly all right with me, and I told her so.

There was a short hiatus in the conversation. Then,

picking Teddy up off the floor where he'd been during the meal, she installed him in her lap and launched out on an account of what she called her *hobby*. In the last year or so she'd taken up drawing and it had become, from what she said, almost an obsession.

Holding Teddy under one arm, she rose and went to the walnut sideboard and returned with a portfolio of drawings for me to look at.

"I do almost all my drawing here in the dining room," she said, "because the light is so good. Tell me, what do you think of *these?*" She handed me fifty or sixty small sheets of drawing paper.

I spread the drawings out on the dining-room table, among the litter of dishes, and examined them carefully. They were all in pencil, though one or two had been touched up with blotches of water color, and they were all of the same subject, four apples in a low china bowl.

They had been labored over; Aunt Muriel had erased and re-erased until the surface of the paper was gritty and miserable. I racked my brains for something nice to say about them.

"You—unh—you've really caught something of the essence of those apples," I forced out after a moment. "Very creditable."

My aunt smiled. "I'm *so* glad you like them," she replied. "Amy said—the maid, you know—that I was silly to work at them so much, but I couldn't stop, I couldn't *bear* to stop, until they were *perfect*." She paused, then added, "Do you know, Charles, I had the biggest difficulty!"

"Yes?"

"The apples kept withering! It was dreadful. I put them in the icebox just as soon as I got through for the day, but still they went bad after two or three weeks. It wasn't until Amy thought of *dipping* them in melted wax that they lasted long enough."

"Good idea."

"Yes, wasn't it? But you know, Charles, I've gotten

rather *tired* of apples lately. I'd like to try something else. . . . I've been thinking, that little tree out on the lawn would make a good subject."

She went over to the window to show me the tree she meant. I followed her. It was a young sapling, just coming into leaf. My aunt said it was a flowering peach.

"*Don't* you think that would be a good subject, Charles? I believe I'll try it this afternoon while you take Teddy for a little walk."

Amy helped bundle my aunt up in several layers of coats and mufflers, and I carried the stool, the easel, the box of pencils and the paper out into the garden for her.

She was rather fussy about the location of the various items, but I finally got them fixed to her satisfaction. Then, though I'd much rather have had an after-luncheon nap upstairs, I snapped the lead on Teddy's objectionable little collar and started out for a survey of the town of Downie.

I soon realized that Downie was the sort of town whose social life centers around the drugstore, but I managed to kill the next two hours by letting Teddy investigate the lamp posts which caught his fancy.

I expected to find Aunt Muriel on the lawn when I got back, hard at work on her drawing, but she had gone in and the easel and stool were gone, too. I looked around for her, but she wasn't in sight, so I let Teddy climb into his box in the dining room and went upstairs for that belated nap.

After all, I couldn't get to sleep. For some irrelevant reason I kept thinking of all those painstaking drawings of the bowl of apples, and I lay on the bed and counted the spots on the wall until dinner time.

The dinner was good, and plentiful. My aunt, however, was definitely snappish. After Amy had cleared away the dishes and my aunt had restored Teddy to his accustomed place on her lap, I found out what the reason was.

"My drawing went *badly*," she complained. "The wind kept whipping those leaves around until I couldn't get a *thing* done."

"I didn't notice much wind, Aunt Muriel," I said rather stupidly.

"You just don't notice things!" she flared. "Why, the leaves weren't still a single *minute*."

I hastened to make amends.

"I can see that a careful craftsman like yourself might be distracted," I placated her. "I'm sorry. I haven't been with artists much."

The reference to herself as an artist pleased my aunt.

"Oh, I'm sure you didn't mean to give offense," she said. "It's just that I can't work with anything unless it's *absolutely* still. That's why I stayed with the apples so long. But I *would* like to draw that tree. I wonder . . ." She went into a brown study which lasted until she had emptied two cups of coffee.

"Charles," she said finally, "I've been thinking. I want you to chop that tree down for me tomorrow and bring it into the house. I'll put it in one of those two-quart milk bottles. That way I can draw it without the wind bothering me."

"But it's such a nice little tree," I protested. "Besides, it won't last long after it's been cut down."

"Oh, it's only a tree," she replied. "I'll get another from the nursery. And about the withering, Amy is wonderful with flowers. She puts aspirin and sugar in the water, and they last forever. Of course, I'll have to work fast. But if I put in two or three hours in the morning and four or five after lunch, I ought to get something done."

As far as she was concerned, the matter was settled.

Immediately after breakfast next morning, Aunt Muriel led me to the tool shed in the rear of the house and gave me a rusty hatchet. She watched with ghoulish interest while I put an edge on the hatchet and then escorted me to the scene of the execution. Feeling like a murderer, I severed the little sapling from its trunk with a couple of chops and then carried it into the house.

I spent the rest of that day, and the next three or four days, working in the garden. I've always liked gardening, and there were some nice things in the place, though they'd been badly neglected. I divided some perennials and fertilized the earth around them with bone meal. Somebody had stocked up the shed with Red Arrow and nicotine sulphate, and I had a good time spraying for aphids and beetles.

Friday morning at breakfast I found a five-dollar bill folded up in my napkin. I raised my eyebrows toward Aunt Muriel. She nodded, yes, it was for me, while a faint flush washed up in her flabby cheeks.

I folded it neatly and put it in my pocket, feeling a warm glow of gratitude for the old girl. It really was extraordinarily decent of her to provide me with cigarette money. I resolved to go shopping for a little present for her that afternoon.

I found that the resources of Downie were limited. After hesitating between a China fawn and a bowl of fan-tailed goldfish, I decided that the goldfish had more verve. I went in after them, and discovered that Drake, the clerk who sold them to me, had been to California, too, and was practically a friend. I made a date with him for a gabfest the following night.

Aunt Muriel seemed genuinely delighted with the fish. She oohed and ahhed over the sinuosity and filminess of their tails and ended by installing the bowl on the little stand beside her easel.

We began to settle into a routine. In the mornings and early afternoons Aunt Muriel drew in the dining room while I worked in the garden. Later in the day I ran errands, walked Teddy, and undertook a bunch of small repairs around the house.

About the middle of my second week with Aunt Muriel, the peach tree withered beyond any hope. She told me at dinner time, with a tone of one announcing a major disaster, that she had had to throw it out. We held a post mortem on the batch of thirty-two drawings she had been able to complete before the catastrophe.

I picked out one of them as having more plastic value than the rest. She admitted it was her favorite, too, and everything was fine. I could see, though, that she was wondering what she could draw next.

The next day she flitted restlessly through the house looking for something to draw. She kept popping out into the yard where I was transplanting antirrhinum seedlings, to ask my opinion of this or that as a subject for her pencil. I noticed, when I went in to lunch, that she kept watching the goldfish bowl speculatively, but I didn't make anything of it at the time.

That night when I returned from Drake's house she met me at the door and led me to the kitchen with an air of mysterious triumph.

"I was a little nervous about it," she said, with her hand on the handle of the refrigerator door. "But really, it came out ever so well!" She opened the refrigerator, fumbled in its depths a moment, and pulled out the goldfish bowl. Moisture began to condense on its surface. I stared at it stupidly.

"I *knew* the fish would never hold still, and yet I was just *aching* to draw them," she went on. "So I thought and I thought—and really, I *do* think it was a splendid idea, even if it was my own! I just turned the cold control way down, and put the bowl in, and came back in a couple of hours, and it was frozen solid!

"I was afraid the bowl would crack when it began to freeze, but it didn't. See, the ice is perfectly clear." She picked up a dish towel and rubbed the moisture away until I could see the two goldfish neatly incased in transparent ice. "And now I'll be able to draw them without any trouble. Isn't it *wonderful?*"

I said yes, it was wonderful and went upstairs as soon as I decently could. The incident left an unpleasant taste in my mouth. Not that I held any especial

brief for the continued existence of the goldfish, but
somehow . . .

She'd seemed to enjoy watching them swimming
about so much, and I'd given them to her, and— Oh,
hell!

I woke up the next morning feeling faintly unhappy
before I could remember what was disturbing me.
When I remembered, I decided that I was acting like
a champion chump. To let the demise of two goggle-
eyed fish upset me was tops in imbecility. Whistling, I
went down to breakfast.

After the meal was over, Aunt Muriel got the bowl
out of the refrigerator and set to work. I went out in
the shed and messed around with the spray gun for a
while.

Looking up at the scaling side of the house, I had an
idea. Why not repaint it? I asked my aunt and she ap-
proved. Accordingly, after some calculation, I brought
home a bucket of paint from the store and started
sloshing it on.

The work proceeded slowly. Days went by and I got
to be a familiar customer at the paint store. Aunt
Muriel had finished her eighty-first study of the frozen
goldfish before I'd given the big house its first coat, and
the surface was so bad it was going to require at least
two.

Spring drifted imperceptibly into early summer, and
I was still painting the house and Aunt Muriel was
still drawing the goldfish, both of us increasingly absorbed in our tasks.

I was having a pretty good time. Drake had introduced me to his sister, a vivid brunette with just the
combination of honey and claws which attracts me
most in a woman, and he'd got another girl for himself. We went out together several nights each week.
My room in the city with the unpaid rent, the hopeless
hunt for a job, and the hunger, seemed a long way off.

I got the painting on the house done the day before

Aunt Muriel decided she had exhausted the goldfish. I felt like celebrating. So I mixed soapsuds and nicotine sulphate, stirred up a mess of Red Arrow, and puttered among the neglected plants to my heart's content.

Aunt Muriel handed me the last of the goldfish studies at dinner the next day and I went over the entire group with her. I was beginning to hate these inquests over the anatomy of whatever she'd been drawing, but I bore up under it as well as I could.

When we'd finished, she said, "Charles, I've been wondering. Do you suppose Teddy would be a good subject for me next?"

I looked down at the little animal where he was lying in her lap and said, yes, I thought he would, but would he hold still enough?

My aunt looked thoughtful.

"I don't know," she said. "I'll have to try to think of something. Perhaps I could give him his dinner right after breakfast. Or . . ." She went off into one of those periods of meditation of hers and, after a while, I left unobtrusively for my date with Virginia, Drake's sister.

We sat in the porch swing in the dark and held hands while the breeze blew the smell of purple lilacs toward us. It was a sweet, sad, sentimental sort of date.

The next day was Saturday. After breakfast my aunt told me to take Teddy for a walk, and to get him thoroughly tired out. She was going to feed him when I got back and she hoped that the exercise, plus the food, might make him comatose enough to serve as a model.

Obediently, we started out. Teddy and I assessed every lamp post in Downie at least twice, and if he wasn't tired out when I brought him back, he should have been. My aunt took the lead from his collar and led him to the pantry where his food dish was waiting, piled high with hamburger.

Teddy ate like a little pig. When he had finished he lay down on the floor of the pantry with a resolute air.

My aunt had to carry him into the dining room and deposit him in a sunny spot near her easel. He was asleep and snoring before I left the room.

We had lunch late that day, almost two-thirty in the afternoon, so Aunt Muriel would be able to take full advantage of Teddy's lethargy. I was hungry, and Amy had prepared a really snazzy meal, centering around fried chicken Southern style. As a result, it wasn't until I had finished with the fresh peach mousse that I paid much attention to my aunt. Then I saw that she was looking distracted and morose.

"Didn't the drawing go well this morning, Aunt Muriel?" I asked.

She shook her head until the pendants of her bright earrings jangled violently.

"No, Charles, it did not. Teddy—" She halted, looking very sad.

"What was the matter? Wouldn't he stay asleep?"

If my aunt had been a different type of woman she would have laughed sardonically. As it was, she gave a tiny, delicate snort.

"Oh, he *slept*," she replied. "Yes, he *slept*. But he kept twitching and jumping and panting in his sleep until—well, really, Charles, it was *quite* impossible. Like trying to draw an aspen in a high wind!"

"That's too bad. I guess you'll have to find another subject."

For a moment my aunt did not answer. Looking at her, I thought I caught the glint of tears in her eyes.

"Yes," she replied slowly, "I guess I will. . . . I think, Charles, I'll go into town this afternoon and buy a few little things for Teddy."

For a moment something cold slid up and down my spine. Then it was gone, and I was thinking it was nice of the old girl, considering how much store she set by her drawing, not to be annoyed at the little dog. . . .

She came up to my room just before dinner and showed me what she'd bought for Teddy. There was a bright red collar with a little bell, a chocolate-flavored rubber bone, and a box of some weird confection called "Dog Treet," which, according to the label, was a wholesome sweetmeat for pets.

She put the collar on Teddy while I watched and then gave him two of the dark brown lozenges out of the "Dog Treet" box. He ate them with a flurry of little growls, and seemed to relish them. . . .

Sunday morning I sat around, nursing the old bones until my watch told me it was time to get going if I didn't want to be late for the all-day hike Drake and I had planned with the girls.

We had a fine time in the country. Drake wandered into a thicket of poison oak, and Virginia, giggling, dropped a woolly caterpillar down my neck.

It was quite dark when I returned to the house. Even before I got inside I noticed that all the lights were on and that there was a general air of confusion.

When I opened the door I found Aunt Muriel standing in the hallway, having what looked like a fit. Amy was standing before her waving a bottle of smelling salts.

"It's *Teddy!*" my aunt gasped when she saw me. "Oh, Charles, he's—"

I put my arm around her comfortingly, and my aunt dissolved into tears. They began to trickle over the coating of talcum powder on her cheeks and drop on the high net collar around her neck.

"It's Teddy," she whimpered. "Oh, Charles, he's dead!"

I'd been expecting it subconsciously, but all the same I jumped.

"What happened?" I asked.

"I let him out in the yard for a little run about three hours ago. He was gone a *long* time, and at last I went out to look for him. I called and called and finally I found him out under the rhododendron. He was *awfully* sick. So I came right in and called the doctor, but when he got here, poor little Teddy—was—was gone.

Somebody must have poisoned him." She began to cry
again.

I stroked my aunt's shoulder and murmured reassur-
ing words while my mind was busy. Some one of the
neighbors? Teddy had been a quiet little beast, but he
did bark once in a while, and some people just don't
like dogs.

"Dr. Jones was ever so nice and *sympathetic* about
it. He took poor little Teddy away in a bag. He's going
to take him to a man he knows and have him *stuffed.*"

Stuffed? I felt sweat break out along my shoulder
blades and under my arms. Mechanically I pulled the
handkerchief out of my hip pocket and handed it to
my aunt.

She took it and began to blot her eyes. "It's such a
comfort to me, anyway," she said, blowing her nose,
"to think that he did—enjoy his—last day—on earth."

I took her up to her room and mixed her a bromide.
I stood over her while she drank and talked to her
soothingly and patted her hand. After a while I got her
calm enough so I could go to my room.

I lay down on the bed and stared up at the spots on
the ceiling for a while. My heart was beating hard and
quick. Pretty soon I reached in my coat pocket for cigarettes and began to smoke.

I emptied the pack while I lay there, looking at the
ceiling, not thinking about anything, keeping my mind
back, with an effort that was barely conscious, from the
edge of something I didn't want to explore. About
twelve I undressed and went to bed.

I felt soggy the next day. I'd slept, but it hadn't done
me any good. Aunt Muriel came in later after I'd
pushed aside my toast. She was red-eyed. I said good
morning and went out into the garden.

The day was muggy and overcast, and I didn't feel
like doing much, anyhow. I disbudded peonies for a
while and clipped off seed pods; then I decided to give
the Oriental cherries a light going-over with the prun-
ing shears. It ought to have been done earlier. When

I'd finished, I went into the shed for some linseed oil and bordeaux to mix a poultice for their wounds.

Reaching for the can of bordeaux, an unfamiliar gleam in the corner behind it caught my eyes. It was a can of arsenate of lead. The label bore the usual skull and crossbones. I opened the can. About a quarter of an inch of the poison was gone.

It might have been in the shed before, of course; I wasn't sure it hadn't been. I held on to that idea: I wasn't sure.

I don't know what I did the rest of the day. I must have pottered around in the garden, trying not to think, until dinner time. Aunt Muriel came to the window once and asked me if I didn't want any lunch, and I said I wasn't hungry.

I guess she spent the day looking at Teddy's box in the living room.

Well, I got over it. Two or three days later, when Teddy came back from the taxidermist's, I'd pushed the whole thing back so far in my mind that my reaction had begun to seem slightly comic as well as inexplicable.

Even when Aunt Muriel got her pencils and started on an endless series of sketches of the little stuffed animal, it was all right with me. If anyone had asked me, I'd have said it was only natural for her to want to draw the pet of which she'd been so fond.

While she drew Teddy over and over again, I started re-roofing the house. It was a rough job because it was full of old-fashioned turrets and cupolas, and the summer was well along before I finished.

Aunt Muriel kept urging me to relax, but I just couldn't be quiet.

After the roof, I started a lath house in back for seedlings. Virginia and I were dating almost every night, and I told myself I was feeling fine. I did notice a slight, steady loss of weight, but I pretended it was due to my smoking too much.

One hot night toward the end of August, my aunt got

out the packet of drawings she'd made of Teddy, and I went over them with her.

"I think I'll try a few more," she said when I'd laid the last sketch aside. "And then—well, I must get something else." She looked sad.

"Yes," I said noncommittally. The subject made me uneasy, somehow. But so thoroughly had I repressed my awareness, I had no idea why.

"Charles," she said after a minute. She was looking more depressed than ever. "You've made an old woman very happy. This Virginia you've been going around with so much—are you *fond* of her?"

"Why—unh—yes. Yes, I am."

"Well, I've been *thinking*. Would you like it, Charles, if—if I were to advance you the money to set up a little nursery business here in Downie? You seem to have a real *talent* for that sort of thing. I'd miss you, of course, but if you *wanted* to—I'm sure you'd be happy with Virginia, and—" She choked up and couldn't go on.

The old darling! I went around to her side of the table and gave her a hug and kiss. I managed to tell her how happy it would make me and how much I'd been wanting to do just what she suggested. A business of my own, and Virginia for a wife! She was better than a fairy godmother!

We sat up late discussing plans for the nursery—location, stock, advertising, policy—items that I found fascinating, and Aunt Muriel seemed to enjoy listening to.

When I went upstairs to bed, I was feeling so elated I didn't think I could ever get to bed. I whistled while I undressed. And, despite my expectations, I corked off almost as soon as my head hit the pillow.

I awoke about three in the morning, my mind filled with an unalterable conviction. It was as if what I'd only suspected, what I'd made myself forget, had added itself up and become, while I slept, an unyielding certainty.

I sat on the edge of the bed in my pajamas, shivering.

Aunt Muriel was going to kill me.

Lovingly, regretfully, she was going to put poison in my food or in my drink. Lovingly, regretfully, she was going to watch my agonies or smooth my pillow.

With tears in her eyes, she would delay calling the doctor until it was too late. She'd be most unhappy over the whole thing. And, after I was dead, she'd give me to the best mortician in Downie to embalm.

A week later, after drawing me for eighteen hours daily, she'd consign me to the earth, still regretfully, but with her regret a little alleviated by the knowledge that my last days on earth had been happy ones. The nursery business and the marriage with Virginia Drake were, you see, to be the equivalent for me of Teddy's red collar and chocolate-flavored bone.

I went over my chain of reasoning rapidly. It was flawless. But there was one thing more—I had to see for myself.

I drew on my bathrobe and tiptoed along the corridor and down the back stairs. When I got into the shed, I lighted matches and looked until I found the spot on the shelf behind the can of bordeaux where the arsenate of lead should have been. It wasn't there.

Back in my room, I dressed, threw things into my suitcase, and exited in the classical way. That is, I knotted sheets together, tied them to the four-poster bed, and slid down them to the ground. I caught the five-thirty train for the city at the station.

I never heard from Aunt Muriel again. After I got to L.A. I wrote a few cards to Virginia, without any address, just to let her know I hadn't forgotten her. After a while I got into private employment and met a nice girl. One thing led to another, and we got married.

But there's one thing I'd give a good deal to know. What did Aunt Muriel draw next?

The Price of the Head

by JOHN RUSSELL

The possessions of Christopher Alexander Pellett were these: his name, which he was always careful to retain intact; a suit of ducks, no longer intact, in which he lived and slept; a continuous thirst for liquor, and a set of red whiskers. Also he had a friend. Now no man can gain friendship, even among the gentle islands of Polynesia, except by virtue of some quality attaching to him. Strength, humor, villainy: he must show some trait by which the friend can catch and hold. How, then, explain the loving devotion lavished upon Christopher Alexander Pellett by Karaki, the company boat boy? This was the mystery at Fufuti.

There was no harm in Pellett. He never quarreled. He never raised his fist. Apparently he had never learned that a white man's foot, though it wabble ever so, is given him wherewith to kick natives out of the road. He never even cursed anyone except himself and the Chinese half-caste who sold him brandy: which was certainly allowable because the brandy was very bad.

On the other hand, there was no perceptible good in him. He had long lost the will to toil, and latterly even the skill to beg. He did not smile, nor dance, nor exhibit any of the amiable eccentricities that sometimes recommend the drunken to a certain toleration. In any other part of the world he must have passed without a struggle. But some chance had drifted him to the beaches where life is as easy as a song and his particular fate had given him a friend. And so he persisted. That was all. He persisted, a sodden lump of flesh preserved in alcohol. . . .

Karaki, his friend, was a heathen from Bougainville, where some people are smoked and others eaten. Being a black, a Melanesian, he was as much an alien in brown Fufuti as any white. He was a serious, efficient little man with deeply sunken eyes, a great mop of kinky hair, and a complete absence of expression. His tastes were simple. He wore a red cotton kerchief belted around his waist and a brass curtain ring suspended from his nose.

Some powerful chief in his home island had sold Karaki into the service of the trading company for three years, annexing his salary of tobacco and beads in advance. When the time should be accomplished, Karaki would be shipped back to Bougainville, a matter of some eight hundred miles, where he would land no richer than before except in experience. This was the custom. Karaki may have had plans of his own.

It is seldom that one of the black races of the Pacific shows any of the virtues for which subject populations are admired. Fidelity and humility can be exacted from other colors between tan and chocolate. But the black remains the inscrutable savage. His secret heart is his own. Hence the astonishment of Fufuti, which knew the ways of black recruits, when Karaki took the worthless beachcomber to his bosom.

"Hy, you, Johnny," called Moy Jack, the Chinese half-caste. "Better you come catch this fella mahster b'long you. He fella plenty too much drunk, galow."

Karaki left the shade of the copra shed where he had been waiting an hour or more and came forward to receive the sagging bulk that was thrust out-of-doors. He took it scientifically by wrist and armpit and swung toward the beach. Moy Jack stood on his threshold watching with cynic interest.

"Hy, you," he said; "what name you make so much bobeley 'long that fella mahster? S'pose you bling me all them fella pearl; me pay you one dam' fella good trade—my word!"

It annoyed Moy Jack that he had to provide the white man with a daily drunk in exchange for the little seed pearls with which Pellett was always flush. He knew where those pearls came from. Karaki did forbidden diving in the lagoon to get them. Moy Jack made a good thing of the traffic, but he could have made a much better thing by trading directly with Karaki for a few sticks of tobacco.

"What name you give that fella mahster all them fella pearl?" demanded Moy Jack offensively. "He plenty too much no good, galow. Close up he die altogether."

Karaki did not reply. He looked at Moy Jack once, and the half-caste trailed off into mutterings. For an instant there showed a strange light in Karaki's dull eyes, like the flat, green flicker of a turning shark glimpsed ten fathoms down. . . .

Karaki bore his charge down the beach to the little thatched shelter of pandanus leaves that was all his home. Tenderly he eased Pellett to a mat, pillowed his head, bathed him with cool water, brushed the filth from his hair and whiskers. Pellett's whiskers were true whiskers, the kind that sprout like the barbels of a catfish, and they were a glorious coppery, sun-gilt red. Karaki combed them out with a sandalwood comb. Later he sat by with a fan and kept the flies from the bloated face of the drunkard.

It was a little past midday when something brought him scurrying into the open. For weeks he had been studying every weather sign. He knew that the change was due when the southeast trade begins to harden through this flawed belt of calms and cross-winds. And now, as he watched, the sharp shadows began to blur along the sands and a film crept over the face of the sun.

All Fufuti was asleep. The house boys snored on the back veranda. Under his netting the agent dreamed happily of big copra shipments and bonuses. Moy Jack dozed among his bottles. Nobody would have been mad enough to stir abroad in the noon hour of repose: nobody but Karaki, the untamed black, who cared nothing for custom nor yet for dreams. The light pad of his steps was lost in the surf drone on the barrier reefs. He flitted to and fro like a wraith. And while Fufuti slept he applied himself to a job for which he had never been hired. . . .

Karaki had long ago ascertained two vital facts: where the key to the trade room was kept and where the rifles and ammunition were hidden. He opened the trade room and selected three bolts of turkey-red cloth, a few knives, two cases of tobacco, and a fine small ax. There was much else he might have taken as well. But Karaki was a man of simple tastes, and efficient.

With the ax he next forced the rifle chest and removed therefrom one Winchester and a big box of cartridges. With the ax again he broke into the boat sheds. Finally with the ax he smashed the bottoms out of the whaleboat and the two cutters so they would be of no use to anyone for many days to come. It was really a very handy little ax, a true tomahawk, ground to a shaving edge. Karaki took a workman's pleasure in its keen, deep strokes. It was almost his chief prize.

On the beach lay a big proa, a stout outrigger canoe of the kind Karaki's own people used at Bougainville, so high of prow and stern as to be nearly crescent shaped. The northwest monsoon of last season had washed it ashore at Fufuti and Karaki had repaired it, by the agent's own order. This proa he now launched in the lagoon, and aboard of it he stored his loot.

Of supplies he had to make a hasty selection. He took a bag of rice and another of sweet potatoes. He took as many coconuts as he could carry in a net in three trips. He took a cask of water and a box of biscuit. And here happened an odd thing.

In his search for the biscuit he came upon the agent's private store of liquor, a dozen bottles of rare Irish whisky. He glanced at them and passed them by. He knew what the stuff was, and he was a savage, a black man. But he passed it by. When Moy Jack heard of that later he remembered what he had seen in Karaki's eyes and ventured the surprising prediction that Karaki would never be taken alive.

When all was ready Karaki went back to his thatch and aroused Christopher Alexander Pellett.

"Hy, mahster, you come 'long me."

Mr. Pellett sat up and looked at him. That is to say, he looked. Whether he saw anything or not belongs among the obscurer questions of psychopathy.

"Too late," said Mr. Pellett profoundly. "This shop is closed. Copy boy! Give all those damned loafers good night. I'm—I'm goin'—bed!"

Whereupon he fell flat on his back.

"Wake up, mahster," insisted Karaki, shaking him. "You too much strong fella sleep. Hy-ah, mahster! Rum! You like'm rum? You catch'm rum any amount—my word! Plenty rum, mahster!"

But even this magic call, which never failed to rouse Pellett from his couch in the mornings, fell now on deaf ears. Pellett had had his skinful, and the fitness of things decreed that he should soak the clock around.

Karaki knelt beside him, pried him up until he could get a shoulder under his middle, and lifted him like a loose bag of meal. Pellett weighed one hundred and fifty pounds; Karaki not much more than a hundred. Yet in some deft coolie fashion of his own the little black man packed his burden, with the feet dragging behind, clear down to the beach. Moreover, he managed to get it aboard the proa. Pellett was half drowned and the proa half swamped. But Karaki managed.

No man saw their departure. Fufuti still dreamed on. Long before the agent awoke to wrath and ruin their queer crescent craft had slipped from the lagoon and faded away on the wings of the trade.

The first day Karaki had all he could do to keep the proa running straight before the wind. Big smoky seas came piling up out of the southeast and would have piled aboard if he had given them the least chance. He was only a heathen who did not know a compass from a degree of latitude. But his forefathers used to people these waters on cockleshell voyages that made the venture of Columbus look like a ride in a ferryboat. Karaki bailed with a tin pan and sailed with a mat and steered with a paddle: but he proceeded.

Along about sunrise Mr. Pellett stirred in the bilge and raised a pea-green face. He took one bewildered glance overside at the seething waste and collapsed with a groan. After a decent interval he tried again, but this was an illusion that would not pass, and he twisted around to Karaki sitting crouched and all aglisten with spray in the stern.

"Rum!" he demanded.

Karaki shook his head, and a haunted look crept into Pellett's eyes.

"Take—take away all that stuff," he begged pathetically, pointing at the ocean. . . .

Thereafter for two days he was very, very sick, and he learned how a small boat in any kind of a sea can move forty-seven different ways within one and the same minute. This was no trifling bit of knowledge, as those who have acquired it can tell. It was nearly fatal to Pellett.

On the third day he awoke with a mouth and a stomach of fumed leather and a great weakness, but otherwise in command of his few faculties. The gale had fallen and Karaki was quietly preparing fresh coconuts.

Pellett quaffed two before he thought to miss the brandy with which his breakfast draught was always laced. But when he remembered the milk choked in his throat.

"Me like'm rum."

"No got'm rum."

Pellett looked forward and aft, to windward and to lee. There was a great deal of horizon in sight, but nothing else. For the first time he was aware of a strangeness in events.

"What name you come so far?" he asked.

"We catch'm one big fella wind," explained Karaki.

Pellett was in no condition to question his statement nor to observe from the careful stocking of the proa that they had not been blown to sea on a casual fishing trip. Pellett had other things to think of. Some of the things were pink and others purple and others were striped like the rainbow in most surprising designs, and all were highly novel and interesting. They came thronging up out of the vasty deep to entertain Christopher Alexander Pellett. Which they did.

You cannot cut off alcohol from a man who has been continuously pickled for two years without results more or less picturesque. These were days when the proa went shouting across the empty southern seas to madrigal and choric song. Tied hand and foot and lashed under a thwart, Pellett raved in the numbers of his innocent youth. It would have been singular hearing had there been any to hear, but there was only Karaki, who did not care for the lesser Cavalier poets and on whom whole pages of "Atalanta in Calydon" were quite wasted. Now and then he threw a dipperful of sea water over the white man, or spread a mat to keep the sun from him, or fed him with coconut milk by force. Karaki was a poor audience, but an excellent nurse. Also, he combed Pellett's whiskers twice every day.

They ran into calms. But the trade picked them up again more gently, so that Karaki ventured to make westing, and they fled under skies as bright as polished brass.

> My heart is within me
>   As an ash in the fire;
> Whosoever hath seen me
>   Without lute, without lyre,
> Shall sing of me grievous things,
>   even things that were ill
>   to desire—

Thus chanted Christopher Alexander Pellett, whose face began to show a little more like flesh and a little less like rotten kelp. . . .

Whenever a fair chance offered, Karaki landed on the lee of some one of the tiny islets with which the Santa Cruz region is peppered, and would make shift to cook rice and potatoes in the tin dipper. This was risky, for one day the islet proved to be inhabited. Two white men in a cutter came out to stop them. Karaki could not hide his resemblance to a runaway nigger, and he did not try to. But when the cutter approached within fifty yards he suddenly announced himself as a runaway nigger with a gun. He left the cutter sinking and one of the men dead.

"There's a bullet hole alongside me here," said Pellett from under the thwart. "You'd better plug it."

Karaki plugged it and released his passenger, who sat up and began stretching himself with a certain naïve curiosity of his own body.

"So you're real," observed Pellett, staring hard at Karaki. "By George, you *are,* and that's comfort."

He was right. Karaki was very real.

"What side you take'm this fella canoe?"

"Balbi," said Karaki, using the native word for Bougainville.

Pellett whistled. An eight-hundred-mile evasion in an open boat was a considerable undertaking. It enlisted his respect. Moreover, he had just had emphatic proof of the efficiency of this little black man.

"Balbi all some home b'long you?"

"Yes."

"All right, commodore," said Pellett. "Lead on. I don't know why you shipped me for supercargo, but I'll see you through."

Strangely—or perhaps not so strangely—the whole Fufuti interval of his history had been fading from his brain while the poison was ebbing from his tissues. The Christopher Alexander Pellett that emerged was one from earlier years: pretty much of a wreck, it was true, and a feckless, indolent, paltry creature at best, but ordinarily human and rather more than ordinarily intelligent.

He was very feeble at first, but Karaki's diet of coco-nuts and sweet potatoes did wonders for him, and the time came when he could rejoice in the good salt taste of the spray on his lips and forget for hours together the crazy craving for stimulant. They made a strange crew, this pair—simple savage and convalescent drunk-ard—but there was never any question as to which was in command. That was well seen in the third week when their food began to fail and Pellett noticed that Karaki ate nothing for a whole day.

"See here, this won't do," he cried. "You've given me the last coconut and kept none for yourself."

"Me no like'm eat," said Karaki shortly.

Christopher Alexander Pellett pondered many mat-ters in long, idle hours while the rush of foam under the proa and the creak and fling of her outriggers were the only sounds between sea and sky. Sometimes his brow was knotted with pain. It is not always pleasant to be wrenched back into level contact with one's mem-ories. Thoughts are no sweeter company for having long been drowned. He had met the horrors of delir-ium. He had now to face the livelier devils of his past. He had fled them before.

But here was no escape of any kind. So he turned and grappled with them and laid them one by one.

When they had been at sea twenty-nine days they had nothing left of their provisions but a little water. Karaki doled it out by moistening a shred of coconut husk and giving Pellett the shred to suck. In spite of Pellett's petulant protest, he would take none himself. Again the heathen nursed the derelict, this time through the last stages of thirst, scraping the staves of the cask and feeding him the ultimate drop of moisture on the point of a knife.

On the thirty-sixth day from Fufuti they sighted Choiseul, a great green wall that built up slowly across the west.

Once fairly under its headlands, Karaki might have indulged a certain triumph. He had taken as his target the whole length of the Solomons, some six hundred miles. But to have fetched the broadside of them anywhere in such a craft as the proa through storm and current, without instrument or chart, was distinctly a feat of navigation. Karaki, however, did no celebrating. Instead, he stared long and anxiously over his shoulder into the east.

The wind had been fitful since morning. By noon it was dead calm on a restless, oily sea. A barometer would have told evil tales, but Karaki must have guessed them anyway, for he staggered forward and unstepped the little mast. Then he bound all his cargo securely under the thwarts and put all his remaining strength into the paddle, heading for a small outpost island where a line of white showed beach. They had been very lucky thus far, but they were still two miles offshore when the first rush of the hurricane caught them.

Karaki himself was reduced to a rattle of bones in a dried skin, and Pellett could scarce lift a hand. But Karaki fought for Pellett among the waves that leaped up like sheets of fire on the reef. Why or how they got through neither could have said. Perhaps because it was written that after drink, illness, madness, and starvation the white man should be saved by the black man again and a last time from ravening waters. When they came ashore on the islet they were both nearly flayed, but they were alive, and Karaki still gripped Pellett's shirt. . . .

For a week they stayed while Pellett fattened on unlimited coconut and Karaki tinkered with the proa. It had landed in a waterlogged tangle, but Karaki's treasures were safe. He got his bearings from a passing native fisherman, and then he knew that *all* his treasures were safe. His home island lay across Bougainville Strait, the stretch of water just beyond.

"Balbi over there?" asked Pellett.

"Yes," said Karaki.

"And a mighty good thing too," cried Pellett heartily. "This is the limit of British authority, old boy. Big fella mahster b'long Beretani stop'm here, no can go that side."

Karaki was quite aware of it. If he feared one thing in the world, he feared the Fiji High Court and its Resident Commissioner for the Southern Solomons, who did sure justice upon all who transgressed in its jurisdiction. Once beyond the strait he might still be liable for the stolen goods and the broken contract. But never—this was the point—never could he be punished for anything he might choose to do over there in Bougainville.

So Karaki was content.

And so was Christopher Alexander Pellett. His body had been wrung and swept and scoured, and he had downed his devils. Sweet air and sunshine were on his lips and in his heart. His bones were sweet in him. As his vigor returned he swam the lagoon or helped Karaki at the proa. He would spend hours hugging the warm sand or rejoicing in the delicate tracery of some tiny seashell, singing softly to himself, while the ground-swell hushed along the beach, savoring life as he never had done.

"Oh, this is good—good!" he said.

Karaki puzzled him. Not that he vexed himself, for a smiling wonder at everything, almost childlike, filled him these days. But he thought of this taciturn savage, how he had capped thankless service with rarest sacrifice. And now that he could consider soberly, the why of it eluded him. Why? Affection? Friendship? It must be so, and he warmed toward the silent little man with the sunken eyes and the expressionless face from which he could never raise a wink.

"Hy, you, Karaki, what name you no laugh all same me? What? You too much fright 'long that fella stuff you steal? Forget it, you old black scamp. If they ever trouble you, I'll square them somehow. By George, I'll say I stole it myself!"

Karaki only grunted and sat down to clean his Winchester with a bit of rag and some drops of oil he had crushed from a dried coconut.

"No, that don't reach him either," murmured Pellett, baffled. "I'd like to know what's going on under that topknot of yours, old chap. You're like Kipling's cat, that walks by himself. God knows I'm not ungrateful. I wish I could show you—"

He sprang up.

"Karaki! He one big fella friend 'long you; savee? You one big fella friend 'long me; savee? We two dam' big fella friend, my word! . . . What?"

"Yes," said Karaki. No other response. He looked at Pellett and he looked away toward Bougainville. "Yes," he said, "my word," and went on cleaning his gun— the black islander, inscrutable, incomprehensible, an enigma always, and to the end.

The end came two days later at Bougainville.

Under a gorgeous dawn they came into a bay that opened before their prow as with jeweled arms of welcome. The land lay lapped in bright garments like a sleeper half awakened, all flushed and smiling, sensuous, intimate, thrilling with life, breathing warm scents—

These were some of the foolish phrases Pellett babbled to himself as he leaped ashore and ran up on a rocky point to see and to feel and to draw all the charm of the place to himself.

Meanwhile Karaki, that simple and efficient little man, was proceeding methodically about his own affairs. He landed his bolts of cloth, his tobacco, his knives, and the other loot. He landed his box of cartridges and his rifle and his fine tomahawk. The goods were somewhat damaged by sea water, but the weapons had been carefully cleaned and polished. . . .

Pellett was declaiming poetry aloud to the alluring solitude when he was aware of a gentle footfall and turned, surprised, to find Karaki standing just behind him with the rifle at his hip and the ax in his hand.

"Well," said Pellett cheerfully, "what d'you want, old chappie?"

"Me like," said Karaki, while there gleamed in his eyes the strange light that Moy Jack had glimpsed there, like the flicker of a turning shark; "me like'm too much one fella head b'long you!"

"What? Head! Whose—my head?"

"Yes," said Karaki simply.

That was the way of it. That was all the mystery. The savage had fallen enamored of the head of the beachcomber, and Christopher Alexander Pellett had been betrayed by his fatal red whiskers. In Karaki's country a white man's head, well smoked, is a thing to be desired above wealth, above lands and chiefship's fame, and the love of women. In all Karaki's country was no head like the head of Pellett. Therefore Karaki had served to win it with the patience and single faith of a Jacob. For this he had schemed and waited, committed theft and murder, expended sweat and cunning, starved and denied himself, nursed, watched, tended, fed, and saved his man that he might bring the head alive and on the hoof—so to speak—to the spot where he could remove it at leisure and enjoy the fruits of his labor in safety.

Pellett saw all this at a flash, understood it so far as any white could understand it: the whole elemental and stupendous simplicity of it. And standing there in his new strength and sanity under the fair promise of the morning, he gave a laugh that pealed across the waters and started the sea birds from their cliffs, the deep-throated laugh of a man who fathoms and accepts the last great jest.

For finally, by corrected list, the possessions of Christopher Alexander Pellett were these: his name still intact; the ruins of some rusty ducks; his precious red whiskers—and a soul which had been neatly recovered, renewed, refurbished, reanimated, and restored to him by his good friend Karaki.

> *Thou shouldst die as he dies,*
>   *For whom none sheddeth tears;*
> *Filling thine eyes*
>   *And fulfilling thine ears*
> *With the brilliance . . . the bloom*
>   *and the beauty . . .*

Thus chanted Christopher Alexander Pellett over the waters of the bay, and then whirled, throwing wide his arms.

"Shoot, damn you! It's cheap at the price!"

Love Comes to Miss Lucy

by Q. PATRICK

They sat around the breakfast table, their black coats
hanging sleevelessly from their shoulders in the Mexican tourist fashion. They looked exactly what they
were—three middle-aged ladies from the most respectable suburbs of Philadelphia.

"*Mas cafe,*" demanded Miss Ellen Yarnell from a
recalcitrant waitress. Miss Ellen had traveled before
and knew how to get service in foreign countries.

"And *mas* hot—*caliente,*" added Mrs. Vera True-
good who was the oldest of the three and found the
mornings in Mexico City chilly.

Miss Lucy Bram didn't say anything. She looked
at her watch to see if it was time for Mario to arrive.

The maid dumped a tin pot of lukewarm coffee on
the table.

"Don't you think, Lucy," put in Ellen, "that it would
be a good idea if we got Mario to come earlier in the
morning? He could take us out somewhere so we could
get a nice hot breakfast."

"Mario does quite enough for us already." Miss
Lucy flushed slightly as she spoke of the young Mexi-

can guide. She flushed because her friends had teased her about him, and because she had just been thinking of his strong, rather cruel Mexican legs as she had seen them yesterday when he rowed them through the floating gardens of Xochimilco.

Miss Lucy Bram had probably never thought about a man's legs (and certainly not at breakfast time) in all her fifty-two years of polite, Quakerish spinsterhood. This was another disturbing indication of the change which had taken place in her since her cautious arrival in Mexico a month before. The change, perhaps, had in fact happened earlier, when the death of an ailing father had left her suddenly and bewilderingly rich, both in terms of bonds and a release from bondage. But Miss Lucy had only grown aware of it later, here in Mexico—on the day when she had found Mario in Taxco.

It had been an eventful day for Miss Lucy. Perhaps the most eventful of all these new Mexican days. Her sense of freedom, which still faintly shocked her sedate soul, had awakened with her in her sunny hotel bedroom. It had hovered over her patio breakfast with her two companions (whose expenses she was discreetly paying). It had been quenched neither by Vera's complaints of the chill mountain air nor by Ellen's travel-snobbish remark that Taxco was sweet, of course, but nowhere near as picturesque as the hill towns of Tuscany.

To Miss Lucy, with only Philadelphia and Bar Harbor behind her, Taxco's pink weathered roofs and pink, feathery-steepled churches was the impossible realization of a dream. "A rose-red city half as old as time. . . ."

The raffish delight of "foreignness," of being her own mistress, had reached a climax when she saw The Ring.

She saw it in one of the little silversmith shops below the leafy public square. It caught her attention while Vera and Ellen were haggling with the proprie-

tor over a burro pin. It wasn't a valuable ring. To her
Quaker eyes, severely trained against the ostentatious,
it was almost vulgar. A large, flamboyant white
sapphire on a slender band of silver. But there was
something tempting in its brash sparkle. She slipped
it on her finger and it flashed the sunlight back at her.
It made her mother's prim engagement ring, which
was worth certainly fifty times as much, fade out of the
picture. Miss Lucy felt unaccountably gay, and then
self-conscious. With a hurried glance at the stuffy
black backs of Vera and Ellen, she tried to take it off
her finger.

It would not come off. And while she was still struggling Vera and Ellen joined her, inspecting it with
little cries of admiration.

"My, Lucy, it's darling."

"Pretty as an engagement ring."

Miss Lucy flushed. "Don't be foolish. It's much too
young for me. I just tried it on. I don't seem to be
able . . ."

She pulled at the ring again. The Mexican who
owned the shop hovered at her side, purring compli-
ments.

"Go on, Lucy," said Ellen daringly. "Buy it."

"Really, it's annoying. But since I can't seem to get
it off, I suppose I'll have to. . . ."

Miss Lucy bought the white sapphire ring for a
sum which was higher than its value, but which was
still negligible to her. While Ellen who handled all
the financial aspects of the trip because she was "so
clever" at those things, settled with the proprietor,
Miss Lucy said to Vera, "I'll get it off with soap and
water back at the hotel."

But she didn't take it off. Somehow her new disturbing happiness had become centered in it.

In Taxco Miss Lucy's energy seemed boundless.
That evening, before dinner, while Vera and Ellen
were resting aching feet in their rooms, she decided
upon a second trip to the Church of Santa Prisca

which dominated the public square. Her first visit had been marred by the guidebook chatter of her companions. She wanted to be alone in that cool, tenebrous interior, to try to get the feeling of its atmosphere, so different from the homespun godliness of her own Quaker meeting-house at home.

As she stepped through the ornate wooden doors, the fantastic Churrigueresque altar of gold-leaf flowers and cherubs gleamed richly at her. An ancient peasant woman, sheathed in black, was offering a guttering candle to an image of the Virgin. A mongrel dog ran past her into the church, looked around and ran out again. The splendor and the small humanities of the scene had a curious effect upon Miss Lucy. This stood for all that was "popish" and alien and yet it seemed to call her. On an impulse which she less than half understood, she dropped to her knees, in imitation of the peasant woman, and crossed herself, the sapphire ring flashing with some of the exotic quality of the church itself.

Miss Lucy remained kneeling only a short time, but before she rose she was conscious of a presence close to her on the right. She glanced around and saw that a Mexican youth in a spotless white suit had entered the church and was kneeling a few yards away, the thick black hair shining on his reverently bent head. As she got up, his gaze met hers. It was only a momentary glance, but she retained a vivid impression of his face. Honey-brown skin and the eyes—particularly the eyes—dark and patient with a gentle, passive beauty. Somehow that brief contact gave her the sensation of seeing a little into the mind of this strange city of strange people. Remembering him, her spontaneous genuflection seemed somehow the right thing to have done. Not, of course, that she would ever speak of it to Vera and Ellen.

She left the church, happy and ready for dinner. The evening light had faded, and as she passed from the crowded Xocalo into the deserted street which led to the hotel, it was almost night. Her footsteps echoed unfamiliarly against the rough cobblestones. The sound seemed to emphasize her loneliness. A single male figure, staggering slightly, was coming up the hill now toward her. Miss Lucy was no coward, but with a tingle of alarm she realized that the on-comer was drunk. She looked around. There was no one else in sight. A weak impulse urged her to return to the Xocalo, but she suppressed it. After all, she was an American, she would not be harmed. She marched steadfastly on.

But the seeds of fear were there, and when she came abreast of the man, he peered at her and swung toward her. He was bearded and shabby and his breath reeked of tequila. He started a stream of Spanish which she couldn't understand. She knew he was begging and, trained to organized charities, Miss Lucy had no sympathy for street beggars. She shook her head firmly and tried to move on. But a dirty hand grabbed her sleeve, and the soft whining words continued. She freed her arm more violently than she intended. Anger glinted in the man's eyes. He raised his arm in an indignant gesture.

Although he was obviously not intending to strike her, Miss Lucy recoiled instinctively and as she did so, caught her high heel in the uneven cobbles and fell rather ungracefully on the ground. She lay there, her ankle twisted underneath her while the man stood threateningly, it seemed, over her.

For a moment, Miss Lucy felt panic—blind over-whelming terror completely unjustified by the almost farcical unpleasantness of the situation.

And then from the shadows, another man appeared. A slight man in a white suit. Miss Lucy could not see his face but she knew that it was the boy from the church. She was conscious of his white-sleeved arm flashing toward the beggar and pushing him away.

She saw the beggar reel backward and shuffle mut-teringly off. Then she was aware of a young face close to her own, and a strong arm was helping her to rise. She could not understand all her rescuer said, but his voice was gentle and concerned.

"*Qué malo*," he said, grinning in the direction of the departing beggar. "*Malo Mexicano.*" The teeth gleamed white in the moonlight. "Me Mario, from the church, yes? Me help the señora, no?"

He almost carried Miss Lucy, who had twisted her ankle painfully, back to the hotel and right into her room where she was turned over to the flustered administrations of Vera and Ellen.

As Mario hovered solicitously around, Ellen grabbed at her pocketbook with a whispered: "How much, Lucy?"

But here Miss Lucy showed a will of her own. "No. Money would be an insult."

And Mario, who seemed to understand, said "*Gracias, Señora.*" And after several sentences, in which Miss Lucy understood only the word "*madre,*" he picked up Miss Lucy's left hand—the one with the new sapphire ring—kissed it and then bowed himself smilingly out.

That was how Mario had come into their lives. And having come in, it was apparent that he intended to stay. Next morning he came to the hotel to inquire for Miss Lucy and she saw him squarely for the first time. He was not really handsome. His long-lashed eyes were perhaps a shade too close together. His slight mustache above the full-lipped mouth was perhaps too long. But his figure, though slight, was powerful, and there was something about him that inspired both affection and confidence.

He was, he explained, a student anxious to make a little money on vacation. He wanted to be a guide to the Señoras, and since Miss Lucy could not walk with her twisted ankle, he suggested that he hire a car and act as their chauffeur. The fee he requested was astonishingly small and he stubbornly refused to accept more.

The next day he hired a car at a low price which more than satisfied even the parsimonious Miss Ellen and from then on he drove the ladies around to points of interest with as much care and consideration as if they had been his three *"madres."*

His daily appearances, always in spotless white, were a constant delight to Miss Lucy—indeed, to all three of them. He was full of plans for their entertainment. One day he drove them around the base of Mount Popocatepetl and for several hours they were able to rhapsodize over what is certainly one of the most beautiful and mysterious mountains in the world. And for a moment when they happened to be alone together, staring at the dazzling whiteness of the mountain's magnificent summit, Miss Lucy felt her hand taken in Mario's firm brown one and softly squeezed.

It was, of course, his way of telling her, despite the difficulties of language, that they were sharing a great Mexican experience and he was glad they were sharing it together. Under his touch the large sapphire in the ring pressed into her finger painfully, but another feeling, different from pain, stirred in her.

After the Popocatepetl trip, Miss Lucy decided that it was time to leave Taxco and take up their quarters in Mexico City.

She instructed Ellen to dismiss Mario—to give him an extra hundred pesos and to let him know politely yet firmly that his services were terminated. But Ellen might as well have tried to dispel Popocatepetl or bid it remove itself into the sea. Mario just laughed at her, waved away the hundred pesos, and referred himself directly to Miss Lucy. There were bad Mexicans in Mexico City. He threw out his strong, honey-gold hands. He would take care of them. No, of no importance was the money of Señora Ellen (the other two women were always Señora to him, Miss Lucy alone was Señorita). The important thing was that he should show them everything. Here ·the strong arms waved to embrace the sun, the sky, the mountains, all of

Mexico. And the dark eyes with the too thick lashes embraced Miss Lucy too.

And Miss Lucy, against some deeply rooted instinct, yielded.

Mario went with them to Mexico City.

It was the second week of their stay in Mexico City and they had decided upon a trip to the pyramids at Teotihuacan. As usual Miss Lucy sat in front with Mario. He was an excellent driver and she loved to watch his profile as he concentrated on the road; loved his occasional murmurs to himself when something pleased or displeased him. She liked it less when he turned to her, flashing his dark eyes caressingly on her face and lowering them to her breast.

His gaze embarrassed her and today something prompted her to say to him in English, "Mario, you are what in America we call a flirt. I imagine you are very popular with the girls here in Mexico."

For a moment he did not seem to understand her remark. Then he burst out, "Girls—*muchachas. Para me, no.*" His hand went into his breast pocket and he brought out a small battered photograph. *"Mi muchacha.* My girl, *mi unica muchacha . . . Una sola . . ."*

Miss Lucy took the photograph. It was of a woman older than herself with gray hair and large sad eyes. There were lines of worry and illness in her face.

"Your mother?" said Miss Lucy gently. "Tell me about her."

Mario rattled on, not in the slow careful Spanish which he generally reserved for the ladies, but in a rapid monologue of which Miss Lucy understood but part. She gathered that Mario's mother was terribly poor, that she had devoted her life in a tiny Guerreros village to raising fatherless children, and was a saint on earth. It was obvious that Mario felt the almost idolatrous love for his mother that is so frequent in young Mexican males.

While he talked excitedly, Miss Lucy reached a decision. Somehow, before her vacation was over, she'd get from Mario his mother's address and she'd write and send her money, enough money to finance Mario at college. A mother surely would accept it even though her son might be too proud to yield to persuasion.

"Is that one of the pyramids?" It was Ellen's disappointed voice that broke the chain of Miss Lucy's thought. "Why, it's nothing compared to the pyramids in Egypt!"

Miss Lucy was thrilled, however, by the Pyramids of the Sun and the Moon. And as she gazed at their somber, ancient magnificence, she felt that strange inner elation which she had felt on the morning when she had genuflected and crossed herself in the church at Taxco.

"I'm not going to climb up all those crumbly steps," said Ellen peevishly. "I'm too old and it's too hot."

And Vera, though never too hot, was far too old. She stood at the foot of the pyramid, her coat hanging sleevelessly over her shoulders, the inevitable cigarette held in her clawlike hand. "You go, Lucy—you're young and active."

Lucy went.

With Mario's help she climbed to the very top of the Pyramid of the Sun and she was hardly out of breath when she reached the summit, so great was her sense of mystic exaltation.

They sat alone and close together on the summit, this cultivated woman past fifty with a degree from Bryn Mawr, and this almost ignorant boy from an adobe hut in the hinterland of Guerreros. They looked over the vast design of the square where the ancient village had been with its Temple of Quetzalcoatl of the Plumed Serpents, gazing down at the Road of the Dead which led from the Temple to the Pyramid of the Moon.

Mario started to tell her of the sacrificial rites of the feast of Toxcatl which, in ancient days, took place once a year.

As he talked, Miss Lucy half-closed her eyes and visualized the scene: the assembled public hushed in the huge square beneath them; the priests, each in his appointed place on the steps of the pyramid; the spotless youth who was, of course, Mario.

And because it was Mario who was being sacrificed in her mind, sacrificed to the futility of life and beauty, she felt a warm human pity for him and instinctively her hand went out—the hand with the cheap sapphire ring that would not come off—and it found his, and was held fast in his warm brown fingers.

Miss Lucy was hardly aware of it when Mario's arm slipped round her, and his dark head dropped against her breast. It was not until she became conscious of a smell like warm brown sugar, which was his skin, and a smell of flowery oil which he used on his hair, that all Philadelphia came rushing back. She jumped up hastily—jumping out of the centuries to this practical moment when two friends would be waiting at the base of the pyramid, hungry for lunch—and there were a great many steps to descend.

On the way home Miss Lucy decided that she and Vera would take the back seat, so Ellen sat in front and argued with the sulky Mario.

When they reached the pension, Miss Lucy said quickly, "It's a Sunday tomorrow, Mario. You'd better take a holiday."

He began to protest. When Lucy repeated, "No, not tomorrow, Mario," his face fell like a disappointed child's. Then his expression changed, and his dark eyes looked squarely, challengingly into hers.

As she turned into the house, Miss Lucy felt her heart pounding. The intimacy of that glance had brought into the open the thing which she had not dared to contemplate before. She was quite certain of it now.

Somehow—for some reason that she did not understand and in some way that her simple mind had never dreamed of—Mario desired her.

He desired her physically.

That night, before she went to bed, Miss Lucy did something she had never done in her life before. She stood in her plain cotton nightgown for several minutes before the long Venetian mirror in the sumptuous room and took stock of herself as a woman.

She saw nothing new or startling—nothing external to balance the startling changes which were going on inside her. Her face was not beautiful. It never had been, even in youth, and now it was uncompromisingly middle-aged. Her hair was almost white but not white enough. It was soft and plentiful and sat rather prettily on her forehead. Her eyes were clear and pleasing in themselves, but surrounded by the lines and shadows natural to her age. Her breasts were firm beneath the cotton nightgown but her figure was in no way remarkable. In fact, there was nothing externally desirable either about her face or her body. And yet she was desired. She knew it. For some reason a handsome Mexican youth found her desirable.

Miss Lucy was sure of that.

There was no nonsense about Miss Lucy and she knew that young men often make up to rich older women in the hopes of eventually obtaining money from them. But Mario, apart from the fact that he'd refused all financial offers, did not even know that Miss Lucy was by far the richest of the three ladies. Only a Philadelphia lawyer or a member of their old Quaker family could possibly know how rich Miss Lucy really was. No, if Mario had wanted money, he would have concentrated on Ellen who held the purse strings and never for a moment let it be known to anyone that it was Miss Lucy's money she was dispensing.

There was nothing about Miss Lucy, drab, black-clad Miss Lucy, to suggest wealth. True, her mother's engagement ring had a rather valuable diamond in it.

But only an expert jeweler would recognize that. As for the flashy white sapphire ring, that wasn't worth anyone's time or energy and Miss Lucy would have gladly given it to Mario out of gratitude if only she could have got it off her finger.

No, there were thousands of other women in Mexico City with far more obvious signs of wealth. There were young, beautiful women and any one of them might have been pleased and proud to have Mario as an escort and—yes, Miss Lucy faced it uncompromisingly—as something else.

And yet . . . suddenly Miss Lucy became frightened at the illogicality of it all.

Some virginal instinct stirred in her and warned her of—danger.

And because there was no nonsense about Miss Lucy, she decided that she must do something final about it. Lying there quietly beneath the sheets, she came to her great resolution.

Miss Lucy and Vera were waiting at the bus station. Both of them hugged their coats around them as if cold. Vera was always cold, of course. But today Miss Lucy was cold, too, despite the splendid warmth of the spring sunshine. Her eyes—and her nose—were red.

They were waiting for Ellen who had been left behind to deliver the final *coup de grâce* to Mario. The bus for Patzcuaro was leaving in twenty minutes.

At last Ellen appeared. Her nose was red too.

"You shouldn't have done it, Lucy," she snapped. "It was cruel." She thrust two one-hundred-peso bills into Lucy's hands. "I thought he was going to hit me when I gave him these." She sniffed. "And he burst into tears like a child when he read your letter."

Miss Lucy did not speak. In fact, she spoke very little during the entire length of the tiring bus journey to Patzcuaro.

The three women had been sitting since dinner around their table on the veranda overlooking the se-

rene expanse of Lake Patzcuaro. Ellen, restlessly vol-
uble, was discussing possible plans for the next day.
Miss Lucy was, apparently, paying no attention. Her
eyes studied the evening gray-green waters of the lake
with its clustering islands and its obscene bald-headed
vultures that squawked and fought greedily over scraps
of carrion on the lake shore.

After a short time she rose, saying, "It's getting a
bit cold. I think I'll go up to my room. Good night."

Miss Lucy's room, with its small veranda, com-
manded a view of the lake from another angle. Below
her, in the growing darkness, the fishermen were pottering with their boats, talking in low, sibilant voices
or singing snatches of Michoacan songs.

Miss Lucy sat watching them. She was thinking of
Mario, missing him with an intensity that was almost
painful. She had thought of him constantly since she
left Mexico City and now was appalled at her harsh-
ness in dismissing him by proxy through Ellen. She
should have spoken to him herself. She would hate
to have him think . . . The thoughts went on with a
goading persistence. She had done him a wrong, hurt
him. . . .

At some indeterminate stage of her reverie she became conscious of a white-clad figure moving among
the fishermen below. Miss Lucy's gaze rested on him
and then her heart turned over. She strained forward
and peered into the darkness. Surely, surely, there was
something familiar about those light, graceful movements—that small, compact form.

But it couldn't be Mario! She had left him hundreds
of miles away in Mexico City, and Ellen had been particularly instructed not to tell him where they were
going.

The figure in white moved away from the lake shore
toward her window. He passed through a shaft of light
from an open door. There was no doubt about it now.
It was Mario.

She bent over the balcony, her heart fluttering like a foolish bird. He was only about fifteen feet below her.

"Oh, Miss Lucy, I have found you." He spoke in the slow careful Spanish which he reserved for her. "I knew I would find you."

"But, Mario, how . . . ?"

"The bus company told me you had come here. I got a ride and I have been waiting."

She saw his teeth gleaming as he smiled at her. "Miss Lucy, why did you go away without saying *adios?*"

She did not answer.

"But I am back now to take care of you. And tomorrow you and I—we will go on the lake. Before the other two ladies are up. You and I alone together. There will be a moon and then the sunrise."

"Yes . . ."

"At five o'clock in the morning I come. I will have a boat. Before even the birds awake I will be waiting here."

"Yes, yes . . ."

"Good night, *carissima.*"

Miss Lucy went back into her room. Her hands were trembling as she undid her dress and slipped into bed.

And she was still trembling when—in the middle of the night, it seemed—a low whistle beneath her window told her that Mario had come for her.

She dressed swiftly, patted her soft gray hair into place, threw a coat over her shoulders and hurried downstairs. The hotel was very quiet. No one saw her as she made her way through the deserted lobby and no one saw her as she went down the slope to where Mario was waiting for her with the boat.

He took her hand and pressed it to his lips. Then he drew her gently toward the boat.

She did not resist. It was as though he were Destiny leading her onward toward the inevitable.

Mario had been right. There was a moon—full and lemon-white, it shed a weird light on the opaque waters of the lake.

Miss Lucy was in the bottom of the boat, lying on her coat. It was cold, but she did not seem to notice it. She was watching Mario as he stood up in the boat, guiding it skillfully past the other craft into the deep waters of the lake. He had rolled his trousers up beyond his knees and his legs looked strong and somehow cruel in the moonlight. He was singing.

Miss Lucy had not realized before what a beautiful voice he had. The song seemed sweet and ineffably sad. Mario's eyes caressed her as his gaze traveled downward from her face and rested on her hands which lay impassive on her lap. The cheap sapphire sparkled in the moonlight.

Miss Lucy was not conscious of time or place as the boat moved slowly toward the secret heart of the lake with its myriad islets. She was not conscious of the dimming stars and the moon paling before the dawn. She felt only a deep, utter tranquillity, as though this gentle almost imperceptible motion must go on forever. She started at the sound of Mario's voice.

"Listen, the birds."

She heard them in the cluster of small islands that were all around her, but she could see only the vultures that hovered silently overhead.

Mario rested from his rowing and produced a parcel. It contained *tortas,* butter, and goat cheese. He also brought out a bottle of red Mexican wine.

He spread butter on a *torta* with his large clasp knife and handed it to Miss Lucy. Suddenly she realized that she was very hungry. She ate wolfishly and drank from the bottle of the sweet Mexican wine. It went to her head and made her feel girlish and happy. She laughed at everything Mario said and he laughed too while his eyes still caressed her.

And so they breakfasted like honeymoon lovers, as

a sunrise splashed red gold over the lake, miles away now from anyone, with only the visible vultures and the invisible songsters to witness them.

When the last *torta* was eaten and the bottle drained, Mario took up his paddle again and propelled the boat deeper into the heart of the lake, on and on without speaking.

As soon as she saw the island, Miss Lucy knew it was the one Mario had chosen. It looked more solitary, more aloof than the rest of them, and there was a fringe of high reeds around its edges.

He steered the boat carefully through the reeds which were so tall that they were completely hidden in a little world of their own. When they reached the shore, he took her hand and raised her gently with the one word, "Come."

She followed him like a child. He found a dry spot and spread out her coat for her. Then, as she lay down, he sat with her head in his lap. She could see his face above hers very close; could see those dark eyes set a little too close together; could feel the warm breath, wine-scented, that came from his lips.

She closed her eyes knowing that this was the moment to which everything had been leading—ever since the day in the church of Santa Prisca when she had first met Mario. She could feel his hands caressing her hair, her face, gently, gently. She felt him take her hand, felt him touch the sapphire ring.

The moment he touched the ring, she knew. She could feel it in his fingers, an outflowing, obsessive desire. The whole pattern which had seemed so complex was plain.

His hands moved upward. His fingers, still gentle, reached her throat. She didn't scream. She wasn't even frightened.

As his hands tightened their grasp, the full mouth came down upon hers, and their lips met in their first and only kiss.

Mario threw the bloodstained knife away. He hated the sight of blood and it had disgusted him that he had .had to cut off a finger to get the ring.

He hadn't even bothered about the engagement ring that had belonged to Miss Lucy's mother. It was a plain, cheap affair, and for weeks now the great beauty of the sapphire had blinded him to anything else.

He spread the coat carefully over Miss Lucy's body. For a moment he considered putting it in the reeds, but it might float away and be discovered by the fishermen.

Here, on the island, it could be years before anyone came, and by that time—he glanced up at the vultures hovering eternally overhead. . . .

Without looking back Mario went to the boat and rowed toward the deserted mainland shore. There he landed, overturned the boat, and pushed it free so that it would drift into deep water.

An American woman had gone out in a boat on the lake with an inexperienced boatman. They had both been drowned. The officials would never drag so big a lake to find the bodies.

Mario made his way in the direction of the railroad track. He could board a freight car and tomorrow perhaps he would be in Guerreros.

He was sure his mother would like the ring.

Sredni Vashtar

by "SAKI" (H. H. MUNRO)

Conradin was ten years old, and the doctor had pronounced his professional opinion that the boy would
not live another five years. The doctor was silky and
effete, and counted for little, but his opinion was en-
dorsed by Mrs. de Ropp, who counted for nearly everything. Mrs. de Ropp was Conradin's cousin and guardian, and in his eyes she represented those three-fifths
of the world that are necessary and disagreeable and
real; the other two-fifths, in perpetual antagonism to
the foregoing, were summed up in himself and his
imagination. One of these days Conradin supposed he
would succumb to the mastering pressure of wearisome
necessary things—such as illnesses and coddling re-
strictions and drawn-out dullness. Without his imagination, which was rampant under the spur of loneliness, he would have succumbed long ago.

Mrs. de Ropp would never, in her honestest moments, have confessed to herself that she disliked Conradin, though she might have been dimly aware that
thwarting him "for his good" was a duty which she

did not find particularly irksome. Conradin hated her with a desperate sincerity which he was perfectly able to mask. Such few pleasures as he could contrive for himself gained an added relish from the likelihood that they would be displeasing to his guardian, and from the realm of his imagination she was locked out— an unclean thing, which should find no entrance.

In the dull, cheerless garden, overlooked by so many windows that were ready to open with a message not to do this or that, or a reminder that medicines were due, he found little attraction. The few fruit trees that it contained were set jealously apart from his plucking, as though they were rare specimens of their kind blooming in an arid waste; it would probably have been difficult to find a market-gardener who would have offered ten shillings for their entire yearly produce. In a forgotten corner, however, almost hidden behind a dismal shrubbery, was a disused toolshed of respectable proportions, and within its walls Conradin found a haven, something that took on the varying aspects of a playroom and a cathedral. He had peopled it with a legion of familiar phantoms, evoked partly from fragments of history and partly from his own brain, but it also boasted two inmates of flesh and blood. In one corner lived a ragged-plumaged Houdan hen, on which the boy lavished an affection that had scarcely another outlet. Further back in the gloom stood a large hutch, divided into two compartments, one of which was fronted with close iron bars. This was the abode of a large polecat-ferret, which a friendly butcherboy had once smuggled, cage and all, into its present quarters, in exchange for a long-secreted hoard of small silver. Conradin was dreadfully afraid of the lithe, sharp-fanged beast, but it was his most treasured possession. Its very presence in the toolshed was a secret and fearful joy, to be kept scrupulously from the knowledge of the Woman, as he privately dubbed his cousin. And one day, out of Heaven knows what material, he spun the beast a wonderful name, and

from that moment it grew into a god and a religion.
The Woman indulged in religion once a week at a
church nearby, and took Conradin with her, but to
him the church service was an alien rite in the House
of Rimmon. Every Thursday, in the dim and musty
silence of the toolshed, he worshiped with mystic and
elaborate ceremonial before the wooden hutch where
dwelt Sredni Vashtar, the great ferret. Red flowers in
their season and scarlet berries in the wintertime were
offered at his shrine, for he was a god who laid some
special stress on the fierce impatient side of things, as
opposed to the Woman's religion, which, as far as
Conradin could observe, went to great lengths in the
contrary direction. And on great festivals powdered
nutmeg was strewn in front of his hutch, an important
feature of the offering being that the nutmeg had to
be stolen. These festivals were of irregular occurrence,
and were chiefly appointed to celebrate some passing
event. On one occasion, when Mrs. de Ropp suffered
from acute toothache for three days, Conradin kept
up the festival during the entire three days, and almost
succeeded in persuading himself that Sredni Vashtar
was personally responsible for the toothache. If the
malady had lasted for another day the supply of nutmeg would have given out.

The Houdan hen was never drawn into the cult of
Sredni Vashtar. Conradin had long ago settled that
she was an Anabaptist. He did not pretend to have
the remotest knowledge as to what an Anabaptist was,
but he privately hoped that it was dashing and not very
respectable. Mrs. de Ropp was the ground plan on
which he based and detested all respectability.

After a while Conradin's absorption in the toolshed
began to attract the notice of his guardian. "It is not
good for him to be pottering down there in all weath-
ers," she promptly decided, and at breakfast one morning she announced that the Houdon hen had been sold
and taken away overnight. With her shortsighted
eyes she peered at Conradin, waiting for an outbreak

of rage and sorrow, which she was ready to rebuke with a flow of excellent precepts and reasoning. But Conradin said nothing: there was nothing to be said. Something perhaps in his white set face gave her a momentary qualm, for at tea that afternoon there was toast on the table, a delicacy which she usually banned on the ground that it was bad for him; also because the making of it "gave trouble," a deadly offense in the middle-class feminine eye.

"I thought you liked toast," she exclaimed, with an injured air, observing that he did not touch it.

"Sometimes," said Conradin.

In the shed that evening there was an innovation in the worship of the hutch-god. Conradin had been wont to chant his praises, tonight he asked a boon.

"Do one thing for me, Sredni Vashtar."

The thing was not specified. As Sredni Vashtar was a god he must be supposed to know. And choking back a sob as he looked at that other empty corner, Conradin went back to the world he so hated.

And every night, in the welcome darkness of his bedroom, and every evening in the dusk of the tool-shed, Conradin's bitter litany went up: "Do one thing for me, Sredni Vashtar."

Mrs. de Ropp noticed that the visits to the shed did not cease, and one day she made a further journey of inspection.

"What are you keeping in that locked hutch?" she asked. "I believe it's guinea pigs. I'll have them all cleared away."

Conradin shut his lips tight, but the Woman ransacked his bedroom till she found the carefully hidden key, and forthwith marched down to the shed to complete her discovery. It was a cold afternoon, and Conradin had been bidden to keep to the house. From the furthest window of the dining room the door of the shed could just be seen beyond the corner of the shrubbery, and there Conradin stationed himself. He saw the Woman enter, and then he imagined her opening the door of the sacred hutch and peering down with her shortsighted eyes into the thick straw bed where his god lay hidden. Perhaps she would prod at the straw in her clumsy impatience. And Conradin fervently breathed his prayer for the last time. But he knew as he prayed that he did not believe. He knew that the Woman would come out presently with that pursed smile he loathed so well on her face, and that in an hour or two the gardener would carry away his wonderful god, a god no longer, but a simple brown ferret in a hutch. And he knew that the Woman would triumph always as she triumphed now, and that he would grow ever more sickly under her pestering and domineering and superior wisdom, till one day nothing would matter much more with him, and the doctor would be proved right. And in the sting and misery of his defeat, he began to chant loudly and defiantly the hymn of his threatened idol:

Sredni Vashtar went forth,
His thoughts were red thoughts and his teeth were
*   white.*
His enemies called for peace, but he brought them
*   death.*
Sredni Vashtar the Beautiful.

And then of a sudden he stopped his chanting and drew closer to the windowpane. The door of the shed still stood ajar as it had been left, and the minutes were slipping by. They were long minutes, but they slipped by nevertheless. He watched the starlings running and flying in little parties across the lawn; he counted them over and over again, with one eye always on that swinging door. A sour-faced maid came in to lay the table for tea, and still Conradin stood and waited and watched. Hope had crept by inches into his heart, and now a look of triumph began to blaze in his eyes that had only known the wistful patience of defeat. Under his breath, with a furtive exultation, he began once again the paean of victory and devastation. And presently his eyes were rewarded: out through that doorway came a long, low, yellow-and-brown beast, with eyes a-blink at the waning daylight, and dark wet stains around the fur of jaws and throat. Conradin dropped on his knees. The great polecat-ferret made its way down to a small brook at the foot of the garden, drank for a moment, then crossed a little plank bridge and was lost to sight in the bushes. Such was the passing of Sredni Vashtar.

"Tea is ready," said the sour-faced maid; "where is the mistress?"

"She went down to the shed some time ago," said Conradin.

And while the maid went to summon her mistress to tea, Conradin fished a toasting fork out of the sideboard drawer and proceeded to toast himself a piece of bread. And during the toasting of it and the buttering of it with much butter and the slow enjoyment of eating it, Conradin listened to the noises and silences which fell in quick spasms beyond the dining-room door. The loud foolish screaming of the maid, the answering chorus of wondering ejaculations from the kitchen region, the scuttering footsteps and hurried embassies for outside help, and then, after a lull, the sacred sobbings and the shuffling tread of those who bore a heavy burden into the house.

"Whoever will break it to the poor child? I couldn't for the life of me!" exclaimed a shrill voice. And while they debated the matter among themselves, Conradin made himself another piece of toast.

Love Lies Bleeding

by PHILIP MACDONALD

Cyprian didn't like rushing over dinner, so they had eaten early. And now, at eight o'clock, he was alone with coffee in Astrid's living room while Astrid herself was in the bedroom out of sight and sound, changing into some frock suitable for the rather tedious party they were going to together.

It was very quiet in Astrid's apartment, very comfortable. The maid had gone as soon as they had finished eating, so there weren't even sounds of movements from dining room and kitchen to disturb the peace. And there was plenty of time. Plenty. Because they needn't arrive at the Ballards' before nine-thirty at the earliest.

Cyprian stretched luxuriously. He picked his coffee cup from the mantel and drained it and set it down again, his fingers momentarily caressing the delicate texture of the thin china.

He strolled about the room, thinking how well Astrid had done with it, taking pleasure in the blendings and contrasts of color under the soft lights, the balance and position of furniture, the choice and subject of the few paintings.

He went back to the mantel, and took the fragile, thistle-shaped liqueur glass from beside his empty coffee cup. He couldn't remember what was in it, and sniffed at it, his thin sensitive nostrils quivering a little as the sharp, bitter-orange aroma stung them pleasantly. He smiled; he should have known that Astrid wouldn't make mistakes.

He sipped slowly, letting the hot stringency slide over his tongue. He turned his back to the room and faced himself in the big mirror over the mantel and was pleased by what he saw. He could find this evening nothing at variance with the appearance of Cyprian Morse as he wished it to be. With absorbed interest he studied Cyprian—the graceful, high-shouldered slenderness so well set off by the dinner jacket of midnight blue; the fine-textured pallor of the odd, high-cheekboned face with its heavy-lidded eyes and chiseled mouth which seemed to lift at one corner in satire perpetual but never overstressed; the long slim fingers of the hand which twitched with languid dexterity at the tie which so properly enhanced the silken snowy richness of the shirt and its collar.

The blue gleam of the carved lapis lazuli in his signet ring made him think of Charles, and the time when Charles had given it to him. He turned away from the mirror and sipped at the liqueur again and wished Charles were here and wondered how long it would be before Charles returned from Venezuela. He was looking forward to Charles and Astrid meeting, though he wasn't too sure what Charles's initial reaction would be. Astrid would be all right, of course— and, after all, Charles would very soon find out what she was like, just an awfully nice girl, and a great, an inspired designer. He toyed with visions of making Charles work too. With Astrid doing the sets, and Charles letting himself go on weird, macabre decor,

Cyprian Morse's *Abanazar* could well be the most sensational production ever seen in the theater.

Cyprian finished the liqueur, and set down the glass. Still musing on the possibilities of *Abanazar*, he dropped into a big low chair, and found himself—his eyes almost level with a coffee table—looking straight at a photograph of Astrid he hadn't seen before. It was an excellent portrait, oddly and interestingly lighted, and the camera had caught and registered that somehow astringent little smile which some people said spoiled her looks, but which had always been for Cyprian a sort of epitome of why he liked her. He went on looking at it now, and thought, as he had thought many times looking at her in life, how necessary a smile it was. Without it there would be no way of knowing that the full-blown and almost aggressive femininity of Astrid's structure was merely an accident in design; no way of telling that in fact she had no nonsense about her but was simply the best of designers and—he was beginning to believe more and more as their association developed—the best of friends.

He stretched again and relaxed in the chair. He was in the after-dinner mood which he liked best, and which only seemed to come when he had had exactly the right amount of a-little-too-much-to-drink. All his senses, all his perceptions, were sharpened to a fine edge beneath a placid sheath of contentment. There was a magazine lying on the table near the photograph, and he reached out a lazy arm and picked it up. It was last month's *Manhattan,* and it fell open in his hands to the theatrical page and the beginning of Burn Heyward's long glowing review of *The Square Triangle*. He knew it nearly by heart, but nevertheless began to read and savor it afresh, starting with the headline, *CYPRIAN MORSE DOES IT AGAIN,* and going through its delicious paeans to the shiny superplum of the very last paragraph, ". . . *There is no doubt left that, despite his youth and (in this instance at least) his dubious choice of subject, Morse is one of the really important playwrights of the day, certainly the most significant in America. . . ."*

He heard the door open behind him, and let the magazine fall shut on his knee and said, "Ready?" without turning around.

"Cyprian!" said Astrid's voice.

There was something strange about the sound, a quality which inexplicably, as if it had been some dreadful psychic emanation, seemed to change the shape of his every thought and sensation, so that where he had been relaxed and warmly content, he was now tense and chill with formless apprehension.

"Cyprian!" said the voice again, and he came to his feet in a single spasmodic movement, turning to face Astrid as he rose.

He stared at her in stunned amazement and a useless hope of disbelief. His flesh crept, and he seemed to feel the hairs on his neck rising like the hackles on a dog.

She came toward him, slowly—and he backed away. She mustn't touch him, she mustn't touch him.

She drew inexorably closer. She held out her arms to him. He didn't know he was still moving away until the edge of the mantelshelf came hard against his shoulders. He could feel sweat clammy cold on his forehead, his upper lip, his neck. Desperately, his mind struggled for mastery over his body. His mind knew that, in reality, this was merely a distressing incident hardly removed from the commonplace. His mind knew that a few simple words, a curl of the lip, a lift of the shoulders—any or all of these would free him not only now but forever. But the words had to be uttered, the gestures made—and his body refused the tasks.

She was close now. Very close. She was going to touch him.

She said, in the same thick voice, "Cyprian! Don't look at me like that." And she said, "I love you, Cyprian, you must know that . . ."

There was a ringing in his ears, and the tight grip of nausea in his stomach. His throat worked as he tried to speak, but no words came from his mouth.

She touched him. She was close against him. His body could feel the dreadful soft warmness of her. There was a mist over his eyes and he could hardly see her through it.

And then her arms were around his neck, soft but implacably strong. His mind screamed something, but the arms tightened their hold. She was speaking, but he couldn't hear through the roaring in his head. Somehow, he tore himself free. Forgetting, he tried to retreat, and thudded against the brick of the mantel. With a scrabbling lunge, he went sideways—and almost fell.

He clutched wildly. His left hand caught the edge of the mantelshelf and checked his fall. His right hand, swinging, struck against something metallic and closed around it.

"Cyprian—" said the voice. *"Cyprian!"*

She was going to touch him again. Through the haze he could see her, the arms reaching.

There was a clatter of metal as the rest of the fire-irons fell, and his right hand, still grasping the logpick it had closed around, raised itself above his head and swung downward, with more than all his force.

Through the rushing in his ears, through the red-flecked haze over his eyes, he heard the sick dull crushing of the first blow, saw the slender shape crumple and collapse. . . .

The haze and the roaring faded, and he found himself standing half-crouched over the thing on the floor—striking down at it again and again. It was as if some outside power had taken charge of him, so that the blows came without his conscious volition—thudding with the broadside of the heavy bar, then thrusting, slashing, tearing with the sharp point of the spike. . . .

Then, piercing the haze and thrusting him back into

knowledge of himself, there was a sharp pain in his shoulder as a muscle twisted and cramped.

The logpick fell from his hands, thudding onto the thick carpet. He looked down at what he had done—and then, an arm flung across his eyes, he turned and ran, stumbling and wavering, for the outer door of the apartment.

He smashed into it—scrabbled with shaking hands for the latch—tore it open—plunged out into the corridor—and, sightless, witless, came into heavy collision with a man and a woman just passing the door.

The woman lurched against the opposite wall. Cursing, the man snarled at Cyprian and caught him by the shoulder and straightened his slim bent body and thrust him back against the door jamb. The woman took one horrified look at Cyprian and screamed. The man stared and said, "What in the name of—"

Cyprian swayed. Everything—the figures facing him, the walls and doors, the lights overhead, the pattern of the corridor carpet—all swung crazily together before his eyes; swung and tilted so that he reeled, and clutched vainly for support—and slid down against the jamb to sit sprawled and ungainly on the floor, clutching at his whirling head.

The woman said, "Look at him. *Look* at him!" in a shaking voice. "That's *blood!*" And the man said heavily, "What goes on around here?"

Cyprian moaned—and began to vomit. Above him the man said, "I'm going to take a look in there," and moved through the open doorway.

The woman went after him, and there glowed in Cyprian's mind the first sudden and frightful awareness of his danger. Even as another spasm shook him, a tiny self-preservatory spark was born, and when the woman began to scream just inside the door, he was already mumbling to himself, " . . . *there was a man . . . he went through the window . . .*"

And then the beginning of the long nightmare.

The man and woman rushing out of the apartment.

Shouting. Doors opening. People. More screaming. Trying to get to his feet and failing. More men, one in shirt sleeves, another in a robe, standing over him like guards. Sirens wailing outside. Whistles. Noise. Voices. Elevator doors clanging and heavy feet tramping down the corridor. New voices, harsh and different. Men in uniform. The other faces going, the new faces staring down at him, looming behind the harsh voices. A hand as ruthless as God's pulling him to his feet. . . .

He wanted help. He craved succor. "*. . . there was a man . . . he went through the window . . .*"

He wanted a friend. He wanted Charles. Charles would know what to do. Charles would deal with these bullying louts.

"*. . . there was a man . . . he went through the window . . .*"

And Charles was thousands of miles away.

The nightmare went on. The questions. First in the room where men—not in uniform now—worked over the horror on the floor, muttering to each other, measuring, flashing lights, pointing cameras, scribbling in notebooks.

Then in another room, after a hellish, siren-screaming journey in a crowded car. Questions, questions. All framed with the certainty, the *knowledge,* that he had done what he must not admit having done.

Questions. And the white light aching in his eyes. His throat stiff and his lips unmanageable. His whole body shaking, shaking. The inside of his head shaking too.

—Why did you kill her?

—What time did you kill her?

—What did you kill her for? What had she done?

—How long after ya killed her before you run out?

—*I didn't. I didn't . . . there was a man . . . he went through the window . . .*

—All right—so there was a man. An' he went outa the window. Whaddud he do? Jump? Fly?

—You don't expect us to swallow that, do you?

—Yeah. How d'ya figure this sorta hooey's goin' to help?

—*I tell you there was a man . . . he went through the window . . . Down the fire escape . . .*

—He did? Leavin' your prints all over the poker?

—Yeah. An' splashin' her blood all over ya?

—Now, listen, Mr. Morse; it's completely certain that you killed this woman. The evidence is overwhelming. Can't you realize that you're doing yourself no good by your attitude?

—*I'm telling the truth. There was a man. I—I was in the bathroom. I heard a noise. I ran in. I saw Astrid. There was a man. He climbed out of the window. I'm telling the truth.*

—Very well. So you're telling the truth. Which window did this man go out?

—Yeah? And how come he locked it behind him?

—Never mind that, Mr. Morse. Answer the other question. Which window?

—*I—I don't know . . . The window in the—the end wall . . . Next the fire escape . . .*

—Which window? The right as you face? Or the left?

—Yeah. Which? One of 'em was locked, bud. Which? Questions. And the light. Questions all around him. Questions from faces. Coarse, brutal faces. Sharp fox-faces. They began to associate themselves with the voices.

And another face with wise gray eyes that watched him always. A face with no voice. A face in the corner. A face more to be feared than all the faces with voices.

Questions. And the light. Time standing still, immobilized. He had always been here. He would always be here. "*. . . there was a man . . . he went through the window . . .*"

It was a pattern, diabolic and infinite: Fear—questions—fear fear—light—fear fear fear—fatigue.

Fatigue. First a dull dead core of exhaustion, but now beginning to reach out all around itself, encroaching more and more on all other feeling.

Until even fear was going . . . going . . . almost gone—

—Why don't we wind this up, Morse?

—Yes. We know you killed her, and you know we know. Why not get it over with?

—Yeah. How's about it, fella? Why doncha come clean, so's we can let up on ya?

Fear flickering again, momentarily reborn.

—*I didn't I didn't I didn't . . . There was a man. When I ran in, he was climbing out of the window . . .*

For an instant a picture forming behind his eyes. An image of Charles—tall, tough, elegant, dangerous, one shoulder lifting higher than the other, a cigarette jutting from the corner of his long mouth, his creased face creasing more in a mastering smile. Charles coming through the door, being suddenly framed in the doorway, standing and looking down at the faces, the stupid crafty animal faces—

Then his eyes closing. His head falling forward. Then nothing. Except the hard scratched feeling of the table-top against his cheek. And a ghost smell of soap and pencils and agony.

A rough hand biting into his shoulder. Shaking. His head lolling, jerking back and forward like a marionette's—

Then a new voice, quiet, sharp, charged with authority.

—That's enough. Let him alone. Schraff, you go find Dr. Innes. This isn't any Bowery bum you're handling.

His head resting on the table again. The voices muttering all around him, not thrusting at him now.

Consciousness of someone standing over him. Not touching him. Just standing.

Opening his eyes. Forcing muscles to roll up the ton-weight lids. Seeing the wise gray eyes looking down at him, contemplating him, understanding everything.

Staring dully up into the gray eyes for a moment, dully wondering. Then letting the heavy lids fold down over his own eyes again.

The door opening, and brisk footsteps. And quick impersonal hands upon him. Doctor's hands. Feeling at his temples, his wrist. Tilting back his unbearably heavy head, with a deft thumb rolling back those eyelids.

Then muttering above his head. His coat being eased off, shirt sleeve rolled up.

Indefinite pause—and then the fingers on his arm, and the sting of the needle . . .

When he waked it was to grayness. A gray blanket over him; gray walls; a door of gray bars; gray light filtering through a small grilled window.

For some timeless interval the drug held memory in check. But at last, with a sick gray emptiness in his stomach, recollection came. And fear again, all the worse because its edges were dulled now and instead of it being so intense that there was no room in him for other emotions, it was now entangled and heightened by remorse and shame and horror.

He threw off the blanket and swung his feet to the floor and propped his elbows on his knees and dropped his face into his hands.

There was a clanging sound, and he started convulsively and raised his head and saw a uniformed guard coming into the cell. The man was carrying a big suitcase which he put down as he closed the barred door. On the side of the case were the initials *C. M.*, and Cyprian saw with dull surprise that it was his own, the one Charles had given him in London. He heard himself saying, "Where did you get that?" and the fellow looked at him and said, "Came from y'r apartment. There's clothes an' shaving tack an' setra." He had a strange manner, at once meaning and noncommittal, official and yet faintly sycophantic.

He came closer to Cyprian and looked down at him. He said, "Mr. Friar fixed it. An' about sendin' out for what you want."

A little faint glow of warmth came to life somewhere in Cyprian's coldness. Trust John Friar, he thought.

The guard said, "You like anything now? Breakfast? Or just coffee?"

Cyprian went on staring at him: it was as if his mind was so full that he didn't hear words until long after they had been spoken.

"Coffee," he said at last. "Just coffee."

The man nodded, and went to the door and opened it again, and paused. "Like to see the papers?" he said over his shoulder.

This time the words penetrated fast. Cyprian recoiled from them as if they were blows. "No!" he said. "No—*no!*"

He closed his eyes and held them screwed shut until he had heard the door open and clang shut, and then receding footsteps echoing. A shudder shook him at the thought of newspapers, and once more he covered his face with his hands. Headlines—as if on an endless ticker-tape—began to unroll behind his eyes, running the gamut from the sober through the sensational to the nadir of the tabloid—

—*FAMOUS PLAYWRIGHT HELD ON MURDER CHARGE. DESIGNER SLAIN . . .*

—*CYPRIAN MORSE ARRAIGNED FOR MURDER. GIRL ASSOCIATE BRUTALLY BATTERED TO DEATH . . .*

—*PARK AVENUE LOVE-FIEND MURDER. FAMOUS THEATER BEAUTY SLASHED. MORSE, BROADWAY FIGURE, JAILED . . .*

He groaned and twisted his body this way and that and desperately pressed the heels of his palms against his eyes until a spark-shot red mist seemed to swim under the lids. But the tape went on unrolling—a ceaseless stream of words.

He jumped up and began to pad about the cell—and

then mercifully heard footsteps in the corridor again and mastered himself and was sitting on the edge of the gray cot when the guard reappeared with a tray.

He mumbled thanks and reached for the coffeepot. But his hand trembled so badly that, without speaking, the man filled a cup for him.

He drank greedily, and felt strength coming back to him. He looked up and said, "Can I—would—is it allowed to send a cablegram?"

"Could be. With an okay from the Warden's office." The fellow reached into a pocket, produced a little memo pad and a stump of pencil. "Want to write it down?"

Cyprian took the things. Once more he mumbled thanks. He didn't look at the man; he didn't like his eyes. He began to write, not having to think, letting the pencil print the words—

—Charles de Lastro Hotel Castilia Venezuela In terrible trouble need you desperately please come Reply care John Friar Cyprian.

He handed the pad and pencil back, and watched while what he had written was read. He said, "Well—?" and met the eyes again as they flickered over him.

"Seems like this'll be okay." The guard turned a blue-clad back and went to the door. "I'll look after it."

Once more the clanging, the footsteps dying away— and Cyprian was alone again. His hand steadier now, he poured himself more coffee. Anything, any action, to keep him from thought.

He drained the cup. He picked up the suitcase and set it on the cot and opened it. Forcing himself to activity, he washed and shaved and put on the clothes he found packed. A suit of dark blue flannel—a white silk shirt—a plain maroon tie.

He felt a little better. It was easier to believe that this was Cyprian Morse—and he gave silent thanks to John Friar.

But there was nothing to do now—and if he weren't

careful he might have to start thinking. He lit a cigarette from the box in the suitcase and began to pace
the cell. There were five steps one way and six the
other. . . .

So this was Cyprian Morse. Perhaps he did feel
better after all. Perhaps—

Footsteps in the corridor again. One, two, three sets.

John Friar himself, with another man and the guard.
Who opened the door, and stood aside to let the visitors in, and clanged the door shut again and stood outside, his back to it.

John Friar took Cyprian's hand in both of his and
gripped hard. He was white-faced, strained. He looked
less like a successful producer than ever, and more
like a truncated and careworn Abe Lincoln. The man
with him towered over him, a lank, loose-limbed,
stooping giant with a thatch of white hair and a
seamed, unlikely face which was neither saint's nor
gargoyle's but something of both.

John Friar said, "Cyprian!" in a voice which wasn't
quite steady. He made a gesture including the third
man. He said, "Julius, meet Cyprian Morse . . . Cyprian, this is Julius Magnussen."

Again Cyprian's hand was taken, and enveloped in
a vast paw which gripped firmly but with surprising
gentleness. And Cyprian found himself looking up,
tall though he was, into dark unreadable eyes which
seemed jet black under the shaggy white brows.

John Friar said, "Julius is taking on your def—
your case, Cyprian. And you know what that means!"

"I most definitely do!" Cyprian hoped they wouldn't
hear the trembling in his throat. "Is there anyone in
America who doesn't?"

Magnussen grunted. He turned away and folded his
length in the middle and sat on the edge of the gray
bed. He looked at Cyprian and said, "Better tell me
about it," then moved a little and added, "Sit down
here."

Cyprian found himself obeying. But he couldn't

keep on meeting the dark eyes, and gave up trying to. He looked up at John Friar and essayed a smile. He said, "Of course," in Magnussen's direction—and then, faintly, all the fear and horror of memory breaking loose in his head again, "Where—where—d'you want me to start?" . . .

"At the beginning, Mr. Morse," Magnussen said, and Cyprian drew a deep breath to still the quaking inside him.

But it wouldn't be stilled. It spread from his body to his mind. He was being thrust into nightmare again—

—I can't . . . I can't . . .

—Would it be easier if I asked you questions?

Questions. The pattern returning. Fear—questions—fear fear—fatigue. But worse now. Hiding from friends not enemies.

—I have to ask you this: did you kill this woman Astrid Halmar?

—No—no—no! . . . *There was a man . . . he went through the window* . . .

—You know of no enemies Miss Halmar might have had?

—No. How should I? I—

—So you think the murderer was a stranger, a prowler?

—How—how do I know what he was! Or who! I don't know anything . . .

Questions. Questions. Fear. Thinking furiously before each answer without letting the pause be evident. Trying to screen the vortex of his mind with caution. Time standing still again. He had always been here. He would always be here.

—So you were in the bathroom for more than an hour?

—Yes—yes. I went there just after dinner. Just as—just after the maid left the apartment.

—Were you feeling unwell? Is that why you stayed so long? Had something you ate upset your stomach?

A straw. A solid straw. Snatch it!

—Yes. That's right. I was sick . . . It was the oysters . . .

More questions. More fear. Feeling the dark eyes always on his face. Not meeting them.

—And you were just about to come out of the bathroom when you heard a cry. Am I right?

Another straw. Snatch it!

—Yes. Yes. Astrid screamed . . .

—And you ran out, and along the passage to the living room?

—Yes.

—While you were running along the passage, did you happen to notice Miss Halmar's robe, lying on the floor?

—Robe? What—no, I don't think—

—Her robe was found by the door to the living room. The killer—however he gained entry to the apartment —must have struggled with her, snatched at her, in the passageway there, pulling off the robe as she fled into the living room. I am wondering—did you notice it?

A straw?

—I think I did. There was something—soft on the floor. It caught my shoe . . .

—Now, Mr. Morse, as you entered the living room, you saw the figure of a man just disappearing out of the window?

—Yes. Yes.

—And you saw Miss Halmar's body on the floor and ran to it?

—Yes. Of course I did. I—I had to try and help her . . .

—Naturally. Now, as your fingerprints are on the logpick, Mr. Morse, you must have handled it? Maybe you touched it—picked it up—when you went to her? It was in your way, was it?

A sudden lightening. As if some frightful pressure were easing. Fear actually receding. Knowing now that

these were no accidental straws, but material for a raft.
A life raft.

—Yes. That was it. I remember now. It—it was lying
across her body. I—I picked it up and—threw it down,
away from her.

—And in your shock and horror, when you found she
was dead, you forgot the telephone and ran blindly
out to seek help, and then collapsed?

—Yes. Yes. That's it exactly. ·

Questions. Questions. But not minding them now.
Being eager for them. And being able to meet the dark
eyes, keeping his own eyes on them.

The pattern had changed. Fear was there, as a per-
manent lowering background, but in front of it was
hope. . . .

The hope persisted, even when he was alone once
more. It seemed to widen the cell, and raise its roof.
It set the blood flowing through his head again, so
that his brain worked fast and clear and he started to
elaborate on the structure Julius Magnussen had begun
to build for him.

This work—and work it was—carried him through
the dragging days and weeks with a surprising mini-
mum of anguish. It even fortified him to some extent
against the shock of the answering cablegram from
Charles, which didn't arrive until several days after
he had expected it.

The cable ran: *Hospitalized bad kickup malaria
Flying back immediately released maybe two weeks
Hang on   Charles.*

And that was bad news. Bad from two angles—that
he would have to wait before Charles could get to him,
that poor Charles was sick.

But whereas, before the first meeting with Julius
Magnussen, Cyprian would have been crushed almost
to extinction by these twin misfortunes, now they
seemed merely to serve as a spur to his fortitude and

his hope and his labor. So that he clenched his teeth and redoubled his efforts to produce appropriate "memories"—until he reached the point of being sure that at least Friar and Magnussen believed him, that he almost believed himself.

But it was as well for him that he wasn't present at any of the several meetings between Julius Magnussen and John Friar alone, or he would have heard talk which would have turned his hope-lightened purgatory into hopeless hell.

—A bad case, John. Don't hide it from yourself. We'll need a miracle.

—Good God, Julius, d'you mean you yourself don't believe—

—Stop. That's not a question I want to be asked. Or answer. Leave it at what I said. A bad case. No case at all.

—But the evidence against him's all circumstantial!

—And therefore the best, in spite of what they say in novels.

—But surely it's all open to two interpretations! Like—like his fingerprints on that poker.

—*And* the splashes of blood on him and his clothing? Have you thought of that, John? *Splashes.* Not smears, which are what should be there from raising her, examining her, trying to help her . . .

—But the boy's *gentle,* Julius! There's no violence in him. He couldn't even kill a fly that was pestering him.

—Maybe not. And don't think that's not going to be used. For more than all it's worth. For God's sake, it's practically all we have! You know the young man, John: tell me, how would he react to the suggestion of an alternative plea?

—You mean "not guilty, or guilty by reason of insanity"!—that gag! Good God, Julius—he wouldn't go for that if you tortured him.

—H'mm. I was afraid that would be the answer.

—Look now, what is all this? What are you trying to do—tell me you won't take the case after all? Is that it?

—Cool off, John. I'm trying to save your prodigy's life, that's all.

—I don't get this! Julius Magnussen, of all people, scared of a setup like this! . . . Remember that police photograph you showed me? Well, think of it. Not the head wounds, the others. Think of 'em! Cyprian could not have been responsible for that frightful *sort* of brutality. Think of what was done to that girl, man! . . . Can't you see—can't you?

—Oh, yes, John, I can see. A great many things. . . .

But Cyprian knew nothing of such conversations, and it seemed to him, every time he saw his counsel, that more and more confidence radiated from that towering, loose-limbed figure; that the penetrating dark eyes looked always more cheerful.

So he rode out the rest of the dragging days and nights and came in good enough order to the morning when the trial was to open. It was a Thursday, and he liked that because he had had a fancy, since an episode in his boyhood, that Thor's was his lucky day. Further, a bright autumnal sun was glittering over New York and even—a rare occurrence in the weeks he had been there—pushing rays through the bars of the small window high up in the wall of the cell.

He dressed with great, almost finicking care. He drank a whole pot of coffee and then sent for more. He even ate a little of his breakfast.

He was ready and waiting a full half-hour before they came for him. He spent it pacing the cell, smoking too much and too fast, glancing occasionally toward the pile of letters which he hadn't read and had no more intention of ever reading than he had of looking in court at any of the reporters' faces. He didn't think of what was before him today. He daren't think of that, in the same way—only infinitely multiplied—that he never thought about what was coming on a first night.

So he considered, with furious intensity, anything and everything except what was coming. The sure hope at the back of his mind must be kept inviolate.

He came naturally to thoughts of Charles. Every day he had been sure this must be the day when he would hear again—and every day he had been disappointed. He had wired again, and he had written—just a note which John Friar had air-mailed for him. But still no answer. Charles must be very ill indeed. Or— a wonderful idea which he dare not dwell upon for more than one delicious instant—Charles was well again and had arrived in New York, and was on his way here.

The third alternative he shuddered away from. The thought of Charles dead was so black, so bleak, so dreadful, that it would have driven him back in escape to thoughts of the immediate future if he hadn't been saved by the arrival of his guard.

For once he was glad to see the fellow. He said, "Do we start now?" and moved toward the door.

But the man shook his head. "They ain't here yet," he said. "Take it easy." He drew a folded yellow envelope from a pocket and held it out to Cyprian. "Sent over from Friar's," he said. "He reckoned you might like to have it right away."

Cyprian almost snatched it from the outstretched hand. His heart was pounding, and sudden color had tinged his pallid face. With fingers which he didn't know were shaking, he fumbled at the flimsy envelope, ripped it open at last, and unfolded the sheet it contained.

And read: *Better   Out next Wednesday will fly arriving Thursday   Charles.*

The new color deepened in Cyprian's face. He read the cable again—and again. Here was the best of all possible omens. Almost as good as his wild daydream of a few moments before—that perhaps Charles would arrive in person. On second thought, perhaps better. Because now he was supremely confident, and he would so far prefer to have all this ugliness behind him when

Charles returned; out of sight and wrapped up and put away, to be disinterred and examined, if ever, at a safe distance in time and then only for personal historic interest.

He moved his shoulders unconsciously, as if in reflex to the removal of a heavy weight. He folded the strip of paper carefully, and stowed it away in his breast pocket. And then looked at the guard and smiled, and said softly, "Thank you. Thank you very much. . . ."

There was a tramping of feet in the corridor—and two uniformed men he had never seen before. One of them pushed the cell door wide and looked at him with no expression and said, "All set?"

Cyprian smiled at this man too, and walked out into the corridor quickly, lightly, almost jauntily. . . .

But there was no lightness in him when he came back eight hours later, and no square of sunshine from the barred window. There was only night outside and here the hard cold light of the single bulb overhead.

His face was lined and wax-white. His shoulders sagged and his body seemed not to fill his clothes. He lurched on his feet while they opened the door of the cell, and one of the men gripped his arm and said, "Take it easy."

They put him inside and he dropped on the edge of his cot and sat there limp and head-hanging, his eyes wide and staring at the floor and not seeing it.

The escort went away and his own guard came, and sometime later the doctor. He couldn't get food down, and they put him to bed and gave him a sedative. He slept almost at once, and they left him.

He lay like a log for three hours, until the deadly numbness of fatigue had gone and the drug had eased its grip. And then he began to murmur and thrash around on the cot—and in a moment gave a harsh choked cry and sat upright, awake.

He remembered. He tried not to, he fought, but he couldn't stop memory from working. He remembered everything—at first in jumbled pictures, then in echoing phrases; at last, concentrated upon the gray-haired, gray-eyed figure of the District Attorney, he recalled the whole of the clear and ruthlessly dispassionate Opening for the Prosecution. The speech which, period by period, point by careful point, had not only stripped Cyprian Morse of all cover but had shattered all remnant of hope in him.

What had happened after the speech didn't matter. The irreparable damage to Cyprian Morse, the conviction of Cyprian Morse, had been brought about; those witnesses, the silly endless procession of them who answered silly endless questions, they were just so many more nails in his coffin. After the speech, which showed such complete, such eerie knowledge and understanding, as if the speaker had not only seen everything that had happened but had seen it with Cyprian's mind and Cyprian's eyes—after that, all else seemed time-prolonging and sadistically anticlimactic . . .

He didn't move. He sat as he was, and stared into the abyss. . . .

Morning came, and daylight, and people he heard and saw as if from a long distance. He moved then but was almost unconscious of moving. It was as if his body were an automaton and his mind a separate entity outside it, which had no concern with the robot movements.

The automaton clothed itself, and ate and drank, and went with his mind and the uniformed men and sat in the crowded courtroom in the same place as his undivided self had sat the day before.

The automaton sat still and went through motions —of listening to friends and Counsel, of answering them when necessary, of looking attentive to the gabber-jab of the unending witnesses, of considering thoughtfully the closing speech for the Prosecution, of hearing the crabbed Judge rule that the Court, this being Friday, should recess until the morning of Monday. . . .

But his mind, his actual self, was in hell without a permit. For sixty-two hours the automaton made all the foolish gestures of living; for uncountable stages of distorted time his mind gazed into the pit.

The Monday came, and the automaton moved accordingly. But the clean-cut edges of the schism between body and mind began to waver before the two parts of him left the cell, as if something had happened which demanded they should be joined again. Resisting the pull, his mind began to wonder what had caused it. His refusal to see John Friar or Magnussen during the recess? The odd, almost excited manner of his guard on bringing a newspaper to the cell and trying to insist on the automaton reading it? The looks which both his escorts cast at the automaton in the car on the way to court?

He didn't want the union. He would break, he felt, if he couldn't keep up the separation. But the pull grew stronger with every foot of the way, and almost irresistible as he entered the courtroom itself, and his mind felt a difference—a strange, disturbing, agitated alteration—in the other minds behind the faces staring at him.

And then, with a shivering, nauseating shock, his resistance went and he was swept back into his body once more, so that he was stripped and next to the world again with no transparent armor between.

It was the face of Magnussen's wizened clerk which brought it about, a face which always before had been harassed and grave and filled with foreboding, but which now was gay and eager and irradiated by a tremendous gnomelike smile. As Cyprian was about to take his seat, this smile was turned full on him, and his hand was surreptitiously taken and earnestly squeezed, and through the smile a voice came whispering something which couldn't be distinguished but all the same was pregnant with the most extreme importance.

Cyprian sat down, weakly. Once again, he had no strength. He looked up into the little clerk's face and muttered something—he wasn't sure of the words himself.

An astonished change came over the puckered visage. "Mr. Morse!" The voice cracked in amazement. "Do you mean to say you haven't *heard!*"

Dumbly Cyprian shook his head, the small movement leaving him exhausted.

"Not about the—the other killings! . . . Mr. Morse! There have been two more murders of unfortunate girls! In every respect the same as Miss Halmar's—even the—the mutilations identical. . . . On Saturday night the first victim was found; and another discovered in the early hours of this morning!"

Cyprian went on staring up into the excited, agitated face.

"D-don't you realize what this m-means!" The voice was stammering now. "All three deaths must be linked. *You* couldn't have caused the others! They're the work of a maniac—a Jack the Ripper!" Fluttering hands produced a newspaper, unfolded it, waved it. "Look here, Mr. Morse!"

There were black heavy headlines. They wavered in front of Cyprian's eyes, then focused sharply and made him catch at his breath.

POLICE CLUELESS IN NEW FIEND SLAYINGS! MORSE RELEASE DEMANDED BY PUBLIC!

"Oh," said Cyprian, his lips barely moving. "Oh, I see . . ." His whole body began to tingle, as if circulation had been withheld from it until now. He said, a little louder, "What—what will happen?"

The clerk sat down beside him. His hoarse whispering was as clear now as a shout in Cyprian's ears. "What will happen? I'll tell you, Mr. Morse. I'll tell you exactly. The D.A. will withdraw—and not long after Mr. Magnussen's opened. He'll withdraw, Mr. Morse, you mark my words!"

The words coincided with a stentorian bellow from the back of the courtroom, followed by a stamping rustle as everyone stood up—and Justice swept to its throne in a dusty black robe. . . .

And Cyprian, life welling up in him, found himself caught in a whirling timeless jumble of fact and feeling and emotion, a maelstrom which was in effect the precise opposite of the long nightmare succeeding his arrest—

Julius Magnussen towering on his feet, speaking of Cyprian Morse's innocence with an almost contemptuous certainty. Julius Magnussen examining detectives on the witness stand, forcing them to prove all three killings had been identical. Julius Magnussen calling more witnesses, then looking around haughtily at the Prosecution when the Court was asked to hear a statement. The District Attorney himself, gray eyes not understanding now but puzzled and confused, muttering that the state withdrew its case against Cyprian Morse. The Judge speaking, bestowing commiseration on Cyprian Morse, laudation on Julius Magnussen, censure upon their opponents—

Then bedlam breaking loose, himself the center. Friends. Strangers. Acquaintances. Reporters. All crowding, jabbering, laughing. Women weeping. Flashbulbs exploding. John Friar pumping both his hands. Magnussen clapping him on the shoulder. Himself the center of a wedge of policemen, struggling for the exit. An odd little instant of comparative quiet in the hallway, and hearing Magnussen say to John Friar behind him, "An apology, John, you were right."

Then John's big car, and the soft cushioned seat supporting him. And quietness, with the tires singing on the road and time to draw breath—and taste freedom. . . .

All horror was behind him and it was Wednesday evening and Charles was coming home. From John Friar's house in Westchester, in John Friar's car, driven by John Friar's chauffeur.

It was deepening dusk when they pulled into the parking lot behind the apartment house. Cyprian peered, and saw no sign of any human being and was pleased. He got out and smiled at the chauffeur and said warmly, "Thank you, Maurice. Thank you very much . . ." and thrust a lavish tip into the man's gloved hand and waved a cheerful salute and walked off toward the rear entrance of the building. His footsteps rang crisply on the concrete, and a faint, wreathlike mist from his breathing hung on the autumn air. He suppressed an impulse to stop and crane his neck to look up to the penthouse and see the warm lights glowing out from it. He knew they were there, because he had heard John Friar telephoning to his servant, telling him when Mr. Morse was to be expected.

Good old John, he thought. Thoughtful John! And then forgot John completely as he entered the service door, and still met no one and found one of the service elevators empty and waiting.

He forgot John. He forgot everyone and everything —except Charles.

And Charles would be here tomorrow. That was why Cyprian had insisted upon coming home tonight—so that he could supervise preparation.

He hurried the elevator with his mind, and when it reached the rear hallway of his penthouse, threw open the gate—and was faced, not by light and an open door and Walter's white-smiling black face, but by cold unwelcoming darkness.

He stepped out of the elevator and groped for the light switch and pressed it and blinked at the sudden glare. Frowning, he tried the door to the kitchen. It wasn't locked, but when he opened it there was more darkness. And no sound. No sound at all.

A chill settled on his mind. The warm excited glow which had been growing inside him evaporated with unnerving suddenness. He switched on more lights and went quickly through the bright-tiled neatness and threw open an inner door and called, "Walter! Walter, where are you?" into more darkness still.

Not such absolute darkness this time, but the more disturbing for that. The curtains across the big windows at the west side of the living room had not been drawn and there was still a sort of gray luminosity in the air.

Cyprian took two or three paces into the room. He called, "Walter!" again, and heard his own voice go up too high at the end of the word.

And another voice spoke from behind him—a cracked and casual voice.

"I sent him out for an hour or two," it said. "Hope you don't mind."

Cyprian started violently. He gasped, *"Charles!"* and wheeled around and saw a tall figure looming in the grayness. His heart pounded in his ears and he felt a swaying in his head.

There was no answering sound—and he said, "Charles!" again and moved toward a table near the figure and reached out for the lamp he knew was on it.

But his shoulder was caught in a grip which checked him completely. Long fingers strong as steel bit into his flesh, and Charles's voice said, "Take it easy. We don't need light just yet."

Cyprian felt cold. His head still whirled. He couldn't understand, and the grip on his shoulder seemed to be paralyzing him and he was afraid with that worst of all fears which hasn't any shape.

He said wildly, "Charles, I don't understand—I—" and couldn't get out any more words. He contorted all the muscles in his face in a useless attempt to see Charles's face.

"You will," said Charles's voice. "Do you remember once telling me you'd never lie to me again?"

"Yes," Cyprian whispered—and then, his mouth drying with fear, "Let me go. You're hurting me . . ."

"Did you mean it?" The hand didn't relax its grip.

"Of course . . . And I never have lied to you since! I don't understand—"

"You will." The grip tightened and Cyprian caught his breath. "I want a truthful answer to one question. Will you give it?"

"Yes. Yes. Of course I will . . ."

"Did you kill that Halmar woman?"

"No—no—*there was a man . . . he went through the window . . .*"

"I thought you weren't going to lie to me. Did you kill her?"

"*No!* I—" The steel fingers bit deeper and Cyprian sobbed.

"Did you kill her? Don't lie to me."

"Yes! *Yes!*" Cyprian's face was writhing. His eyes stung with tears and his lips were trembling. "Yes, I killed her! I killed her—*I killed her! . . .*"

The grip eased. The hand lifted from his shoulder. He tottered on uncertain feet, and the lamp on the table jumped suddenly into life and through the mist over his eyes he saw Charles for the first time—and then heard Charles's voice say, easily and softly and with the old-time chuckle hidden somewhere in it, "Well, that's that. Just so long as we know . . . I'd like a drink." He turned away from Cyprian and crossed with his lounging walk to the bar—the lounging walk which always reminded Cyprian of the stalking of a cat—

And suddenly Cyprian knew.

He knew, and in the same moment that understanding flooded his mind, he thought—for the first time actively thought—of those other two deaths which had saved him from death.

A scream came to his throat and froze there. He shrank into himself as he stood there—and Charles turned, glass in hand, and looked at him.

His eyes burned in his head. He couldn't move their

gaze from Charles's face. He said, "You did it. You killed those two women. You weren't ill. You got someone else to send those cables. You heard about Astrid and you flew back without anyone knowing. And you plotted and planned and stalked—and did that. As if they were animals. You did that!"

His voice died in his throat. All strength went out of him and he tottered to a chair and doubled up in it and sat crumpled.

"Don't fret, my dear Cyprian." Charles drank, looking at him over the rim of the glass. "We sit tight—and live happily ever after. . . ."

Cyprian dropped his head into his hands.

"Oh, my God!" he said. "Oh, my God!"

The Dancing Partner

by JEROME K. JEROME

"This story," commenced MacShaugnassy, "comes from Furtwangen, a small town in the Black Forest. There lived there a very wonderful old fellow named Nicholas Geibel. His business was the making of mechanical toys, at which work he had acquired an almost European reputation. He made rabbits that would emerge from the heart of a cabbage, flop their ears, smooth their whiskers, and disappear again; cats that would

Reprinted by permission of the executrix, Miss Rowena Jerome.

wash their faces, and mew so naturally that dogs would mistake them for real cats, and fly at them; dolls, with phonographs concealed within them, that would raise their hats and say, 'Good morning; how do you do?' and some that would even sing a song.

"But he was something more than a mere mechanic; he was an artist. His work was with him a hobby, almost a passion. His shop was filled with all manner of strange things that never would, or could, be sold—things he had made for the pure love of making them. He had contrived a mechanical donkey that would trot for two hours by means of stored electricity, and trot, too, much faster than the live article, and with less need for exertion on the part of the driver; a bird that would shoot up into the air, fly round and round in a circle, and drop to earth at the exact spot from where it started; a skeleton that, supported by an upright iron bar, would dance a hornpipe; a life-sized lady doll that could play the fiddle; and a gentleman with a hollow inside who could smoke a pipe and drink more lager beer than any three average German students put together, which is saying much.

"Indeed, it was the belief of the town that old Geibel could make a man capable of doing everything that a respectable man need want to do. One day he made a man who did too much, and it came about in this way:

"Young Doctor Follen had a baby, and the baby had a birthday. Its first birthday put Doctor Follen's household into somewhat of a flurry, but on the occasion of its second birthday, Mrs. Doctor Follen gave a ball in honor of the event. Old Geibel and his daughter Olga were among the guests.

"During the afternoon of the next day some three or four of Olga's bosom friends, who had also been present at the ball, dropped in to have a chat about it. They naturally fell to discussing the men, and to criticizing their dancing. Old Geibel was in the room, but he appeared to be absorbed in his newspaper, and the girls took no notice of him.

" 'There seem to be fewer men who can dance at every ball you go to,' said one of the girls.

" 'Yes, and don't the ones who can give themselves airs,' said another; 'they make quite a favor of asking you.'

" 'And how stupidly they talk,' added a third. 'They always say exactly the same things: "How charming you are looking tonight." "Do you often go to Vienna? Oh, you should, it's delightful." "What a charming dress you have on." "What a warm day it has been." "Do you like Wagner?" I do wish they'd think of something new.'

" 'Oh, I never mind how they talk,' said a fourth. 'If a man dances well he may be a fool for all I care.'

" 'He generally is,' slipped in a thin girl, rather spitefully.

" 'I go to a ball to dance,' continued the previous speaker, not noticing the interruption. 'All I ask of a partner is that he shall hold me firmly, take me round steadily, and not get tired before I do.'

" 'A clockwork figure would be the thing for you,' said the girl who had interrupted.

" 'Bravo!' cried one of the others, clapping her hands, 'what a capital idea!'

" 'What's a capital idea?' they asked.

" 'Why, a clockwork dancer, or, better still, one that would go by electricity and never run down.'

"The girls took up the idea with enthusiasm.

" 'Oh, what a lovely partner he would make,' said one; 'he would never kick you, or tread on your toes.'

" 'Or tear your dress,' said another.

" 'Or get out of step.'

" 'Or get giddy and lean on you.'

" 'And he would never want to mop his face with his handkerchief. I do hate to see a man do that after every dance.'

" 'And wouldn't want to spend the whole evening in the supper room.'

" 'Why, with a phonograph inside him to grind out

all the stock remarks, you would not be able to tell him from a real man,' said the girl who had first suggested the idea.

" 'Oh, yes, you would,' said the thin girl, 'he would be so much nicer.'

"Old Geibel had laid down his paper, and was listening with both his ears. On one of the girls glancing in his direction, however, he hurriedly hid himself again behind it.

"After the girls were gone, he went into his workshop, where Olga heard him walking up and down, and every now and then chuckling to himself; and that night he talked to her a good deal about dancing and dancing men—asked what they usually said and did—what dances were most popular—what steps were gone through, with many other questions bearing on the subject.

"Then for a couple of weeks he kept much to his factory, and was very thoughtful and busy, though prone at unexpected moments to break into a quiet low laugh, as if enjoying a joke that nobody else knew of.

"A month later another ball took place in Furtwangen. On this occasion it was given by old Wenzel, the wealthy timber merchant, to celebrate his niece's betrothal, and Geibel and his daughter were again among the invited.

"When the hour arrived to set out, Olga sought her father. Not finding him in the house, she tapped at the door of his workshop. He appeared in his shirt sleeves, looking hot but radiant.

" 'Don't wait for me,' he said, 'you go on, I'll follow you. I've got something to finish.'

"As she turned to obey he called after her, 'Tell them I'm going to bring a young man with me—such a nice young man, and an excellent dancer. All the girls will like him.' Then he laughed and closed the door.

"Her father generally kept his doings secret from everybody, but she had a pretty shrewd suspicion of what he had been planning, and so, to a certain extent, was able to prepare the guests for what was coming. Anticipation ran high, and the arrival of the famous mechanist was eagerly awaited.

"At length the sound of wheels was heard outside, followed by a great commotion in the passage, and old Wenzel himself, his jolly face red with excitement and suppressed laughter, burst into the room and announced in stentorian tones:

" 'Herr Geibel—and a friend.'

"Herr Geibel and his 'friend' entered, greeted with shouts of laughter and applause, and advanced to the center of the room.

" 'Allow me, ladies and gentlemen,' said Herr Geibel, 'to introduce you to my friend, Lieutenant Fritz. Fritz, my dear fellow, bow to the ladies and gentlemen.'

"Geibel placed his hand encouragingly on Fritz's shoulder, and the lieutenant bowed low, accompanying the action with a harsh clicking noise in his throat, unpleasantly suggestive of a death rattle. But that was only a detail.

" 'He walks a little stiffly' (old Geibel took his arm and walked him forward a few steps. He certainly did walk stiffly.) 'but then, walking is not his forte. He is essentially a dancing man. I have only been able to teach him the waltz as yet, but at that he is faultless. Come, which of you ladies may I introduce him to as a partner? He keeps perfect time; he never gets tired; he won't kick you or tread on your dress; he will hold you as firmly as you like, and go as quickly or as slowly as you please; he never gets giddy; and he is full of conversation. Come, speak up for yourself, my boy.'

"The old gentleman twisted one of the buttons at the back of his coat, and immediately Fritz opened his mouth, and in thin tones that appeared to proceed from the back of his head, remarked suddenly, 'May I have the pleasure?' and then shut his mouth again with a snap.

"That Lieutenant Fritz had made a strong impression on the company was undoubted, yet none of the girls seemed inclined to dance with him. They looked askance at his waxen face, with his staring eyes and fixed smile, and shuddered. At last old Geibel came to the girl who had conceived the idea.

"It is your own suggestion, carried out to the letter,' said Geibel, 'an electric dancer. You owe it to the gentleman to give him a trial.'

"She was a bright, saucy little girl, fond of a frolic. Her host added his entreaties, and she consented.

"Herr Geibel fixed the figure to her. Its right arm was screwed round her waist, and held her firmly; its delicately jointed left hand was made to fasten itself upon her right. The old toymaker showed her how to regulate its speed, and how to stop it and release herself.

" 'It will take you round in a complete circle,' he explained; 'be careful that no one knocks against you, and alters its course.'

"The music struck up. Old Geibel put the current in motion, and Annette and her strange partner began to dance.

"For a while everyone stood watching them. The figure performed its purpose admirably. Keeping perfect time and step, and holding its little partner tight clasped in an unyielding embrace, it revolved steadily, pouring forth at the same time a constant flow of squeaky conversation, broken by brief intervals of grinding silence.

" 'How charming you are looking tonight,' it remarked in its thin, faraway voice. 'What a lovely day it has been. Do you like dancing? How well our steps agree. You will give me another, won't you? Oh, don't be so cruel. What a charming gown you have on. Isn't waltzing delightful? I could go on dancing forever— with you. Have you had supper?'

"As she grew more familiar with the uncanny creature, the girl's nervousness wore off, and she entered into the fun of the thing.

" 'Oh, he's just lovely,' she cried, laughing. 'I could go on dancing with him all my life.'

"Couple after couple now joined them, and soon all the dancers in the room were whirling round behind them. Nicholas Geibel stood looking on, beaming with childish delight at his success.

"Old Wenzel approached him, and whispered something in his ear. Geibel laughed and nodded, and the two worked their way quietly toward the door.

" 'This is the young people's house tonight,' said Wenzel, so soon as they were outside; 'you and I will have a quiet pipe and a glass of hock, over in the counting house.'

"Meanwhile the dancing grew more fast and furious. Little Annette loosened the screw regulating her partner's rate of progress, and the figure flew round with her swifter and swifter. Couple after couple dropped out exhausted, but they only went the faster, till at length they remained dancing alone.

"Madder and madder became the waltz. The music lagged behind: the musicians, unable to keep the pace, ceased, and sat staring. The younger guests applauded, but the older faces began to grow anxious.

" 'Hadn't you better stop, dear,' said one of the women, 'you'll make yourself so tired.'

"But Annette did not answer.

" 'I believe she's fainted,' cried out a girl who had caught sight of her face as it was swept by.

"One of the men sprang forward and clutched at the figure, but its impetus threw him down onto the floor, where its steel-cased feet laid bare his cheek. The thing evidently did not intend to part with its prize easily.

"Had anyone retained a cool head, the figure, one cannot help thinking, might easily have been stopped. Two or three men acting in concert might have lifted it bodily off the floor, or have jammed it into a corner. But few human heads are capable of remaining cool under excitement. Those who are not present think how stupid must have been those who were; those who are reflect afterward how simple it would have been to do this, that, or the other, if only they had thought of it at the time.

"The women grew hysterical. The men shouted contradictory directions to one another. Two of them made a bungling rush at the figure, which had the result of forcing it out of its orbit in the center of the room, and sending it crashing against the walls and furniture. A stream of blood showed itself down the girl's white frock, and followed her along the floor. The affair was becoming horrible. The women rushed screaming from the room. The men followed them.

"One sensible suggestion was made: 'Find Geibel—fetch Geibel.'

"No one had noticed him leave the room, no one knew where he was. A party went in search of him. The others, too unnerved to go back into the ballroom, crowded outside the door and listened. They could hear the steady whir of the wheels upon the polished floor as the thing spun round and round; the dull thud as every now and again it dashed itself and its burden against some opposing object and ricocheted off in a new direction.

"And everlastingly it talked in that thin ghostly voice, repeating over and over the same formula: 'How charming you are looking tonight. What a lovely day it has been. Oh, don't be so cruel. I could go on dancing forever—with you. Have you had supper?'

"Of course they sought for Geibel everywhere but where he was. They looked in every room in the house, then rushed off in a body to his own place, and spent precious minutes in waking up his deaf old housekeeper. At last it occurred to one of the party that Wenzel was missing also, and then the idea of the counting house across the yard presented itself to them, and there they found him.

"He rose up, very pale, and followed them; and he

and old Wenzel forced their way through the crowd of guests gathered outside, and entered the room and locked the door behind them.

"From within there came the muffled sound of low voices and quick steps, followed by a confused scuffling noise, the silence, then the low voices again.

"After a time the door opened, and those near it pressed forward to enter, but old Wenzel's broad shoulders barred the way.

"'I want you—and you, Bekler,' he said, addressing a couple of the elder men. His voice was calm, but his face was deadly white. 'The rest of you, please go—get the women away as quickly as you can.'

"From that day old Nicholas Geibel confined himself to the making of mechanical rabbits, and cats that mewed and washed their faces."

Casting the Runes

by M. R. JAMES

April 15th, 190–

DEAR SIR,—I am requested by the Council of the —— Association to return to you the draft of a paper on *The Truth of Alchemy,* which you have been good enough to offer to read at our forthcoming meeting,

From *The Collected Ghost Stories of M. R. James.* Reprinted by permission of the publisher, Edward Arnold, Ltd., London.

and to inform you that the Council do not see their way to including it in the program.

> I am,
>
> > Yours faithfully,
> >
> > > —— *Secretary*

April 18th

DEAR SIR,—I am sorry to say that my engagements do not permit of my affording you an interview on the subject of your proposed paper. Nor do our laws allow of your discussing the matter with a Committee of our Council, as you suggest. Please allow me to assure you that the fullest consideration was given to the draft which you submitted, and that it was not declined without having been referred to the judgment of a most competent authority. No personal question (it can hardly be necessary for me to add) can have had the slightest influence on the decision of the Council.

> > Believe me (*ut supra*)

April 20th

The Secretary of the —— Association begs respectfully to inform Mr. Karswell that it is impossible for him to communicate the name of any person or persons to whom the draft of Mr. Karswell's paper may have been submitted; and further desires to intimate that he cannot undertake to reply to any further letters on this subject.

"And who *is* Mr. Karswell?" inquired the Secretary's wife. She had called at his office, and (perhaps unwarrantably) had picked up the last of these three letters, which the typist had just brought in.

"Why, my dear, just at present Mr. Karswell is a very angry man. But I don't know much about him otherwise, except that he is a person of wealth, his address is Lufford Abbey, Warwickshire, and he's an alchemist, apparently, and wants to tell us all about it; and that's about all—except that I don't want to meet him for the next week or two. Now, if you're ready to leave this place, I am."

"What have you been doing to make him angry?" asked Mrs. Secretary.

"The usual thing, my dear, the usual thing: he sent in a draft of a paper he wanted to read at the next meeting, and we referred it to Edward Dunning—almost the only man in England who knows about these things—and he said it was perfectly hopeless, so we declined it. So Karswell has been pelting me with letters ever since. The last thing he wanted was the name of the man we referred his nonsense to; you saw my answer to that. But don't you say anything about it, for goodness' sake."

"I should think not, indeed. Did I ever do such a thing? I do hope, though, he won't get to know that it was poor Mr. Dunning."

"Poor Mr. Dunning? I don't know why you call him that; he's a very happy man, is Dunning. Lots of hobbies and a comfortable home, and all his time to himself."

"I only meant I should be sorry for him if this man got hold of his name, and came and bothered him."

"Oh, ah! yes. I dare say he would be poor Mr. Dunning then."

The Secretary and his wife were lunching out, and the friends to whose house they were bound were Warwickshire people. So Mrs. Secretary had already settled it in her own mind that she would question them judiciously about Mr. Karswell. But she was saved the trouble of leading up to the subject, for the hostess said to the host, before many minutes had passed, "I saw the Abbot of Lufford this morning." The host whistled. "*Did* you? What in the world brings him up to town?" "Goodness knows; he was coming out of the British Museum gate as I drove past." It was not unnatural that Mrs. Secretary should inquire whether this was a real Abbot who was being spoken of. "Oh no, my dear:

only a neighbor of ours in the country who bought Lufford Abbey a few years ago. His real name is Karswell." "Is he a friend of yours?" asked Mr. Secretary, with a private wink to his wife. The question let loose a torrent of declamation. There was really nothing to be said for Mr. Karswell. Nobody knew what he did with himself; his servants were a horrible set of people; he had invented a new religion for himself, and practised no one could tell what appalling rites; he was very easily offended, and never forgave anybody; he had a dreadful face (so the lady insisted, her husband somewhat demurring); he never did a kind action, and whatever influence he did exert was mischievous. "Do the poor man justice, dear," the husband interrupted. "You forget the treat he gave the school children." "Forget it, indeed! But I'm glad you mentioned it, because it gives an idea of the man. Now, Florence, listen to this. The first winter he was at Lufford this delightful neighbor of ours wrote to the clergyman of his parish (he's not ours, but we know him very well) and offered to show the school children some magic-lantern slides. He said he had some new kinds, which he thought would interest them. Well, the clergyman was rather surprised, because Mr. Karswell had shown himself inclined to be unpleasant to the children—complaining of their trespassing, or something of the sort; but of course he accepted, and the evening was fixed, and our friend went himself to see that everything went right. He said he never had been so thankful for anything as that his own children were all prevented from being there: they were at a children's party at our house, as a matter of fact. Because this Mr. Karswell had evidently set out with the intention of frightening these poor village children out of their wits, and I do believe, if he had been allowed to go on, he would actually have done so. He began with some comparatively mild things. Red Riding Hood was one, and even then, Mr. Farrer said, the wolf was so dreadful that several of the smaller children had to be taken out; and he

said Mr. Karswell began the story by producing a noise
like a wolf howling in the distance, which was the most
gruesome thing he had ever heard. All the slides he
showed, Mr. Farrer said, were most clever; they were
absolutely realistic, and where he had got them or how
he worked them he could not imagine. Well, the show
went on, and the stories kept on becoming a little more
terrifying each time, and the children were mesmer-
ized into complete silence. At last he produced a series
which represented a little boy passing through his own
park—Lufford, I mean—in the evening. Every child in
the room could recognize the place from the pictures.
And this poor boy was followed, and at last pursued
and overtaken, and either torn in pieces or somehow
made away with, by a horrible hopping creature in
white, which you saw first dodging about among the
trees, and gradually it appeared more and more plainly.
Mr. Farrer said it gave him one of the worst nightmares
he ever remembered, and what it must have meant to
the children doesn't bear thinking of. Of course this
was too much, and he spoke very sharply indeed to Mr.
Karswell, and said it couldn't go on. All *he* said was,
'Oh, you think it's time to bring our little show to an
end and send them home to their beds? *Very* well!'
And then, if you please, he switched on another slide,
which showed a great mass of snakes, centipedes, and
disgusting creatures with wings, and somehow or other
he made it seem as if they were climbing out of the
picture and getting in amongst the audience; and this
was accompanied by a sort of dry rustling noise which
sent the children nearly mad, and of course they stam-
peded. A good many of them were rather hurt in getting out of the room, and I don't suppose one of them
closed an eye that night. There was the most dreadful
trouble in the village afterward. Of course the mothers
threw a good part of the blame on poor Mr. Farrer,
and, if they could have got past the gates, I believe the
fathers would have broken every window in the Abbey.
Well, now, that's Mr. Karswell; that's the Abbot of

Lufford, my dear, and you can imagine how we covet *his* society."

"Yes, I think he has all the possibilities of a distinguished criminal, has Karswell," said the host. "I should be sorry for anyone who got into his bad books."

"Is he the man, or am I mixing him up with someone else?" asked the Secretary (who for some minutes had been wearing the frown of the man who is trying to recollect something). "Is he the man who brought out a *History of Witchcraft* some time back—ten years or more?"

"That's the man; do you remember the reviews of it?"

"Certainly I do; and what's equally to the point, I knew the author of the most incisive of the lot. So did you: you must remember John Harrington; he was at John's in our time."

"Oh, very well indeed, though I don't think I saw or heard anything of him between the time I went down and the day I read the account of the inquest on him."

"Inquest?" said one of the ladies. "What happened to him?"

"Why, what happened was that he fell out of a tree and broke his neck. But the puzzle was, what could have induced him to get up there. It was a mysterious business, I must say. Here was this man—not an athletic fellow, was he? and with no eccentric twist about him that was ever noticed—walking home along a country road late in the evening—no tramps about—well known and liked in the place—and he suddenly begins to run like mad, loses his hat and stick, and finally shins up a tree—quite a difficult tree—growing in the hedgerow; a dead branch gives way, and he comes down with it and breaks his neck, and there he's found next morning with the most dreadful face of fear on him that could be imagined. It was pretty evident, of course, that he had been chased by something, and people talked of savage dogs, and beasts escaped out of menageries; but there was nothing to be made of that. That was in '89, and I believe his brother Henry (whom I remember as well at Cambridge, but *you* probably don't) has been trying to get on the track of an explanation ever since. He, of course, insists there was malice in it, but I don't know. It's difficult to see how it could have come in."

After a time the talk reverted to the *History of Witchcraft*. "Did you ever look into it?" asked the host.

"Yes, I did," said the Secretary. "I went so far as to read it."

"Was it as bad as it was made out to be?"

"Oh, in point of style and form, quite hopeless. It deserved all the pulverizing it got. But, besides that, it was an evil book. The man believed every word of what he was saying, and I'm very much mistaken if he hadn't tried the greater part of his receipts."

"Well, I only remember Harrington's review of it, and I must say if I'd been the author it would have quenched my literary ambition for good. I should never have held up my head again."

"It hasn't had that effect in the present case. But come, it's half-past three; I must be off."

On the way home the Secretary's wife said, "I do hope that horrible man won't find out that Mr. Dunning had anything to do with the rejection of his paper." "I don't think there's much chance of that," said the Secretary. "Dunning won't mention it himself, for these matters are confidential, and none of us will for the same reason. Karswell won't know his name, for Dunning hasn't published anything on the same subject yet. The only danger is that Karswell might find out, if he was to ask the British Museum people who was in the habit of consulting alchemical manuscripts: I can't very well tell them not to mention Dunning, can I? It would set them talking at once. Let's hope it won't occur to him."

However, Mr. Karswell was an astute man.

This much is in the way of prologue. On an evening rather later in the same week, Mr. Edward Dunning was returning from the British Museum, where he had been engaged in research, to the comfortable house in a suburb where he lived alone, tended by two excellent women who had been long with him. There is nothing to be added by way of description of him to what we have heard already. Let us follow him as he takes his sober course homeward.

A train took him to within a mile or two of his house, and an electric tram a stage farther. The line ended at a point some three hundred yards from his front door. He had had enough of reading when he got into the car, and indeed the light was not such as to allow him to do more than study the advertisements on the panes of glass that faced him as he sat. As was not unnatural, the advertisements in this particular line of cars were objects of his frequent contemplation, and, with the possible exception of the brilliant and convincing dialogue between Mr. Lamplough and an eminent K.C. on the subject of Pyretic Saline, none of them afforded much scope to his imagination. I am wrong: there was one at the corner of the car farthest from him which did not seem familiar. It was in blue letters on a yellow ground, and all that he could read of it was a name—John Harrington—and something like a date. It could be of no interest to him to know more; but for all that, as the car emptied, he was just curious enough to move along the seat until he could read it well. He felt to a slight extent repaid for his trouble; the advertisement was *not* of the usual type. It ran thus: "In memory of John Harrington, F.S.A., of The Laurels, Ashbrooke. Died Sept. 18th, 1889. Three months were allowed."

The car stopped. Mr. Dunning, still contemplating the blue letters on the yellow ground, had to be stimulated to rise by a word from the conductor. "I beg your pardon," he said, "I was looking at that advertisement; it's a very odd one, isn't it?" The conductor read it slowly. "Well, my word," he said, "I never see that one before. Well, that is a cure, ain't it? Someone bin up to their jokes 'ere, I should think." He got out a duster and applied it, not without saliva, to the pane and then to the outside. "No," he said, returning, "that ain't no transfer; seems to me as if it was reg'lar *in* the glass, what I mean in the substance, as you may say. Don't you think so, sir?" Mr. Dunning examined it and rubbed it with his glove, and agreed. "Who looks after these advertisements, and gives leave for them to be put up? I wish you would inquire. I will just take a note of the words." At this moment there came a call from the driver: "Look alive, George, time's up." "All right, all right; there's somethink else what's up at this end. You come and look at this 'ere glass." "What's gorn with the glass?" said the driver, approaching. "Well, and oo's 'Arrington? What's it all about?" "I was just asking who was responsible for putting the advertisements up in your cars, and saying it would be as well to make some inquiry about this one." "Well, sir, that's all done at the Company's orfice, that work is: it's our Mr. Timms, I believe, looks into that. When we put up tonight I'll leave word, and per'aps I'll be able to tell you tomorrer if you 'appen to be coming this way."

This was all that passed that evening. Mr. Dunning did just go to the trouble of looking up Ashbrooke, and found that it was in Warwickshire.

Next day he went to town again. The car (it was the same car) was too full in the morning to allow of his getting a word with the conductor; he could only be sure that the curious advertisement had been made away with. The close of the day brought a further element of mystery into the transaction. He had missed the tram, or else preferred walking home, but at a rather late hour, while he was at work in his study, one of the maids came to say that two men from the tramways were very anxious to speak to him. This was a reminder of the advertisement, which he had, he says, nearly forgotten. He had the men in—they were the conductor and driver of the car—and when the matter of refreshment had been attended to, asked what Mr. Timms had had to say about the advertisement. "Well, sir, that's what we took the liberty to step round about," said the conductor. "Mr. Timms 'e give William 'ere the rough side of his tongue about that; 'cord-in' to 'im there warn't no advertisement of that descrip-tion sent in, nor ordered, nor paid for, nor put up, nor nothink, let alone not bein' there, and we was playing the fool takin' up his time. 'Well,' I says, 'if that's the case, all I ask of you, Mr. Timms,' I says, 'is to take and look at it for yourself,' I says. 'Of course if it ain't there,' I says, 'you may take and call me what you like.' 'Right,' he says, 'I will'; and we went straight off. Now, I leave it to you, sir, if that ad, as we term 'em, with 'Arrington on it warn't as plain as ever you see anythink—blue letters on yeller glass, and as I says at the time, and you borne me out, reg'lar *in* the glass, because, if you remember, you recollect of me swabbing it with my duster." "To be sure I do, quite clearly—well?" "You may say well, I don't think. Mr. Timms he gets in that car with a light—no, he told William to 'old the light outside. 'Now,' he says, 'where's your precious ad what we've 'eard so much about?' ' 'Ere it is,' I says, 'Mr. Timms,' and I laid my 'and on it." The conductor paused.

"Well," said Mr. Dunning, "it was gone, I suppose. Broken?"

"Broke!—not it. There warn't, if you'll believe me, no more trace of them letters—blue letters they was—on that piece o' glass, than—well, it's no good *me* talk-in'. *I* never see such a thing. I leave it to William here if—but there, as I says, where's the benefit in me going on about it?"

"And what did Mr. Timms say?"

"Why 'e did what I give 'im leave to—called us pretty much anythink he liked, and I don't know as I blame him so much neither. But what we thought, William and me did, was as we seen you take down a bit of a note about that—well, that letterin'—"

"I certainly did that, and I have it now. Did you wish me to speak to Mr. Timms myself, and show it to him? Was that what you came in about?"

"There, didn't I say as much?" said William. "Deal with a gent if you can get on the track of one, that's my word. Now perhaps, George, you'll allow as I ain't took you very far wrong tonight."

"Very well, William, very well; no need for you to go on as if you'd 'ad to frog's-march me 'ere. I come quiet, didn't I? All the same for that, we 'adn't ought to take up your time this way, sir; but if it so 'appened you could find time to step round to the Company's orfice in the morning and tell Mr. Timms what you seen for yourself, we should lay under a very 'igh obligation to you for the trouble. You see it ain't bein' called—well, one thing and another, as we mind, but if they got it into their 'ead at the orfice as we seen things as warn't there, why, one thing leads to another, and where we should be a twelvemunce 'ence—well, you can understand what I mean."

Amid further elucidations of the proposition, George, conducted by William, left the room.

The incredulity of Mr. Timms (who had a nodding acquaintance with Mr. Dunning) was greatly modified on the following day by what the latter could tell and show him; and any bad mark that might have been attached to the names of William and George was not suffered to remain on the Company's books; but explanation there was none.

Mr. Dunning's interest in the matter was kept alive by an incident of the following afternoon. He was walking from his club to the train, and he noticed some way ahead a man with a handful of leaflets such as are distributed to passers-by by agents of enterprising firms. This agent had not chosen a very crowded street for his operations: in fact, Mr. Dunning did not see him get rid of a single leaflet before he himself reached the spot. One was thrust into his hand as he passed: the hand that gave it touched his, and he experienced a sort of little shock as it did so. It seemed unnaturally rough and hot. He looked in passing at the giver, but the impression he got was so unclear that, however much he tried to reckon it up subsequently, nothing would come. He was walking quickly, and as he went on glanced at the paper. It was a blue one. The name of Harrington in large capitals caught his eye. He stopped, startled, and felt for his glasses. The next instant the leaflet was twitched out of his hand by a man who hurried past, and was irrecoverably gone. He ran back a few paces, but where was the passer-by? and where the distributor?

It was in a somewhat pensive frame of mind that Mr. Dunning passed on the following day into the Select Manuscript Room of the British Museum, and filled out tickets for Harley 3586, and some other volumes. After a few minutes they were brought to him, and he was settling the one he wanted first upon the desk, when he thought he heard his own name whispered behind him. He turned round hastily, and in doing so, brushed his little portfolio of loose papers onto the floor. He saw no one he recognized except one of the staff in charge of the room, who nodded to him, and he proceeded to pick up his papers. He thought he had them all and was turning to begin work, when a stout gentleman at the table behind him, who was just rising to leave, and had collected his own belongings, touched him on the shoulder, saying, "May I give you this? I think it should be yours," and handed him a missing quire. "It is mine, thank you," said Mr. Dunning. In another moment the man had left the room. Upon finishing his work for the afternoon, Mr. Dunning had some conversation with the assistant in charge, and took occasion to ask who the stout gentleman was. "Oh, he's a man named Karswell," said the assistant; "he was asking me a week ago who were the great authorities on alchemy, and of course I told him you were the only one in the country. I'll see if I can't catch him; he'd like to meet you, I'm sure."

"For heaven's sake, don't dream of it!" said Mr. Dunning, "I'm particularly anxious to avoid him."

"Oh! very well," said the assistant, "he doesn't come here often; I dare say you won't meet him."

More than once on the way home that day Mr. Dunning confessed to himself that he did not look forward with his usual cheerfulness to a solitary evening. It seemed to him that something ill defined and impalpable had stepped in between him and his fellow-men —had taken him in charge, as it were. He wanted to sit close up to his neighbors in the train and in the tram, but as luck would have it both train and car were markedly empty. The conductor George was thoughtful, and appeared to be absorbed in calculations as to the number of passengers. On arriving at his house he found Dr. Watson, his medical man, on his doorstep. "I've had to upset your household arrangements, I'm sorry to say, Dunning. Both your servants *hors de combat*. In fact, I've had to send them to the Nursing Home."

"Good heavens! what's the matter?"

"It's something like ptomaine poisoning, I should think; you've not suffered yourself, I can see, or you wouldn't be walking about. I think they'll pull through all right."

"Dear, dear! Have you any idea what brought it on?"

"Well, they tell me they bought some shellfish from a hawker at their dinnertime. It's odd. I've made inquiries, but I can't find that any hawker has been to other houses in the street. I couldn't send word to you; they won't be back for a bit yet. You come and dine with me tonight, anyhow, and we can make arrangements for going on. Eight o'clock. Don't be too anxious."

The solitary evening was thus obviated; at the expense of some distress and inconvenience, it is true. Mr. Dunning spent the time pleasantly enough with the doctor (a rather recent settler), and returned to his lonely home at about 11:30. The night he passed is not one on which he looks back with any satisfaction. He was in bed and the light was out. He was wondering if the charwoman would come early enough to get him hot water next morning, when he heard the unmistakable sound of his study door opening. No step followed it on the passage floor, but the sound must mean mischief, for he knew that he had shut the door that evening after putting his papers away in his desk. It was rather shame than courage that induced him to slip out into the passage and lean over the banister in his nightgown, listening. No light was visible; no further sound came; only a gust of warm, or even hot air played for an instant round his shins. He went back and decided to lock himself into his room. There was more unpleasantness, however. Either an economical suburban company had decided that their light would not be required in the small hours, and had stopped working, or else something was wrong with the meter; the effect was in any case that the electric light was off. The obvious course was to find a match, and also to consult his watch; he might as well know how many hours of discomfort awaited him. So he put his hand into the well-known nook under the pillow; only, it did not get so far. What he touched was, according to his account, a mouth, with teeth, and with hair about it, and, he declares, not the mouth of a human being. I do not think it is any use to guess what he said or did; but he was in a spare room with the door locked and his ear to it before he was clearly conscious again. And there he spent the rest of a most miserable night, looking every moment for some fumbling at the door; but nothing came.

The venturing back to his own room in the morning was attended with many listenings and quiverings. The door stood open, fortunately, and the blinds were up (the servants had been out of the house before the hour of drawing them down); there was, to be short, no trace of an inhabitant. The watch, too, was in its usual place; nothing was disturbed, only the wardrobe door had swung open, in accordance with its confirmed habit. A ring at the back door now announced the charwoman, who had been ordered the night before, and nerved Mr. Dunning, after letting her in, to continue his search in other parts of the house. It was equally fruitless.

The day thus begun went on dismally enough. He dared not go to the Museum; in spite of what the assistant had said, Karswell might turn up there, and Dunning felt he could not cope with a probably hostile stranger. His own house was odious; he hated sponging on the doctor. He spent some little time in a call at the Nursing Home, where he was slightly cheered by a good report of his housekeeper and maid. Toward lunch time he betook himself to his club, again experiencing a gleam of satisfaction at seeing the Secretary of the Association. At luncheon Dunning told his friend the more material of his woes, but could not bring himself to speak of those that weighed most heavily on his spirits. "My poor dear man," said the Secretary, "what an upset! Look here; we're alone at home, absolutely. You must put up with us. Yes! no excuse; send your things in this afternoon." Dunning was unable to stand out; he was, in truth, becoming acutely anxious, as the hours went on, as to what that night might have waiting for him. He was almost happy as he hurried home to pack up.

His friends, when they had time to take stock of him, were rather shocked at his lorn appearance, and did their best to keep him up to the mark. Not altogether without success; but, when the two men were smoking alone later, Dunning became dull again. Suddenly he said, "Gayton, I believe that alchemist man knows it was I who got his paper rejected." Gayton whistled. "What makes you think that?" he said. Dunning told of his conversation with the Museum assistant, and Gayton could only agree that the guess seemed likely

to be correct. "Not that I care much," Dunning went
on, "only it might be a nuisance if we were to meet.
He's a bad-tempered party, I imagine." Conversation
dropped again; Gayton became more and more
strongly impressed with the desolateness that came
over Dunning's face and bearing, and finally—though
with a considerable effort—he asked him point-blank
whether something serious was not bothering him.
Dunning gave an exclamation of relief. "I was perish-
ing to get it off my mind," he said. "Do you know anything about a man named John Harrington?" Gayton
was thoroughly startled, and at the moment could only
ask why. Then the complete story of Dunning's experiences came out—what had happened in the tram-
car, in his own house, and in the street, the troubling
of spirit that had crept over him, and still held him;
and he ended with the question he had begun with.
Gayton was at a loss how to answer him. To tell the
story of Harrington's end would perhaps be right; only,
Dunning was in a nervous state, the story was a grim
one, and he could not help asking himself whether
there were not a connecting link between these two
cases, in the person of Karswell. It was a difficult con-
cession for a scientific man, but it could be eased by
the phrase "hypnotic suggestion." In the end he decided that his answer tonight should be guarded; he
would talk the situation over with his wife. So he said
that he had known Harrington at Cambridge, and believed he had died suddenly in 1889, adding a few details about the man and his published work. He did
talk over the matter with Mrs. Gayton, and, as he had
anticipated, she leaped at once to the conclusion which
had been hovering before him. It was she who reminded him of the surviving brother, Henry Harrington, and she also who suggested that he might be got
hold of by means of their hosts of the day before. "He
might be a hopeless crank," objected Gayton. "That
could be ascertained from the Bennetts, who knew

him," Mrs. Gayton retorted; and she undertook to see the Bennetts the very next day.

It is not necessary to tell in further detail the steps by which Henry Harrington and Dunning were brought together.

The next scene that does require to be narrated is a conversation that took place between the two. Dunning had told Harrington of the strange ways in which the dead man's name had been brought before him, and had said something, besides, of his own subsequent experiences. Then he had asked if Harrington was disposed, in return, to recall any of the circumstances connected with his brother's death. Harrington's surprise at what he heard can be imagined: but his reply was readily given.

"John," he said, "was in a very odd state, undeniably, from time to time, during some weeks before, though not immediately before, the catastrophe. There were several things; the principal notion he had was that he thought he was being followed. No doubt he was an impressionable man, but he never had had such fancies as this before. I cannot get it out of my mind that there was ill will at work, and what you tell me about yourself reminds me very much of my brother. Can you think of any possible connecting link?"

"There is just one that has been taking shape vaguely in my mind. I've been told that your brother reviewed a book very severely not long before he died, and just lately I have happened to cross the path of the man who wrote that book in a way he would resent."

"Don't tell me the man was called Karswell."

"Why not? that is exactly his name."

Henry Harrington leaned back. "That is final to my mind. Now I must explain further. From something he said, I feel sure that my brother John was beginning to believe—very much against his will—that Karswell was at the bottom of his trouble. I want to tell you

what seems to me to have a bearing on the situation.
My brother was a great musician, and used to run up
to concerts in town. He came back, three months before he died, from one of these, and gave me his program to look at—an analytical program: he always
kept them. 'I nearly missed this one,' he said. 'I suppose I must have dropped it; anyhow, I was looking for
it under my seat and in my pockets and so on, and my
neighbor offered me his; said "might he give it me, he
had no further use for it," and he went away just
afterward. I don't know who he was—a stout, clean-
shaven man. I should have been sorry to miss it; of
course I could have bought another, but this cost me
nothing.' At another time he told me that he had been
very uncomfortable both on the way to his hotel and
during the night. I piece things together now in thinking it over. Then, not very long after, he was going
over these programs, putting them in order to have
them bound up, and in this particular one (which by
the way I had hardly glanced at), he found quite near
the beginning a strip of paper with some very odd
writing on it in red and black—most carefully done—
it looked to me more like Runic letters than anything
else. 'Why,' he said, 'this must belong to my fat neighbor. It looks as if it might be worth returning to him;
it may be a copy of something; evidently someone has
taken trouble over it. How can I find his address?' We
talked it over for a little and agreed that it wasn't
worth advertising about, and that my brother had better look out for the man at the next concert, to which
he was going very soon. The paper was lying on the
book and we were both by the fire; it was a cold, windy
summer evening. I suppose the door blew open, though
I didn't notice it; at any rate a gust—a warm gust it
was—came quite suddenly between us, took the paper
and blew it straight into the fire; it was light, thin
paper, and flared and went up the chimney in a single
ash. 'Well,' I said, 'you can't give it back now.' He
said nothing for a minute; then rather crossly, 'No, I

can't; but why you should keep on saying so I don't know.' I remarked that I didn't say it more than once. 'Not more than four times, you mean,' was all he said. I remember all that very clearly, without any good reason; and now to come to the point. I don't know if you looked at that book of Karswell's which my unfortunate brother reviewed. It's not likely that you should; but I did, both before his death and after it. The first time we made game of it together. It was written in no style at all—split infinitives, and every sort of thing that makes an Oxford gorge rise. Then there was nothing that the man didn't swallow: mixing up classical myths, and stories out of the *Golden Legend* with reports of savage customs of today—all very proper, no doubt, if you know how to use them, but he didn't; he seemed to put the *Golden Legend* and the *Golden Bough* exactly on a par, and to believe both: a pitiable exhibition, in short. Well, after the misfortune, I looked over the book again. It was no better than before, but the impression which it left this time on my mind was different. I suspected—as I told you—that Karswell had borne ill will to my brother, even that he was in some way responsible for what had happened; and now his book seemed to me to be a very sinister performance indeed. One chapter in particular struck me, in which he spoke of 'casting the Runes' on people, either for the purpose of gaining their affection or of getting them out of the way—perhaps more especially the latter; he spoke of all this in a way that really seemed to me to imply actual knowledge. I've not time to go into details, but the upshot is that I am pretty sure from information received that the civil man at the concert was Karswell; I suspect—I more than suspect—that the paper was of importance; and I do believe that if my brother had been able to give it back, he might have been alive now. Therefore, it occurs to me to ask you whether you have anything to put beside what I have told you."

By way of answer, Dunning had the episode in the

Manuscript Room at the British Museum to relate. "Then he did actually hand you some papers; have you examined them? No? Because we must, if you'll allow it, look at them at once, and very carefully."

They went to the still empty house—empty, for the two servants were not yet able to return to work. Dunning's portfolio of papers was gathering dust on the writing table. In it were the quires of small-sized scribbling paper which he used for his transcripts; and from one of these, as he took it up, there slipped and fluttered out into the room with uncanny quickness, a strip of thin light paper. The window was open, but Harrington slammed it to, just in time to intercept the paper, which he caught. "I thought so," he said; "it might be the identical thing that was given to my brother. You'll have to look out, Dunning; this may mean something quite serious for you."

A long consultation took place. The paper was narrowly examined. As Harrington had said, the characters on it were more like Runes than anything else, but not decipherable by either man, and both hesitated to copy them, for fear, as they confessed, of perpetuating whatever evil purpose they might conceal. So it has remained impossible (if I may anticipate a little) to ascertain what was conveyed in this curious message or commission. Both Dunning and Harrington are firmly convinced that it had the effect of bringing its possessors into very undesirable company. That it must be returned to the source whence it came they were agreed, and further, that the only safe and certain way was that of personal service; and here contrivance would be necessary, for Dunning was known by sight to Karswell. He must, for one thing, alter his appearance by shaving his beard. But then might not the blow fall first? Harrington thought they could time it. He knew the date of the concert at which the "black spot" had been put on his brother: it was June 18. The death had followed on September 18. Dunning reminded him that three months had been mentioned in the inscription on the car window. "Perhaps," he added, with a cheerless laugh, "mine may be a bill at three months too. I believe I can fix it by my diary. Yes, April 23 was the day at the Museum; that brings us to July 23. Now, you know, it becomes extremely important to me to know anything you will tell me about the progress of your brother's trouble, if it is possible for you to speak of it." "Of course. Well, the sense of being watched whenever he was alone was the most distressing thing to him. After a time I took to sleeping in his room, and he was the better for that; still, he talked a great deal in his sleep. What about? Is it wise to dwell on that, at least before things are straightened out? I think not, but I can tell you this: two things came for him by post during those weeks, both with a London postmark, and addressed in a commercial hand. One was a woodcut of Bewick's, roughly torn out of the page: one which shows a moonlit road and a man walking along it, followed by an awful demon creature. Under it were written the lines out of *The Ancient Mariner* (which I suppose the cut illustrates) about one who, having once looked round—

> *walks on,*
> *And turns no more his head;*
> *Because he knows a frightful fiend*
> *Doth close behind him tread.*

The other was a calendar, such as tradesmen often send. My brother paid no attention to this, but I looked at it after his death, and found that everything after September 18 had been torn out. You may be surprised at his having gone out alone the evening he was killed, but the fact is that during the last ten days or so of his life he had been quite free from the sense of being followed or watched."

The end of the consultation was this. Harrington, who knew a neighbor of Karswell's, thought he saw a way of keeping a watch on his movements. It would be

Dunning's part to be in readiness to try to cross Karswell's path at any moment, to keep the paper safe and in a place of ready access.

They parted. The next weeks were no doubt a severe strain upon Dunning's nerves; the intangible barrier which had seemed to rise about him on the day when he received the paper, gradually developed into a brooding blackness that cut him off from the means of escape to which one might have thought he might resort. No one was at hand who was likely to suggest them to him, and he seemed robbed of all initiative. He waited with inexpressible anxiety as May, June, and early July passed on, for a mandate from Harrington. But all this time Karswell remained immovable at Lufford.

At last, less than a week before the date he had come to look upon as the end of his earthly activities, came a telegram: "LEAVES VICTORIA BY BOAT TRAIN THURSDAY NIGHT. DO NOT MISS. I COME TO YOU TONIGHT. HARRINGTON."

He arrived accordingly, and they concocted plans. The train left Victoria at nine and its last stop before Dover was Croydon West. Harrington would mark down Karswell at Victoria, and look out for Dunning at Croydon, calling to him if need were by a name agreed upon. Dunning, disguised as far as might be, was to have no label or initials on any hand luggage, and must at all costs have the paper with him.

Dunning's suspense as he waited on the Croydon platform I need not attempt to describe. His sense of danger during the last days had only been sharpened by the fact that the cloud about him had perceptibly been lighter; but relief was an ominous symptom, and, if Karswell eluded him now, hope was gone; and there were so many chances of that. The rumor of the journey might be itself a device. The twenty minutes in which he paced the platform and persecuted every porter with inquires as to the boat train were as bitter as any he had spent. Still, the train came, and Harrington was at the window. It was important, of course, that there should be no recognition; so Dunning got in at the farther end of the corridor carriage, and only gradually made his way to the compartment where Harrington and Karswell were. He was pleased, on the whole, to see that the train was far from full.

Karswell was on the alert, but gave no sign of recognition. Dunning took the seat not immediately facing him, and attempted, vainly at first, then with increasing command of his faculties, to reckon the possibilities of making the desired transfer. Opposite to Karswell, and next to Dunning, was a heap of Karswell's coats on the seat. It would be of no use to slip the paper into these—he would not be safe, or would not feel so, unless in some way it could be proffered by him and accepted by the other. There was a handbag open, and with papers in it. Could he manage to conceal this (so that perhaps Karswell might leave the carriage without it), and then find and give it to him? This was the plan that suggested itself. If he could only have counseled with Harrington! but that could not be. The minutes went on. More than once Karswell rose and went out into the corridor. The second time Dunning was on the point of attempting to make the bag fall off the seat, but he caught Harrington's eye, and read in it a warning. Karswell, from the corridor, was watching; probably to see if the two men recognized each other. He returned, but was evidently restless; and, when he rose the third time, hope dawned, for something did slip off his seat and fall with hardly a sound to the floor. Karswell went out once more, and passed out of range of the corridor window. Dunning picked up what had fallen, and saw that the key was in his hands in the form of one of Cook's ticket cases, with tickets in it. These cases have a pocket in the cover, and within very few seconds the paper of which we have heard was in the pocket of this one. To make the operation more secure, Harrington stood in the doorway of the compartment and fiddled with the blind. It was done, and done at the right time, for the train was now slowing down toward Dover.

In a moment more Karswell re-entered the compartment. As he did so, Dunning, managing, he knew not how, to suppress the tremble in his voice, handed him the ticket case, saying, "May I give you this, sir? I believe it is yours." After a brief glance at the ticket inside, Karswell uttered the hoped-for response, "Yes, it is; much obliged to you, sir," and he placed it in his breast pocket.

Even in the few moments that remained—moments of tense anxiety, for they knew not to what a premature finding of the paper might lead—both men noticed that the carriage seemed to darken about them and to grow warmer; that Karswell was fidgety and oppressed; that he drew the heap of loose coats near to him and cast it back as if it repelled him; and that he then sat upright and glanced anxiously at both. They, with sickening anxiety, busied themselves in collecting their belongings; but they both thought that Karswell was on the point of speaking when the train stopped at Dover Town. It was natural that in the short space between town and pier they should both go into the corridor.

At the pier they got out, but so empty was the train that they were forced to linger on the platform until Karswell should have passed ahead of them with his porter on the way to the boat, and only then was it safe for them to exchange a pressure of the hand and a word of concentrated congratulation. The effect upon Dunning was to make him almost faint. Harrington made him lean up against the wall, while he himself went forward a few yards within sight of the gangway to the boat, at which Karswell had now arrived. The man at the head of it examined his ticket, and, laden with coats, he passed down into the boat. Suddenly the official called after him, "You, sir, beg pardon, did the other gentleman show his ticket?" "What the devil do you mean by the other gentleman?" Karswell's snarling voice called back from the deck. The man bent over and looked at him. "The devil? Well, I don't know, I'm sure," Harrington heard him say to himself, and then aloud, "My mistake, sir; must have been your rugs! ask your pardon." And then, to a subordinate near him, " 'Ad he got a dog with him, or what? Funny thing; I could 'a' swore 'e wasn't alone. Well, whatever it was, they'll 'ave to see to it aboard. She's off now. Another week and we shall be gettin' the 'oliday customers." In five minutes more there was nothing but the lessening lights of the boat, the long line of the Dover lamps, the night breeze, and the moon.

Long and long the two sat in their room at the Lord Warden. In spite of the removal of their greatest anxiety, they were oppressed with a doubt, not of the lightest. Had they been justified in sending a man to his death, as they believed they had? Ought they not to warn him, at least? "No," said Harrington; "if he is the murderer I think him, we have done no more than is just. Still, if you think it better—but how and where can you warn him?" "He was booked to Abbeville only," said Dunning. "I saw that. If I wired to the hotels there in Joanne's Guide, 'Examine your ticket case, Dunning,' I should feel happier. This is the twenty-first; he will have a day. But I am afraid he has gone into the dark." So telegrams were left at the hotel office.

It is not clear whether these reached their destination, or whether if they did, they were understood. All that is known is that, on the afternoon of the twenty-third, an English traveler, examining the front of St. Wulfram's Church at Abbeville, then under extensive repair, was struck on the head and instantly killed by a stone falling from the scaffold erected round the northwestern tower, there being, as was clearly proved, no workman on the scaffold at that moment; and the traveler's papers identified him as Mr. Karswell.

Only one detail shall be added. At Karswell's sale a set of Bewick, sold with all faults, was acquired by Harrington. The page with the woodcut of the traveler and the demon was, as he had expected, mutilated. Also, after a judicious interval, Harrington repeated to Dunning something of what he had heard his brother say in his sleep; but it was not long before Dunning stopped him.

The Voice in the Night

by WILLIAM HOPE HODGSON

It was a dark, starless night. We were becalmed in the Northern Pacific. Our exact position I do not know; for the sun had been hidden during the course of a weary, breathless week, by a thin haze which had seemed to float above us, about the height of our mastheads, at whiles descending and shrouding the surrounding sea.

With there being no wind, we had steadied the tiller, and I was the only man on deck. The crew, consisting of two men and a boy, were sleeping forward in their den; while Will—my friend, and the master of our little craft—was aft in his bunk on the port side of the little cabin.

Reprinted by permission of Miss Lissie S. Hodgson.

Suddenly, from out of the surrounding darkness, there came a hail: "Schooner, ahoy!"

The cry was so unexpected that I gave no immediate answer, because of my surprise.

It came again—a voice curiously throaty and inhuman, calling from somewhere upon the dark sea away on our port broadside.

"Schooner, ahoy!"

"Hullo!" I sang out, having gathered my wits somewhat. "What are you? What do you want?"

"You need not be afraid," answered the queer voice, having probably noticed some trace of confusion in my tone. "I am only an old—man."

The pause sounded oddly; but it was only afterward that it came back to me with any significance.

"Why don't you come alongside, then?" I queried somewhat snappishly; for I liked not his hinting at my having been a trifle shaken.

"I—I—can't. It wouldn't be safe. I—" The voice broke off, and there was silence.

"What do you mean?" I asked, growing more and more astonished. "What not safe? Where are you?"

I listened for a moment; but there came no answer. And then, a sudden indefinite suspicion, of I knew not what, coming to me, I stepped swiftly to the binnacle, and took out the lighted lamp. At the same time, I knocked on the deck with my heel to waken Will. Then I was back at the side, throwing the yellow funnel of light out into the silent immensity beyond our rail. As I did so, I heard a slight, muffled cry, and then the sound of a splash as though someone had dipped oars abruptly. Yet I cannot say that I saw anything with certainty; save, it seemed to me, that in the first flash of the light, there had been something upon the waters, where now there was nothing.

"Hullo, there!" I called. "What foolery is this!"

But there came only the indistinct sounds of a boat being pulled away into the night.

Then I heard Will's voice, from the direction of the after scuttle.

"What's up, George?"

"Come here, Will!" I said.

"What is it?" he asked, coming across the deck.

I told him the queer thing which had happened. He put several questions; then, after a moment's silence, he raised his hands to his lips, and hailed, "Boat, ahoy!"

From a long distance away there came back to us a faint reply, and my companion repeated his call. Presently, after a short period of silence, there grew on our hearing the muffled sound of oars; at which Will hailed again.

This time there was a reply.

"Put away the light."

"I'm damned if I will," I muttered; but Will told me to do as the voice bade, and I shoved it down under the bulwarks.

"Come nearer," he said, and the oar strokes continued. Then, when apparently some half-dozen fathoms distant, they again ceased.

"Come alongside," exclaimed Will. "There's nothing to be frightened of aboard here!"

"Promise that you will not show the light?"

"What's to do with you," I burst out, "that you're so infernally afraid of the light?"

"Because—" began the voice, and stopped short.

"Because what?" I asked quickly.

Will put his hand on my shoulder.

"Shut up a minute, old man," he said in a low voice. "Let me tackle him."

He leaned more over the rail.

"See here, mister," he said, "this is a pretty queer business, you coming upon us like this, right out in the middle of the blessed Pacific. How are we to know what sort of a hanky-panky trick you're up to? You say there's only one of you. How are we to know, unless we get a squint at you—eh? What's your objection to the light, anyway?"

As he finished, I heard the noise of the oars again, and then the voice came; but now from a greater distance, and sounding extremely hopeless and pathetic.

"I am sorry—sorry! I would not have troubled you, only I am hungry, and—so is she."

The voice died away, and the sound of the oars, dipping irregularly, was borne to us.

"Stop!" sung out Will. "I don't want to drive you away. Come back! We'll keep the light hidden, if you don't like it."

He turned to me.

"It's a damned queer rig, this; but I think there's nothing to be afraid of?"

There was a question in his tone, and I replied.

"No, I think the poor devil's been wrecked around here, and gone crazy."

The sound of the oars drew nearer.

"Shove that lamp back in the binnacle," said Will; then he leaned over the rail and listened. I replaced the lamp, and came back to his side. The dipping of the oars ceased some dozen yards distant.

"Won't you come alongside now?" asked Will in an even voice. "I have had the lamp put back in the binnacle."

"I—I cannot," replied the voice. "I dare not come nearer. I dare not even pay you for the—the provisions."

"That's all right," said Will, and hesitated. "You're welcome to as much grub as you can take—" Again he hesitated.

"You are very good," exclaimed the voice. "May God, Who understands everything, reward you—" It broke off huskily.

"The—the lady?" said Will abruptly. "Is she—"

"I have left her behind upon the island," came the voice.

"What island?" I cut in.

"I know not its name," returned the voice. "I would to God—!" it began, and checked itself as suddenly.

"Could we not send a boat for her?" asked Will at this point.

"No!" said the voice, with extraordinary emphasis. "My God! No!" There was a moment's pause; then it added, in a tone which seemed a merited reproach, "It was because of our want I ventured—because her agony tortured me."

"I am a forgetful brute," exclaimed Will. "Just wait a minute, whoever you are, and I will bring you up something at once."

In a couple of minutes he was back again, and his arms were full of various edibles. He paused at the rail.

"Can't you come alongside for them?" he asked.

"No—I *dare not*," replied the voice, and it seemed to me that in its tones I detected a note of stifled craving—as though the owner hushed a mortal desire. It came to me then in a flash that the poor old creature out there in the darkness was *suffering* for actual need of that which Will held in his arms; and yet, because of some unintelligible dread, refraining from dashing to the side of our schooner, and receiving it. And with the lightning-like conviction, there came the knowledge that the Invisible was not mad; but sanely facing some intolerable horror.

"Damn it, Will!" I said, full of many feelings, over which predominated a vast sympathy. "Get a box. We must float off the stuff to him in it."

This we did—propelling it away from the vessel, out into the darkness, by means of a boathook. In a minute, a slight cry from the Invisible came to us, and we knew that he had secured the box.

A little later, he called out a farewell to us, and so heartful a blessing that I am sure we were the better for it. Then, without more ado, we heard the ply of oars across the darkness.

"Pretty soon off," remarked Will, with perhaps just a little sense of injury.

"Wait," I replied. "I think somehow he'll come back. He must have been badly needing that food."

"And the lady," said Will. For a moment he was silent; then he continued, "It's the queerest thing ever I've tumbled across, since I've been fishing."

"Yes," I said, and fell to pondering.

And so the time slipped away—an hour, another, and still Will stayed with me; for the queer adventure had knocked all desire for sleep out of him.

The third hour was three parts through, when we heard again the sound of oars across the silent ocean.

"Listen!" said Will, a low note of excitement in his voice.

"He's coming, just as I thought," I muttered.

The dipping of the oars grew nearer, and I noted that the strokes were firmer and longer. The food had been needed.

They came to a stop a little distance off the broadside, and the queer voice came again to us through the darkness.

"Schooner, ahoy!"

"That you?" asked Will.

"Yes," replied the voice. "I left you suddenly; but—but there was great need."

"The lady?" questioned Will.

"The—lady is grateful now on earth. She will be more grateful soon in—in heaven."

Will began to make some reply, in a puzzled voice; but became confused, and broke off short. I said nothing. I was wondering at the curious pauses, and, apart from my wonder, I was full of a great sympathy.

The voice continued.

"We—she and I, have talked, as we shared the result of God's tenderness and yours—"

Will interposed; but without coherence.

"I beg of you not to—to belittle your deed of Christian charity this night," said the voice. "Be sure that it has not escaped His notice."

It stopped, and there was a full minute's silence. Then it came again.

"We have spoken together upon that which—which has befallen us. We had thought to go out, without telling any, of the terror which has come into our—lives. She is with me in believing that tonight's happenings are under a special ruling, and that it is God's wish that we should tell to you all that we have suffered since—since—"

"Yes?" said Will softly.

"Since the sinking of the *Albatross*."

"Ah!" I exclaimed involuntarily. "She left Newcastle for 'Frisco some six months ago, and hasn't been heard of since."

"Yes," answered the voice. "But some few degrees to the north of the line she was caught in a terrible storm, and dismasted. When the day came, it was found that she was leaking badly, and presently, it falling to a calm, the sailors took to the boats, leaving—leaving a young lady—my fiancée—and myself upon the wreck.

"We were below, gathering together a few of our belongings, when they left. They were entirely callous, through fear, and when we came up upon the decks, we saw them only as small shapes afar off upon the horizon. Yet we did not despair, but set to work and constructed a small raft. Upon this we put such few matters as it would hold, including a quantity of water and some ship's biscuit. Then, the vessel being very deep in the water, we got ourselves on to the raft, and pushed off.

"It was later when I observed that we seemed to be in the way of some tide or current, which bore us from the ship at an angle; so that in the course of three hours, by my watch, her hull became invisible to our sight, her broken masts remaining in view for a somewhat longer period. Then, toward evening, it grew misty, and so through the night. The next day we were still encompassed by the mist, the weather remaining quiet.

"For four days we drifted through this strange haze, until, on the evening of the fourth day, there grew upon our ears the murmur of breakers at a distance. Gradually it became plainer, and, somewhat after midnight, it appeared to sound upon either hand at no very great space. The raft was raised upon a swell several times, and then we were in smooth water, and the noise of the breakers was behind.

"When the morning came, we found that we were in a sort of great lagoon; but of this we noticed little at the time; for close before us, through the enshrouding mist, loomed the hull of a large sailing vessel. With one accord, we fell upon our knees and thanked God; for we thought that here was an end to our perils. We had much to learn.

"The raft drew near to the ship, and we shouted at them to take us aboard; but none answered. Presently the raft touched against the side of the vessel, and, seeing a rope hanging downward, I seized it and began to climb. Yet I had much ado to make my way up, because of a kind of gray, lichenous fungus which had seized upon the rope, and which blotched the side of the ship lividly.

"I reached the rail and clambered over it, on to the deck. Here I saw that the decks were covered, in great patches, with the gray masses, some of them rising into nodules several feet in height; but at the time I thought less of this matter than of the possibility of there being people aboard the ship. I shouted; but none answered. Then I went to the door below the poop deck. I opened it, and peered in. There was a great smell of staleness, so that I knew in a moment that nothing living was within, and with the knowledge, I shut the door quickly; for I felt suddenly lonely.

"I went back to the side where I had scrambled up. My—my sweetheart was still sitting quietly upon the raft. Seeing me look down she called up to know whether there were any aboard of the ship. I replied that the vessel had the appearance of having been long deserted; but that if she would wait a little I would see whether there was anything in the shape of a ladder by which she could ascend to the deck. Then we would make a search through the vessel together. A little later, on the opposite side of the decks, I found a rope side ladder. This I carried across, and a minute afterward she was beside me.

"Together we explored the cabins and apartments in the after part of the ship; but nowhere was there any sign of life. Here and there, within the cabins themselves, we came across odd patches of that queer fungus; but this, as my sweetheart said, could be cleansed away.

"In the end, having assured ourselves that the after portion of the vessel was empty, we picked our way to the bows, between the ugly gray nodules of that strange growth; and here we made a further search, which told us that there was indeed none aboard but ourselves.

"This being now beyond any doubt, we returned to the stern of the ship and proceeded to make ourselves as comfortable as possible. Together we cleared out and cleaned two of the cabins; and after that I made examination whether there was anything eatable in the ship. This I soon found was so, and thanked God in my heart for His goodness. In addition to this I discovered the whereabouts of the fresh-water pump, and having fixed it I found the water drinkable, though somewhat unpleasant to the taste.

"For several days we stayed aboard the ship, without attempting to get to the shore. We were busily engaged in making the place habitable. Yet even thus early we became aware that our lot was even less to be desired than might have been imagined; for though, as a first step, we scraped away the odd patches of growth that studded the floors and walls of the cabins and saloon, yet they returned almost to their original size within the space of twenty-four hours, which not only discouraged us, but gave us a feeling of vague unease.

"Still we would not admit ourselves beaten, so set to work afresh, and not only scraped away the fungus, but soaked the places where it had been, with carbolic, a canful of which I had found in the pantry. Yet, by the end of the week the growth had returned in full strength, and, in addition it had spread to other places, as though our touching it had allowed germs from it to travel elsewhere.

"On the seventh morning, my sweetheart woke to find a small patch of it growing on her pillow, close to her face. At that, she came to me, so soon as she could get her garments upon her. I was in the galley at the time lighting the fire for breakfast.

" 'Come here, John,' she said, and led me aft. When I saw the thing upon her pillow I shuddered, and then and there we agreed to go right out of the ship and see whether we could not fare to make ourselves more comfortable ashore.

"Hurriedly we gathered together our few belongings, and even among these I found that fungus had been at work; for one of her shawls had a little lump of it growing near one edge. I threw the whole thing over the side, without saying anything to her.

"The raft was still alongside, but it was too clumsy to guide, and I lowered down a small boat that hung across the stern, and in this we made our way to the shore. Yet, as we drew near to it, I became gradually aware that here the vile fungus, which had driven us from the ship, was growing riot. In places it rose into horrible, fantastic mounds, which seemed almost to quiver, as with a quiet life, when the wind blew across them. Here and there it took on the forms of vast fingers, and in others it just spread out flat and smooth and treacherous. Odd places, it appeared as grotesque stunted trees, seeming extraordinarily kinked and gnarled—the whole quaking vilely at times.

"At first, it seemed to us that there was no single

portion of the surrounding shore which was not hidden beneath the masses of the hideous lichen; yet, in this, I found we were mistaken; for somewhat later, coasting along the shore at a little distance, we descried a smooth white patch of what appeared to be fine sand, and there we landed. It was not sand. What it was I do not know. All that I have observed is that upon it the fungus will not grow; while everywhere else, save where the sandlike earth wanders oddly, pathwise, amid the gray desolation of the lichen, there is nothing but that loathsome grayness.

"It is difficult to make you understand how cheered we were to find one place that was absolutely free from the growth, and here we deposited our belongings. Then we went back to the ship for such things as it seemed to us we should need. Among other matters, I managed to bring ashore with me one of the ship's sails, with which I constructed two small tents, which, though exceedingly rough shaped, served the purposes for which they were intended. In these we lived and stored our various necessities, and thus for a matter of some four weeks all went smoothly and without particular unhappiness. Indeed, I may say with much of happiness—for—we were together.

"It was on the thumb of her right hand that the growth first showed. It was only a small circular spot, much like a little gray mole. My God! how the fear leaped to my heart when she showed me the place. We cleansed it, between us, washing it with carbolic and water. In the morning of the following day she showed her hand to me again. The gray warty thing had returned. For a little while, we looked at one another in silence. Then, still wordless, we started again to remove it. In the midst of the operation she spoke suddenly.

" 'What's that on the side of your face, dear?' Her voice was sharp with anxiety. I put my hand up to feel.

" 'There! Under the hair by your ear. A little to the

front a bit.' My finger rested upon the place, and then I knew.

"'Let us get your thumb done first,' I said. And she submitted, only because she was afraid to touch me until it was cleansed. I finished washing and disinfecting her thumb, and then she turned to my face. After it was finished we sat together and talked awhile of many things; for there had come into our lives sudden, very terrible thoughts. We were, all at once, afraid of something worse than death. We spoke of loading the boat with provisions and water and making our way out onto the sea; yet we were helpless, for many causes, and—and the growth had attacked us already. We decided to stay. God would do with us what was His will. We would wait.

"A month, two months, three months passed and the places grew somewhat, and there had come others. Yet we fought so strenuously with the fear that its headway was but slow, comparatively speaking.

"Occasionally we ventured off to the ship for such stores as we needed. There we found that the fungus grew persistently. One of the nodules on the main deck became soon as high as my head.

"We had now given up all thought or hope of leaving the island. We had realized that it would be unallowable to go among healthy humans, with the thing from which we were suffering.

"With this determination and knowledge in our minds we knew that we should have to husband our food and water; for we did not know, at that time, but that we should possibly live for many years.

"This reminds me that I have told you that I am an old man. Judged by years this is not so. But—but—"

He broke off; then continued somewhat abruptly.

"As I was saying, we knew that we should have to use care in the matter of food. But we had no idea then how little food there was left, of which to take care. It was a week later that I made the discovery that all the other bread tanks—which I had supposed full—were empty, and that (beyond odd tins of vegetables and meat, and some other matters) we had nothing on which to depend, but the bread in the tank which I had already opened.

"After learning this I bestirred myself to do what I could, and set to work at fishing in the lagoon; but with no success. At this I was somewhat inclined to feel desperate until the thought came to me to try outside the lagoon, in the open sea.

"Here, at times, I caught odd fish; but so infrequently that they proved of but little help in keeping us from the hunger which threatened. It seemed to me that our deaths were likely to come by hunger, and not by the growth of the thing which had seized upon our bodies.

"We were in this state of mind when the fourth month wore out. Then I made a very horrible discovery. One morning, a little before midday, I came off from the ship with a portion of the biscuits which were left. In the mouth of her tent I saw my sweetheart sitting, eating something.

" 'What is it, my dear?' I called out as I leaped shore. Yet, on hearing my voice, she seemed confused, and, turning, slyly threw something toward the edge of the little clearing. It fell short, and a vague suspicion having arisen within me, I walked across and picked it up. It was a piece of the gray fungus.

"As I went to her with it in my hand, she turned deadly pale; then a rose red.

"I felt strangely dazed and frightened.

" 'My dear! My dear!' I said, and could say no more. Yet at my words she broke down and cried bitterly. Gradually, as she calmed, I got from her the news that she had tried it the preceding day, and—and liked it. I got her to promise on her knees not to touch it again, however great our hunger. After she had promised she told me that the desire for it had come suddenly, and that, until the moment of desire, she had experienced nothing toward it but the most extreme repulsion.

"Later in the day, feeling strangely restless, and much shaken with the thing which I had discovered, I made my way along one of the twisted paths—formed by the white, sandlike substance—which led among the fungoid growth. I had, once before, ventured along there; but not to any great distance. This time, being involved in perplexing thought, I went much further than hitherto.

"Suddenly I was called to myself by a queer hoarse sound on my left. Turning quickly I saw there was movement among an extraordinarily shaped mass of fungus, close to my elbow. It was swaying uneasily, as though it possessed life of its own. Abruptly, as I stared, the thought came to me that the thing had a grotesque resemblance to the figure of a distorted human creature. Even as the fancy flashed into my brain, there was a slight, sickening noise of tearing, and I saw that one of the branchlike arms was detaching itself from the surrounding gray masses, and coming toward me. The head of the thing—a shapeless gray ball, inclined in my direction. I stood stupidly, and the vile arm brushed across my face. I gave out a frightened cry, and ran back a few paces. There was a sweetish taste upon my lips where the thing had touched me. I licked them, and was immediately filled with an inhuman desire. I turned and seized a mass of the fungus. Then more, and—more. I was insatiable. In the midst of devouring, the remembrance of the morning's discovery swept into my amazed brain. It was sent by God. I dashed the fragment I held to the ground. Then, utterly wretched and feeling a dreadful guiltiness, I made my way back to the little encampment.

"I think she knew, by some marvelous intuition which love must have given, so soon as she set eyes on me. Her quiet sympathy made it easier for me, and

I told her of my sudden weakness; yet omitted to mention the extraordinary thing which had gone before. I desired to spare her all unnecessary terror.

"But, for myself, I had added an intolerable knowledge, to breed an incessant terror in my brain; for I doubted not but that I had seen the end of one of these men who had come to the island in the ship in the lagoon; and in that monstrous ending I had seen our own.

"Thereafter we kept from the abominable food, though the desire for it had entered into our blood. Yet our drear punishment was upon us; for, day by day, with monstrous rapidity, the fungoid growth took hold of our poor bodies. Nothing we could do would check it materially, and so—and so—we who had been human, became— Well, it matters less each day. Only—only we had been man and maid!

"And day by day the fight is more dreadful, to withstand the hunger-lust for the terrible lichen.

"A week ago we ate the last of the biscuit, and since that time I have caught three fish. I was out here fishing tonight when your schooner drifted upon me out of the mist. I hailed you. You know the rest, and may God, out of His great heart, bless you for your goodness to a—a couple of poor outcast souls."

There was the dip of an oar—another. Then the voice came again, and for the last time, sounding through the slight surrounding mist, ghostly and mournful.

"God bless you! Good-by!"

"Good-by," we shouted together, hoarsely, our hearts full of many emotions.

I glanced about me. I became aware that the dawn was upon us.

The sun flung a stray beam across the hidden sea; pierced the mist dully, and lit up the receding boat with a gloomy fire. Indistinctly I saw something nodding between the oars. I thought of a sponge—a great, gray nodding sponge— The oars continued to ply.

They were gray—as was the boat—and my eyes searched a moment vainly for the conjunction of hand and oar. My gaze flashed back to the—head. It nodded forward as the oars went backward for the stroke. Then the oars were dipped, the boat shot out of the patch of light, and the—the thing went nodding into the mist.

How Love Came to Professor Guildea

by ROBERT S. HICHENS

I

Dull people often wondered how it came about that Father Murchison and Professor Frederic Guildea were intimate friends. The one was all faith, the other all skepticism. The nature of the Father was based on love. He viewed the world with an almost child-like tenderness above his long, black cassock; and his mild, yet perfectly fearless, blue eyes seemed always to be watching the goodness that exists in humanity, and rejoicing at what they saw. The Professor, on the other hand, had a hard face like a hatchet, tipped with an aggressive black goatee beard. His eyes were quick, piercing and irreverent. The lines about his small,

From *Tongues of Conscience* by Robert S. Hichens. Reprinted by permission of the author's executors and Methuen & Co., Ltd. London.

thin-lipped mouth were almost cruel. His voice was harsh and dry, sometimes, when he grew energetic, almost soprano. It fired off words with a sharp and clipping utterance. His habitual manner was one of distrust and investigation. It was impossible to suppose that, in his busy life, he found any time for love, either of humanity in general or of an individual.

Yet his days were spent in scientific investigations which conferred immense benefits upon the world.

Both men were celibates. Father Murchison was a member of an Anglican order which forbade him to marry. Professor Guildea had a poor opinion of most things, but especially of women. He had formerly held a post as lecturer at Birmingham. But when his fame as a discoverer grew, he removed to London. There, at a lecture he gave in the East End, he first met Father Murchison. They spoke a few words. Perhaps the bright intelligence of the priest appealed to the man of science, who was inclined, as a rule, to regard the clergy with some contempt. Perhaps the transparent sincerity of this devotee, full of common sense, attracted him. As he was leaving the hall he abruptly asked the Father to call on him at his house in Hyde Park Place. And the Father, who seldom went into the West End, except to preach, accepted the invitation.

"When will you come?" said Guildea.

He was folding up the blue paper on which his notes were written in a tiny, clear hand. The leaves rustled dryly in accompaniment to his sharp, dry voice.

"On Sunday week I am preaching in the evening at St. Saviour's, not far off," said the Father.

"I don't go to church."

"No," said the Father, without any accent of surprise or condemnation.

"Come to supper afterward?"

"Thank you, I will.

"What time will you come?"

The Father smiled.

"As soon as I have finished my sermon. The service is at six-thirty."

"About eight then, I suppose. Don't make the sermon too long. My number in Hyde Park Place is 100. Good night to you."

He snapped an elastic band round his papers and strode off without shaking hands.

On the appointed Sunday, Father Murchison preached to a densely crowded congregation at St. Saviour's. The subject of his sermon was sympathy, and the comparative uselessness of man in the world unless he can learn to love his neighbor as himself. The sermon was rather long, and when the preacher, in his flowing, black cloak, and his hard, round hat, with a straight brim over which hung the ends of a black cord, made his way toward the Professor's house, the hands of the illuminated clock disc at the Marble Arch pointed to twenty minutes past eight.

The Father hurried on, pushing his way through the crowd of standing soldiers, chattering women and giggling street boys in their Sunday best. It was a warm April night, and when he reached number 100 Hyde Park Place, he found the Professor bareheaded on his doorstep, gazing out toward the Park railings, and enjoying the soft, moist air, in front of his lighted passage.

"Ha, a long sermon!" he exclaimed. "Come in."

"I fear it was," said the Father, obeying the invitation. "I am that dangerous thing—an extempore preacher."

"More attractive to speak without notes, if you can do it. Hang your hat and coat—oh, cloak—here. We'll have supper at once. This is the dining room."

He opened a door on the right and they entered a long, narrow room, with gold paper and a black ceiling, from which hung an electric lamp with a gold-colored shade. In the room stood a small oval table with covers laid for two. The Professor rang the bell. Then he said, "People seem to talk better at an oval table than at a square one."

"Really. Is that so?"

"Well, I've had precisely the same party twice, once at a square table, once at an oval table. The first dinner was a dull failure, the second a brilliant success. Sit down, won't you?"

"How d'you account for the difference?" said the Father, sitting down, and pulling the tail of his cassock well under him.

"H'm. I know how you'd account for it."

"Indeed. How then?"

"At an oval table, since there are no corners, the chain of human sympathy—the electric current, is much more complete. Eh! Let me give you some soup."

"Thank you."

The Father took it, and, as he did so, turned his beaming blue eyes on his host. Then he smiled.

"What!" he said, in his pleasant, light tenor voice. "You do go to church sometimes, then?"

"Tonight is the first time for ages. And, mind you, I was tremendously bored."

The Father still smiled, and his blue eyes gently twinkled.

"Dear, dear!" he said, "what a pity!"

"But not by the sermon," Guildea added. "I don't pay a compliment. I state a fact. The sermon didn't bore me. If it had, I should have said so, or said nothing."

"And which would you have done?"

The Professor smiled almost genially.

"Don't know," he said. "What wine d'you drink?"

"None, thank you. I'm a teetotaler. In my profession and *milieu* it is necessary to be one. Yes, I will have some soda water. I think you would have done the first."

"Very likely, and very wrongly. You wouldn't have minded much."

"I don't think I should."

They were intimate already. The Father felt most pleasantly at home under the black ceiling. He drank some soda water and seemed to enjoy it more than the Professor enjoyed his claret.

"You smile at the theory of the chain of human sympathy, I see," said the Father. "Then what is your explanation of the failure of your square party with corners, the success of your oval party without them?"

"Probably on the first occasion the wit of the assembly had a chill on his liver, while on the second he was in perfect health. Yet, you see, I stick to the oval table."

"And that means—"

"Very little. By the way, your omission of any allusion to the notorious part liver plays in love was a serious one tonight."

"Your omission of any desire for close human sympathy in your life is a more serious one."

"How can you be sure I have no such desire?"

"I divine it. Your look, your manner, tell me it is so. You were disagreeing with my sermon all the time I was preaching. Weren't you?"

"Part of the time."

The servant changed the plates. He was a middle-aged, blond, thin man, with a stony white face, pale, prominent eyes, and an accomplished manner of service. When he had left the room the Professor continued.

"Your remarks interested me, but I thought them exaggerated."

"For instance?"

"Let me play the egoist for a moment. I spend most of my time in hard work, very hard work. The results of this work, you will allow, benefit humanity."

"Enormously," assented the Father, thinking of more than one of Guildea's discoveries.

"And the benefit conferred by this work, undertaken merely for its own sake, is just as great as if it were undertaken because I loved my fellow man, and sentimentally desired to see him more comfortable than he is at present. I'm as useful precisely in my present condition of—in my present nonaffectional condition— as I should be if I were as full of gush as the sentimentalists who want to get murderers out of prison, or to put a premium on tyranny—like Tolstoi—by preventing the punishment of tyrants."

"One may do great harm with affection; great good without it. Yes, that is true. Even *le bon motif* is not everything, I know. Still I contend that, given your powers, you would be far more useful in the world with sympathy, affection for your kind, added to them than as you are. I believe even that you would do still more splendid work."

The Professor poured himself out another glass of claret.

"You noticed my butler?" he said.

"I did."

"He's a perfect servant. He makes me perfectly comfortable. Yet he has no feeling of liking for me. I treat him civilly. I pay him well. But I never think about him, or concern myself with him as a human being. I know nothing of his character except what I read of it in his last master's letter. There are, you may say, no truly human relations between us. You would affirm that his work would be better done if I had made him personally like me as man—of any class—can like man— of any other class?"

"I should, decidedly."

"I contend that he couldn't do his work better than he does it at present."

"But if any crisis occurred?"

"What?"

"Any crisis, change in your condition. If you needed his help, not only as a man and a butler, but as a man and a brother? He'd fail you then, probably. You would never get from your servant that finest service which can only be prompted by an honest affection."

"You have finished?"

"Quite."

"Let us go upstairs then. Yes, those are good prints. I picked them up in Birmingham when I was living there. This is my workroom."

They came to a double room lined entirely with books, and brilliantly, rather hardly, lit by electricity. The windows at one end looked onto the Park, at the other onto the garden of a neighboring house. The door by which they entered was concealed from the inner and smaller room by the jutting wall of the outer room, in which stood a huge writing table loaded with letters, pamphlets and manuscripts. Between the two windows of the inner room was a cage in which a large, gray parrot was clambering, using both beak and claws to assist him in his slow and meditative peregrinations.

"You have a pet," said the Father, surprised.

"I possess a parrot," the Professor answered dryly. "I got him for a purpose when I was making a study of the imitative powers of birds, and I have never got rid of him. A cigar?"

"Thank you."

They sat down. Father Murchison glanced at the parrot. It had paused in its journey, and, clinging to the bars of its cage, was regarding them with attentive round eyes that looked deliberately intelligent, but by no means sympathetic. He looked away from it to Guildea, who was smoking, with his head thrown back, his sharp, pointed chin, on which the small black beard bristled, upturned. He was moving his under lip up and down rapidly. This action caused the beard to stir and look peculiarly aggressive. The Father suddenly chuckled softly.

"Why's that?" cried Guildea, letting his chin drop down on his breast and looking at his guest sharply.

"I was thinking it would have to be a crisis indeed that could make you cling to your butler's affection for assistance."

Guildea smiled too.

"You're right. It would. Here he comes."

The man entered with coffee. He offered it gently, and retired like a shadow retreating on a wall.

"Splendid, inhuman fellow," remarked Guildea.

"I prefer the East End lad who does my errands in Bird Street," said the Father. "I know all his worries. He knows some of mine. We are friends. He's more noisy than your man. He even breathes hard when he is especially solicitous, but he would do more for me than put the coals on my fire, or black my square-toed boots."

"Men are differently made. To me the watchful eye of affection would be abominable."

"What about that bird?"

The Father pointed to the parrot. It had got up on its perch and, with one foot uplifted in an impressive, almost benedictory, manner, was gazing steadily at the Professor.

"That's a watchful eye of imitation, with a mind at the back of it, desirous of reproducing the peculiarities of others. No, I thought your sermon tonight very fresh, very clever. But I have no wish for affection. Reasonable liking, of course, one desires—" he tugged sharply at his beard, as if to warn himself against sentimentality—"but anything more would be most irksome, and would push me, I feel sure, toward cruelty. It would also hamper one's work."

"I don't think so."

"The sort of work I do. I shall continue to benefit the world without loving it, and it will continue to accept the benefits without loving me. That's all as it should be."

He drank his coffee. Then he added rather aggressively, "I have neither time nor inclination for sentimentality."

When Guildea let Father Murchison out, he followed the Father onto the doorstep and stood there for a moment. The Father glanced across the damp road into the Park.

"I see you've got a gate just opposite you," he said idly.

"Yes. I often slip across for a stroll to clear my brain. Good night to you. Come again some day."

"With pleasure. Good night."

The priest strode away, leaving Guildea standing on the step.

Father Murchison came many times again to number 100 Hyde Park Place. He had a feeling of liking for most men and women whom he knew, and of tenderness for all, whether he knew them or not, but he grew to have a special sentiment toward Guildea. Strangely enough, it was a sentiment of pity. He pitied this hard-working, eminently successful man of big brain and bold heart, who never seemed depressed, who never wanted assistance, who never complained of the twisted skein of life or faltered in his progress along its way. The Father pitied Guildea, in fact, because Guildea wanted so little. He had told him so, for the intercourse of the two men, from the beginning, had been singularly frank.

One evening, when they were talking together, the Father happened to speak of one of the oddities of life, the fact that those who do not want things often get them, while those who seek them vehemently are disappointed in their search.

"Then I ought to have affection poured upon me," said Guildea smiling rather grimly. "For I hate it."

"Perhaps some day you will."

"I hope not, most sincerely."

Father Murchison said nothing for a moment. He was drawing together the ends of the broad band round his cassock. When he spoke he seemed to be answering someone.

"Yes," he said slowly, "yes, that *is* my feeling—pity."

"For whom?" said the Professor.

Then, suddenly, he understood. He did not say that he understood, but Father Murchison felt, and saw, that it was quite unnecessary to answer his friend's question. So Guildea, strangely enough, found himself closely acquainted with a man—his opposite in all ways—who pitied him.

The fact that he did not mind this, and scarcely ever thought about it, shows perhaps as clearly as anything could, the peculiar indifference of his nature.

II

One autumn evening, a year and half after Father Murchison and the Professor had first met, the Father called in Hyde Park Place and inquired of the blond and stony butler—his name was Pitting—whether his master was at home.

"Yes, sir," replied Pitting. "Will you please come this way?"

He moved noiselessly up the rather narrow stairs, followed by the Father, tenderly opened the library door, and in his soft, cold voice, announced, "Father Murchison."

Guildea was sitting in an armchair, before a small fire. His thin, long-fingered hands lay outstretched upon his knees, his head was sunk down on his chest. He appeared to be pondering deeply. Pitting very slightly raised his voice.

"Father Murchison to see you, sir," he repeated.

The Professor jumped up rather suddenly and turned sharply round as the Father came in.

"Oh," he said. "It's you, is it? Glad to see you. Come to the fire."

The Father glanced at him and thought him looking unusually fatigued.

"You don't look well tonight," the Father said.

"No?"

"You must be working too hard. That lecture you are going to give in Paris is bothering you?"

"Not a bit. It's all arranged. I could deliver it to you at this moment verbatim. Well, sit down."

The Father did so, and Guildea sank once more into his chair and stared hard into the fire without another word. He seemed to be thinking profoundly. His friend did not interrupt him, but quietly lit a pipe and began to smoke reflectively. The eyes of Guildea were fixed upon the fire. The Father glanced about the room, at the walls of soberly bound books, at the crowded writing table, at the windows, before which hung heavy, dark blue curtains of old brocade, at the cage, which stood between them. A green baize covering was thrown over it. The Father wondered why. He had never seen Napoleon—so the parrot was named—covered up at night before. While he was looking at the baize Guildea suddenly jerked up his head and, taking his hands from his knees and clasping them, said abruptly, "D'you think I'm an attractive man?"

Father Murchison jumped. Such a question coming from such a man astounded him.

"Bless me!" he ejaculated. "What makes you ask? Do you mean attractive to the opposite sex?"

"That's what I don't know," said the Professor gloomily, and staring again into the fire. "That's what I don't know."

The Father grew more astonished.

"Don't know!" he exclaimed.

And he laid down his pipe.

"Let's say—d'you think I'm attractive, that there's anything about me which might draw a—a human being, or an animal irresistibly to me?"

"Whether you desired it or not?"

"Exactly—or—no, let us say definitely—if I did not desire it."

Father Murchison pursed up his rather full, cherubic lips, and little wrinkles appeared about the corners of his blue eyes.

"There might be, of course," he said, after a pause. "Human nature is weak, engagingly weak, Guildea. And you're inclined to flout it. I could understand a certain class of lady—the lion-hunting, the intellectual lady, seeking you. Your reputation, your great name—"

"Yes, yes," Guildea interrupted, rather irritably, "I know all that, I know."

He twisted his long hands together, bending the palms outward till his thin, pointed fingers cracked. His forehead was wrinkled in a frown.

"I imagine," he said—he stopped and coughed dryly, almost shrilly—"I imagine it would be very disagreeable to be liked, to be run after—that is the usual expression, isn't it—by anything one objected to."

And now he half turned in his chair, crossed his legs one over the other, and looked at his guest with an unusual, almost piercing interrogation.

"Anything?" said the Father.

"Well—well, anyone. I imagine nothing could be more unpleasant."

"To you—no," answered the Father. "But—forgive me, Guildea, I cannot conceive your permitting such intrusion. You don't encourage adoration."

Guildea nodded his head gloomily.

"I don't," he said, "I don't. That's just it. That's the curious part of it, that I—"

He broke off deliberately, got up and stretched.

"I'll have a pipe, too," he said.

He went over to the mantelpiece, got his pipe, filled it and lighted it. As he held the match to the tobacco, bending forward with an inquiring expression, his eyes fell upon the green baize that covered Napoleon's cage. He threw the match into the grate, and puffed at the pipe as he walked forward to the cage. When he reached it he put out his hand, took hold of the baize and began to pull it away. Then suddenly he pushed it back over the cage.

"No," he said, as if to himself, "no."

He returned rather hastily to the fire and threw himself once more into his armchair.

"You're wondering," he said to Father Murchison.

"So am I. I don't know at all what to make of it. I'll just tell you the facts and you must tell me what you think of them. The night before last, after a day of hard work—but no harder than usual—I went to the front door to get a breath of air. You know I often do that."

"Yes, I found you on the doorstep when I first came here."

"Just so. I didn't put on hat or coat. I just stood on the step as I was. My mind, I remember, was still full of my work. It was rather a dark night, not very dark. The hour was about eleven, or a quarter past. I was staring at the Park, and presently I found that my eyes were directed toward somebody who was sitting, back to me, on one of the benches. I saw the person—if it was a person—through the railings."

"If it was a person!" said the Father. "What do you mean by that?"

"Wait a minute. I say that because it was too dark for me to know. I merely saw some blackish object on the bench, rising into view above the level of the back of the seat. I couldn't say it was man, woman or child. But something there was, and I found that I was looking at it."

"I understand."

"Gradually, I also found that my thoughts were becoming fixed upon this thing or person. I began to wonder, first, what it was doing there; next, what it was thinking; lastly, what it was like."

"Some poor creature without a home, I suppose," said the Father.

"I said that to myself. Still, I was taken with an extraordinary interest about this object, so great an interest that I got my hat and crossed the road to go into the Park. As you know, there's an entrance almost opposite to my house. Well, Murchison, I crossed the road, passed through the gate in the railings, went up to the seat, and found that there was—nothing on it."

"Were you looking at it as you walked?"

"Part of the time. But I removed my eyes from it just as I passed through the gate, because there was a row going on a little way off, and I turned for an instant in that direction. When I saw that the seat was vacant I was seized by a most absurd sensation of disappointment, almost of anger. I stopped and looked about me to see if anything was moving away, but I could see nothing. It was a cold night and misty, and there were few people about. Feeling, as I say, foolishly and unnaturally disappointed, I retraced my steps to this house. When I got here I discovered that during my short absence I had left the hall door open—half open."

"Rather imprudent in London."

"Yes. I had no idea, of course, that I had done so, till I got back. However, I was only away three minutes or so."

"Yes."

"It was not likely that anybody had gone in."

"I suppose not."

"Was it?"

"Why do you ask me that, Guildea?"

"Well, well!"

"Besides, if anybody had gone in, on your return you'd have caught him, surely."

Guildea coughed again. The Father, surprised, could not fail to recognize that he was nervous and that his nervousness was affecting him physically.

"I must have caught cold that night," he said, as if he had read his friend's thought and hastened to contradict it. Then he went on, "I entered the hall, or passage, rather."

He paused again. His uneasiness was becoming very apparent.

"And you did catch somebody?" said the Father.

Guildea cleared his throat.

"That's just it," he said, "now we come to it. I'm not imaginative, as you know."

"You certainly are not."

"No, but hardly had I stepped into the passage before I felt certain that somebody had got into the house during my absence. I felt convinced of it, and not only that, I also felt convinced that the intruder was the very person I had dimly seen sitting upon the seat in the Park. What d'you say to that?"

"I begin to think you are imaginative."

"H'm! It seemed to me that the person—the occupant of the seat—and I, had simultaneously formed the project of interviewing each other, had simultaneously set out to put that project into execution. I became so certain of this that I walked hastily upstairs into this room, expecting to find the visitor awaiting me. But there was no one. I then came down again and went into the dining room. No one. I was actually astonished. Isn't that odd?"

"Very," said the Father, quite gravely.

The Professor's chill and gloomy manner, and uncomfortable, constrained appearance kept away the humor that might well have lurked round the steps of such a discourse.

"I went upstairs again," he continued, "sat down and thought the matter over. I resolved to forget it, and took up a book. I might perhaps have been able to read, but suddenly I thought I noticed—"

He stopped abruptly. Father Murchison observed that he was staring toward the green baize that covered the parrot's cage.

"But that's nothing," he said. "Enough that I couldn't read. I resolved to explore the house. You know how small it is, how easily one can go all over it. I went all over it. I went into every room without exception. To the servants, who were having supper, I made some excuse. They were surprised at my advent, no doubt."

"And Pitting?"

"Oh, he got up politely when I came in, stood while I was there, but never said a word. I muttered 'Don't disturb yourselves,' or something of the sort, and came

out. Murchison, I found nobody new in the house—
yet I returned to this room entirely convinced that
somebody had entered while I was in the Park."

"And gone out again before you came back?"

"No, had stayed, and was still in the house."

"But, my dear Guildea," began the Father, now in
great astonishment. "Surely—"

"I know what you want to say—what I should want
to say in your place. Now, do wait. I am also convinced
that this visitor has not left the house and is at this
moment in it."

He spoke with evident sincerity, with extreme gravity. Father Murchison looked him full in the face, and
met his quick, keen eyes.

"No," he said, as if in reply to an uttered question,
"I'm perfectly sane, I assure you. The whole matter
seems almost as incredible to me as it must to you.
But, as you know, I never quarrel with facts, however
strange. I merely try to examine into them thoroughly.
I have already consulted a doctor and been pronounced
in perfect bodily health."

He paused, as if expecting the Father to say something.

"Go on, Guildea," he said, "you haven't finished."

"No. I felt that night positive that somebody had
entered the house, and remained in it, and my conviction grew. I went to bed as usual, and, contrary to my
expectation, slept as well as I generally do. Yet directly I woke up yesterday morning I knew that my
household had been increased by one."

"May I interrupt you for one moment? How did you
know it?"

"By my mental sensation. I can only say that I was
perfectly conscious of a new presence within my house,
close to me."

"How very strange," said the Father. "And you feel
absolutely certain that you are not overworked? Your
brain does not feel tired? Your head is quite clear?"

"Quite. I was never better. When I came down to

breakfast that morning I looked sharply into Pitting's
face. He was as coldly placid and inexpressive as usual.
It was evident to me that his mind was in no way dis-
tressed. After breakfast I sat down to work, all the time
ceaselessly conscious of the fact of this intruder upon
my privacy. Nevertheless, I labored for several hours,
waiting for any development that might occur to clear
away the mysterious obscurity of this event. I lunched.
About half-past two I was obliged to go out to attend
a lecture. I therefore took my coat and hat, opened my
door, and stepped onto the pavement. I was instantly
aware that I was no longer intruded upon, and this although I was now in the street, surrounded by people.
Consequently, I felt certain that the thing in my house
must be thinking of me, perhaps even spying upon
me."

"Wait a moment," interrupted the Father. "What
was your sensation? Was it one of fear?"

"Oh, dear no. I was entirely puzzled—as I am now—
and keenly interested, but not in any way alarmed. I
delivered my lecture with my usual ease and returned
home in the evening. On entering the house again I
was perfectly conscious that the intruder was still there.
Last night I dined alone and spent the hours after dinner in reading a scientific work in which I was deeply
interested. While I read, however, I never for one moment lost the knowledge that some mind—very attentive to me—was within hail of mine. I will say more
than this—the sensation constantly increased, and, by
the time I got up to go to bed, I had come to a very
strange conclusion."

"What? What was it?"

"That whoever—or whatever—had entered my house
during my short absence in the Park was more than
interested in me."

"More than interested in you?"

"Was fond, or was becoming fond, of me."

"Oh!" exclaimed the Father. "Now I understand
why you asked me just now whether I thought there

was anything about you that might draw a human being or an animal irresistibly to you."

"Precisely. Since I came to this conclusion, Murchison, I will confess that my feeling of strong curiosity
has become tinged with another feeling."

"Of fear?"

"No, of dislike, or irritation. No—not fear, not fear."

As Guildea repeated unnecessarily this asseveration
he looked again toward the parrot's cage.

"What is there to be afraid of in such a matter?" he
added. "I am not a child to tremble before bogies."

In saying the last words he raised his voice sharply;
then he walked quickly to the cage, and, with an abrupt
movement, pulled the baize covering from it. Napoleon
was disclosed, apparently dozing upon his perch with
his head held slightly on one side. As the light reached
him, he moved, ruffled the feathers about his neck,
blinked his eyes, and began slowly to sidle to and fro,
thrusting his head forward and drawing it back with
an air of complacent, though rather unmeaning, energy. Guildea stood by the cage, looking at him closely,
and indeed with an attention that was so intense as to
be remarkable, almost unnatural.

"How absurd these birds are!" he said at length,
coming back to the fire.

"You have no more to tell me?" asked the Father.

"No. I am still aware of the presence of something
in my house. I am still conscious of its close attention
to me. I am still irritated, seriously annoyed—I confess
it—by that attention."

"You say you are aware of the presence of something
at this moment?"

"At this moment—yes."

"Do you mean in this room, with us, now?"

"I should say so—at any rate, quite near us."

Again he glanced quickly, almost suspiciously, toward the cage of the parrot. The bird was sitting still
on its perch now. Its head was bent down and cocked

sideways, and it appeared to be listening attentively to something.

"That bird will have the intonations of my voice more correctly than ever by tomorrow morning," said the Father, watching Guildea closely with his mild blue eyes. "And it has always imitated me very cleverly."

The Professor started slightly.

"Yes," he said. "Yes, no doubt. Well, what do you make of this affair?"

"Nothing at all. It is absolutely inexplicable. I can speak quite frankly to you, I feel sure."

"Of course. That's why I have told you the whole thing."

"I think you must be overworked, overstrained, without knowing it."

"And that the doctor was mistaken when he said I was all right?"

"Yes."

Guildea knocked his pipe out against the chimney piece.

"It may be so," he said, "I will not be so unreasonable as to deny the possibility, although I feel as well as I ever did in my life. What do you advise then?"

"A week of complete rest away from London, in good air."

"The usual prescription. I'll take it. I'll go tomorrow to Westgate and leave Napoleon to keep house in my absence."

For some reason, which he could not explain to himself, the pleasure which Father Murchison felt in hearing the first part of his friend's final remark was lessened, was almost destroyed, by the last sentence.

He walked toward the City that night, deep in thought, remembering and carefully considering the first interview he had with Guildea in the latter's house a year and a half before.

On the following morning Guildea left London.

III

Father Murchison was so busy a man that he had little time for brooding over the affairs of others. During Guildea's week at the sea, however, the Father thought about him a great deal, with much wonder and some dismay. The dismay was soon banished, for the mild-eyed priest was quick to discern weakness in himself, quicker still to drive it forth as a most undesirable inmate of the soul. But the wonder remained. It was destined to a crescendo. Guildea had left London on a Thursday. On a Thursday he returned, having previously sent a note to Father Murchison to mention that he was leaving Westgate at a certain time. When his train ran into Victoria Station, at five o'clock in the evening, he was surprised to see the cloaked figure of his friend standing upon the gray platform behind a line of porters.

"What, Murchison!" he said. "You here! Have you seceded from your order that you are taking this holiday?"

They shook hands.

"No," said the Father. "It happened that I had to be in this neighborhood today, visiting a sick person. So I thought I would meet you."

"And see if I were still a sick person, eh?"

The Professor glanced at him kindly, but with a dry little laugh.

"Are you?" replied the Father gently, looking at him with interest. "No, I think not. You appear very well."

The sea air had, in fact, put some brownish red into Guildea's always thin cheeks. His keen eyes were shining with life and energy, and he walked forward in his loose gray suit and fluttering overcoat with a vigor that was noticeable, carrying easily in his left hand his well-filled Gladstone bag.

The Father felt completely reassured.

"I never saw you look better," he said.

"I never was better. Have you an hour to spare?"

"Two."

"Good. I'll send my bag up by cab, and we'll walk across the Park to my house and have a cup of tea there. What d'you say?"

"I shall enjoy it."

They walked out of the station yard, past the flower girls and newspaper sellers toward Grosvenor Place.

"And you have had a pleasant time?" the Father said.

"Pleasant enough, and lonely. I left my companion behind me in the passage at number 100, you know."

"And you'll not find him there now, I feel sure."

"H'm!" ejaculated Guildea. "What a precious weakling you think me, Murchison."

As he spoke he strode forward more quickly, as if moved to emphasize his sensation of bodily vigor.

"A weakling—no. But anyone who uses his brain as persistently as you do yours must require an occasional holiday."

"And I required one very badly, eh?"

"You required one, I believe."

"Well, I've had it. And now we'll see."

The evening was closing in rapidly. They crossed the road at Hyde Park Corner, and entered the Park, in which were a number of people going home from work; men in corduroy trousers, caked with dried mud, and carrying tin cans slung over their shoulders, and flat panniers, in which lay their tools. Some of the younger ones talked loudly or whistled shrilly as they walked.

"Until the evening," murmured Father Murchison to himself.

"What?" asked Guildea.

"I was only quoting the last words of the text, which seems written upon life, especially upon the life of pleasure: 'Man goeth forth to his work, and to his labor.'"

"Ah, those fellows are not half bad fellows to have in an audience. There were a lot of them at the lecture

I gave when I first met you, I remember. One of them tried to heckle me. He had a red beard. Chaps with red beards are always hecklers. I laid him low on that occasion. Well, Murchison, and now we're going to see."

"What?"

"Whether my companion has departed."

"Tell me—do you feel any expectation of—well—of again thinking something is there?"

"How carefully you choose language. No, I merely wonder."

"You have no apprehension?"

"Not a scrap. But I confess to feeling curious."

"Then the sea air hasn't taught you to recognize that the whole thing came from overstrain."

"No," said Guildea, very dryly.

He walked on in silence for a minute. Then he added, "You thought it would?"

"I certainly thought it might."

"Make me realize that I had a sickly, morbid, rotten imagination—eh? Come now, Murchison, why not say frankly that you packed me off to Westgate to get rid of what you considered an acute form of hysteria?"

The Father was quite unmoved by this attack.

"Come now, Guildea," he retorted, "what did you expect me to think? I saw no indication of hysteria in you. I never have. One would suppose you the last man likely to have such a malady. But which is more natural—for me to believe in your hysteria or in the truth of such a story as you told me?"

"You have me there. No, I mustn't complain. Well, there's no hysteria about me now, at any rate."

"And no stranger in your house, I hope."

Father Murchison spoke the last words with earnest gravity, dropping the half-bantering tone—which they had both assumed.

"You take the matter very seriously, I believe," said Guildea, also speaking more gravely.

"How else can I take it? You wouldn't have me laugh at it when you tell it me seriously?"

"No. If we find my visitor still in the house, I may even call upon you to exorcise it. But first I must do one thing."

"And that is?"

"Prove to you, as well as to myself, that it is still there."

"That might be difficult," said the Father, considerably surprised by Guildea's matter-of-fact tone.

"I don't know. If it has remained in my house I think I can find a means. And I shall not be at all surprised if it is still there—despite the Westgate air."

In saying the last words the Professor relapsed into his former tone of dry chaff. The Father could not quite make up his mind whether Guildea was feeling unusually grave or unusually gay. As the two men drew near to Hyde Park Place their conversation died away and they walked forward silently in the gathering darkness.

"Here we are!" said Guildea at last.

He thrust the key into the door, opened it and let Father Murchison into the passage, following him closely, and banging the door.

"Here we are!" he repeated in a louder voice.

The electric light was turned on in anticipation of his arrival. He stood still and looked round.

"We'll have some tea at once," he said. "Ah, Pitting!"

The pale butler, who had heard the door bang, moved gently forward from the top of the stairs that led to the kitchen, greeted his master respectfully, took his coat and Father Murchison's cloak, and hung them on two pegs against the wall.

"All's right, Pitting? All's as usual?" said Guildea.

"Quite so, sir."

"Bring us up some tea to the library."

"Yes, sir."

Pitting retreated. Guildea waited till he had disappeared, then opened the dining-room door, put his head into the room and kept it there for a moment, standing perfectly still. Presently he drew back into the passage, shut the door, and said, "Let's go upstairs."

Father Murchison looked at him inquiringly, but made no remark. They ascended the stairs and came into the library. Guildea glanced rather sharply round. A fire was burning on the hearth. The blue curtains were drawn. The bright gleam of the strong electric light fell on the long rows of books, on the writing table—very orderly in consequence of Guildea's holiday —and on the uncovered cage of the parrot. Guildea went up to the cage. Napoleon was sitting humped up on his perch with his feathers ruffled. His long toes, which looked as if they were covered with crocodile skin, clung to the bar. His round and blinking eyes were filmy, like old eyes. Guildea stared at the bird very hard, and then clucked with his tongue against his teeth. Napoleon shook himself, lifted one foot, extended his toes, sidled along the perch to the bars nearest to the Professor and thrust his head against them. Guildea scratched it with his forefinger two or three times, still gazing attentively at the parrot; then he returned to the fire just as Pitting entered with the tea tray.

Father Murchison was already sitting in an armchair on one side of the fire. Guildea took another chair and began to pour out tea, as Pitting left the room, closing the door gently behind him. The Father sipped his tea, found it hot and set the cup down on a little table at his side.

"You're fond of that parrot, aren't you?" he asked his friend.

"Not particularly. It's interesting to study sometimes. The parrot mind and nature are peculiar."

"How long have you had him?"

"About four years. I nearly got rid of him just before I made your acquaintance. I'm very glad now I kept him."

"Are you? Why is that?"

"I shall probably tell you in a day or two."

The Father took his cup again. He did not press Guildea for an immediate explanation, but when they had both finished their tea he said, "Well, has the sea air had the desired effect?"

"No," said Guildea.

The Father brushed some crumbs from the front of his cassock and sat up higher in his chair.

"Your visitor is still here?" he asked, and his blue eyes became almost ungentle and piercing as he gazed at his friend.

"Yes," answered Guildea calmly.

"How do you know it, when did you know it—when you looked into the dining room just now?"

"No. Not until I came into this room. It welcomed me here."

"Welcomed you! In what way?"

"Simply by being here, by making me feel that it is here, as I might feel that a man was if I came into the room when it was dark."

He spoke quietly, with perfect composure in his usual dry manner.

"Very well," the Father said, "I shall not try to contend against your sensation, or to explain it away. Naturally, I am in amazement."

"So am I. Never has anything in my life surprised me so much. Murchison, of course I cannot expect you to believe more than that I honestly suppose—imagine, if you like—that there is some intruder here, of what kind I am totally unaware. I cannot expect you to believe that there really is anything. If you were in my place, I in yours, I should certainly consider you the victim of some nervous delusion. I could not do otherwise. But—wait. Don't condemn me as a hysteria patient, or as a madman, for two or three days. I feel convinced that—unless I am indeed unwell, a mental invalid, which I don't think is possible—I shall be able very shortly to give you some proof that there is a newcomer in my house."

"You don't tell me what kind of proof?"

"Not yet. Things must go a little farther first. But, perhaps even tomorrow I may be able to explain myself more fully. In the meanwhile, I'll say this, that if, eventually, I can't bring any kind of proof that I'm not dreaming, I'll let you take me to any doctor you like, and I'll resolutely try to adopt your present view—that I'm suffering from an absurd delusion. That is your view, of course?"

Father Murchison was silent for a moment. Then he said, rather doubtfully, "It ought to be."

"But isn't it?" asked Guildea, surprised.

"Well, you know, your manner is enormously convincing. Still, of course, I doubt. How can I do otherwise? The whole thing must be fancy."

The Father spoke as if he were trying to recoil from a mental position he was being forced to take up.

"It must be fancy," he repeated.

"I'll convince you by more than my manner, or I'll not try to convince you at all," said Guildea.

When they parted that evening, he said, "I'll write to you in a day or two probably. I think the proof I am going to give you has been accumulating during my absence. But I shall soon know."

Father Murchison was extremely puzzled as he sat on the top of the omnibus going homeward.

IV

In two days' time he received a note from Guildea asking him to call, if possible, the same evening. This he was unable to do as he had an engagement to fulfill at some East End gathering. The following day was Sunday. He wrote saying he would come on the Monday, and got a wire shortly afterward: "YES, MONDAY COME TO DINNER SEVEN-THIRTY GUILDEA." At half-past seven he stood on the doorstep of number 100.

Pitting let him in.

"Is the Professor quite well, Pitting?" the Father inquired as he took off his cloak.

"I believe so, sir. He has not made any complaint," the butler formally replied. "Will you come upstairs, sir?"

Guildea met them at the door of the library. He was very pale and somber, and shook hands carelessly with his friend.

"Give us dinner," he said to Pitting.

As the butler retired, Guildea shut the door rather cautiously. Father Murchison had never before seen him look so disturbed.

"You're worried, Guildea," the Father said. "Seriously worried."

"Yes, I am. This business is beginning to tell on me a good deal."

"Your belief in the presence of something here continues then?"

"Oh, dear, yes. There's no sort of doubt about the matter. The night I went across the road into the Park something got into the house, though what the devil it is I can't yet find out. But now, before we go down to dinner, I'll just tell you something about that proof I promised you. You remember?"

"Naturally."

"Can't you imagine what it might be?"

Father Murchison moved his head to express a negative reply.

"Look about the room," said Guildea. "What do you see?"

The Father glanced round the room, slowly and carefully.

"Nothing unusual. You do not mean to tell me there is any appearance of—"

"Oh, no, no, there's no conventional, white-robed, cloudlike figure. Bless my soul, no! I haven't fallen so low as that."

He spoke with considerable irritation.

"Look again."

Father Murchison looked at him, turned in the direction of his fixed eyes and saw the gray parrot clambering in its cage, slowly and persistently.

"What?" he said, quickly. "Will the proof come from there?"

The Professor nodded.

"I believe so," he said. "Now let's go down to dinner. I want some food badly."

They descended to the dining room. While they ate and Pitting waited upon them, the Professor talked about birds, their habits, their curiosities, their fears and their powers of imitation. He had evidently studied this subject with the thoroughness that was characteristic of him in all that he did.

"Parrots," he said presently, "are extraordinarily observant. It is a pity that their means of reproducing what they see are so limited. If it were not so, I have little doubt that their echo of gesture would be as remarkable as their echo of voice often is."

"But hands are missing."

"Yes. They do many things with their heads, however. I once knew an old woman near Goring on the Thames. She was afflicted with the palsy. She held her head perpetually sideways and it trembled, moving from right to left. Her sailor son brought her home a parrot from one of his voyages. It used to reproduce the old woman's palsied movement of the head exactly. Those gray parrots are always on the watch."

Guildea said the last sentence slowly and deliberately, glancing sharply over his wine at Father Murchison, and, when he had spoken it, a sudden light of comprehension dawned in the priest's mind. He opened his lips to make a swift remark. Guildea turned his bright eyes toward Pitting, who at the moment was tenderly bearing a cheese meringue from the lift that connected the dining room with the lower regions. The Father closed his lips again. But presently, when the butler had placed some apples on the table, had meticulously arranged the decanters, brushed away the crumbs and evaporated, he said, quickly, "I begin to understand. You think Napoleon is aware of the intruder?"

"I know it. He has been watching my visitant ever since the night of that visitant's arrival."

Another flash of light came to the priest.

"That was why you covered him with green baize one evening?"

"Exactly. An act of cowardice. His behavior was beginning to grate upon my nerves."

Guildea pursed up his thin lips and drew his brows down, giving to his face a look of sudden pain.

"But now I intend to follow his investigations," he added, straightening his features. "The week I wasted at Westgate was not wasted by him in London, I can assure you. Have an apple."

"No, thank you; no, thank you."

The Father repeated the words without knowing that he did so. Guildea pushed away his glass.

"Let us come upstairs, then."

"No, thank you," reiterated the Father.

"Eh?"

"What am I saying?" exclaimed the Father, getting up. "I was thinking over this extraordinary affair."

"Ah, you're beginning to forget the hysteria theory?"

They walked out into the passage.

"Well, you are so very practical about the whole matter."

"Why not? Here's something very strange and abnormal come into my life. What should I do but investigate it closely and calmly?"

"What, indeed?"

The Father began to feel rather bewildered, under a sort of compulsion which seemed laid upon him to give earnest attention to a matter that ought to strike him—so he felt—as entirely absurd. When they came into the library his eyes immediately turned, with profound curiosity, toward the parrot's cage. A slight smile curled the Professor's lips. He recognized the effect he was producing upon his friend. The Father saw the smile.

"Oh, I'm not won over yet," he said in answer to it.

"I know. Perhaps you may be before the evening is over. Here comes the coffee. After we have drunk it we'll proceed to our experiment. Leave the coffee, Pitting, and don't disturb us again."

"No, sir."

"I won't have it black tonight," said the Father, "plenty of milk, please. I don't want my nerves played upon."

"Suppose we don't take coffee at all?" said Guildea. "If we do, you may trot out the theory that we are not in a perfectly normal condition. I know you, Murchison, devout priest and devout skeptic."

The Father laughed and pushed away his cup.

"Very well, then. No coffee."

"One cigarette, and then to business."

The gray-blue smoke curled up.

"What are we going to do?" said the Father.

He was sitting bolt upright as if ready for action. Indeed there was no suggestion of repose in the attitudes of either of the men.

"Hide ourselves, and watch Napoleon. By the way— that reminds me."

He got up, went to a corner of the room, picked up a piece of green baize and threw it over the cage.

"I'll pull that off when we are hidden."

"And tell me first if you have had any manifestation of this supposed presence during the last few days?"

"Merely an increasingly intense sensation of something here, perpetually watching me, perpetually attending to all my doings."

"Do you feel that it follows you about?"

"Not always. It was in this room when you arrived. It is here now—I feel. But, in going down to dinner, we seemed to get away from it. The conclusion is that it remained here. Don't let us talk about it just now."

They spoke of other things till their cigarettes were

finished. Then, as they threw away the smoldering ends, Guildea said, "Now, Murchison, for the sake of this experiment, I suggest that we should conceal ourselves behind the curtains on either side of the cage, so that the bird's attention may not be drawn toward us and so distracted from that which we want to know more about. I will pull away the green baize when we are hidden. Keep perfectly still, watch the bird's proceedings, and tell me afterward how you feel about them, how you explain them. Tread softly."

The Father obeyed, and they stole toward the curtains that fell before the two windows. The Father concealed himself behind those on the left of the cage, the Professor behind those on the right. The latter, as soon as they were hidden, stretched out his arm, drew the baize down from the cage, and let it fall on the floor.

The parrot, which had evidently fallen asleep in the warm darkness, moved on its perch as the light shone upon it, ruffled the feathers round its throat, and lifted first one foot and then the other. It turned its head round on its supple, and apparently elastic, neck, and, diving its beak into the down upon its back, made some searching investigations with, as it seemed, a satisfactory result, for it soon lifted its head again, glanced around its cage, and began to address itself to a nut which had been fixed between the bars for its refreshment. With its curved beak it felt and tapped the nut, at first gently, then with severity. Finally it plucked the nut from the bars, seized it with its rough, gray toes, and, holding it down firmly on the perch, cracked it and pecked out its contents, scattering some on the floor of the cage and letting the fractured shell fall into the china bath that was fixed against the bars. This accomplished, the bird paused meditatively, extended one leg backward, and went through an elaborate process of wing-stretching that made it look as if it were lopsided and deformed. With its head reversed, it again applied itself to a subtle and exhaustive search among the feathers of its wing. This time its investigation seemed interminable, and Father Murchison had time to realize the absurdity of the whole position, and to wonder why he had lent himself to it. Yet he did not find his sense of humor laughing at it. On the contrary, he was smitten by a sudden gust of horror. When he was talking to his friend and watching him, the Professor's manner, generally so calm, even so prosaic, vouched for the truth of his story and the well-adjusted balance of his mind. But when he was hidden this was not so. And Father Murchison, standing behind his curtain, with his eyes upon the unconcerned Napoleon, began to whisper to himself the word—madness, with a quickening sensation of pity and of dread.

The parrot sharply contracted one wing, ruffled the feathers around its throat again, then extended its other leg backward, and proceeded to the cleaning of its other wing. In the still room the dry sound of the feathers being spread was distinctly audible. Father Murchison saw the blue curtains behind which Guildea stood tremble slightly, as if a breath of wind had come through the window they shrouded. The clock in the far room chimed, and a coal dropped into the grate, making a noise like dead leaves stirring abruptly on hard ground. And again a gust of pity and of dread swept over the Father. It seemed to him that he had behaved very foolishly, if not wrongly, in encouraging what must surely be the strange dementia of his friend. He ought to have declined to lend himself to a proceeding that, ludicrous, even childish in itself, might well be dangerous in the encouragement it gave to a diseased expectation. Napoleon's protruding leg, extended wing and twisted neck, his busy and unconscious devotion to the arrangement of his person, his evident sensation of complete loneliness, most comfortable solitude, brought home with vehemence to the Father the undignified buffoonery of his conduct; the more piteous buffoonery of his friend. He seized the curtains with his hand and was about to thrust them

aside and issue forth, when an abrupt movement of
the parrot stopped him. The bird, as if sharply attracted by something, paused in its pecking, and, with
its head still bent backward and twisted sideways on
its neck, seemed to listen intently. Its round eye looked
glistening and strained, like the eye of a disturbed
pigeon. Contracting its wing, it lifted its head and sat
for a moment erect on its perch, shifting its feet mechanically up and down, as if a dawning excitement
produced in it an uncontrollable desire of movement.
Then it thrust its head forward in the direction of the
further room and remained perfectly still. Its attitude
so strongly suggested the concentration of its attention
on something immediately before it, that Father
Murchison instinctively stared about the room, half
expecting to see Pitting advance softly, having entered
through the hidden door. He did not come, and there
was no sound in the chamber. Nevertheless, the parrot
was obviously getting excited and increasingly attentive. It bent its head lower and lower, stretching out its
neck until, almost falling from the perch, it half extended its wings, raising them slightly from its back, as
if about to take flight, and fluttering them rapidly up
and down. It continued this fluttering movement for
what seemed to the Father an immense time. At length,
raising its wings as far as possible, it dropped them
slowly and deliberately down to its back, caught hold
of the edge of its bath with its beak, hoisted itself onto
the floor of the cage, waddled to the bars, thrust its
head against them, and stood quite still in the exact
attitude it always assumed when its head was being
scratched by the Professor. So complete was the suggestion of this delight conveyed by the bird, that
Father Murchison felt as if he saw a white finger gently
pushed among the soft feathers of its head, and he was
seized by a most strong conviction that something, un-
seen by him but seen and welcomed by Napoleon,
stood immediately before the cage.

The parrot presently withdrew its head, as if the

coaxing finger had been lifted from it, and its pronounced air of acute physical enjoyment faded into
one of marked attention and alert curiosity. Pulling itself up by the bars it climbed again upon its perch,
sidled to the left side of the cage, and began apparently
to watch something with profound interest. It bowed
its head oddly, paused for a moment, then bowed its
head again. Father Murchison found himself conceiving
—from this elaborate movement of the head—a distinct
idea of a personality. The bird's proceedings suggested
extreme sentimentality combined with that sort of
weak determination which is often the most persistent.
Such weak determination is a very common attribute
of persons who are partially idiotic. Father Murchison
was moved to think of these poor creatures who will
often, so strangely and unreasonably, attach themselves with persistence to those who love them least.
Like many priests, he had had some experience of
them, for the amorous idiot is peculiarly sensitive to
the attraction of preachers. This bowing movement of
the parrot recalled to his memory a terrible, pale
woman who for a time haunted all churches in which
he ministered, who was perpetually endeavoring to
catch his eye, and who always bent her head with an
obsequious and cunningly conscious smile when she
did so. The parrot went on bowing, making a short
pause between each genuflection, as if it waited for a
signal to be given that called into play its imitative
faculty.

"Yes, yes, it's imitating an idiot," Father Murchison
caught himself saying as he watched.

And he looked again about the room, but saw nothing; except the furniture, the dancing fire, and the ser-
ried ranks of the books. Presently the parrot ceased
from bowing, and assumed the concentrated and
stretched attitude of one listening very keenly. He
opened his beak, showing his black tongue, shut it,
then opened it again. The Father thought he was going

to speak, but he remained silent, although it was obvious that he was trying to bring out something. He bowed again two or three times, paused, and then, again opening his beak, made some remark. The Father could not distinguish any words, but the voice was sickly and disagreeable, a cooing and, at the same time, querulous voice, like a woman's, he thought. And he put his ear nearer to the curtain, listening with almost feverish attention. The bowing was resumed, but this time Napoleon added to it a sidling movement, affectionate and affected, like the movement of a silly and eager thing, nestling up to someone, or giving someone a gentle and furtive nudge. Again the Father thought of that terrible, pale woman who had haunted churches. Several times he had come upon her waiting for him after evening services. Once she had hung her head smiling, and lolled out her tongue and pushed against him sideways in the dark. He remembered how his flesh had shrunk from the poor thing, the sick loathing of her that he could not banish by remembering that her mind was all astray. The parrot paused, listened, opened his beak, and again said something in the same dovelike, amorous voice, full of sickly suggestion and yet hard, even dangerous, in its intonation. A loathsome voice, the Father thought it. But this time, although he heard the voice more distinctly than before, he could not make up his mind whether it was like a woman's voice or a man's—or perhaps a child's. It seemed to be a human voice, and yet oddly sexless. In order to resolve his doubt he withdrew into the darkness of the curtains, ceased to watch Napoleon and simply listened with keen attention, striving to forget that he was listening to a bird, and to imagine that he was overhearing a human being in conversation. After two or three minutes' silence the voice spoke again, and at some length, apparently repeating several times an affectionate series of ejaculations with a cooing emphasis that was unutterably mawkish and offensive. The sickliness of the voice, its falling intonations and its strange indelicacy, combined with a die-away softness and meretricious refinement, made the Father's flesh creep. Yet he could not distinguish any words, nor could he decide on the voice's sex or age. One thing alone he was certain of as he stood still in the darkness—that such a sound could only proceed from something peculiarly loathsome, could only express a personality unendurably abominable to him, if not to everybody. The voice presently failed, in a sort of husky gasp, and there was a prolonged silence. It was broken by the Professor, who suddenly pulled away the curtains that hid the Father and said to him, "Come out now, and look."

The Father came into the light, blinking, glanced toward the cage, and saw Napoleon poised motionless on one foot with his head under his wing. He appeared to be asleep. The Professor was pale, and his mobile lips were drawn into an expression of supreme disgust.

"Faugh!" he said.

He walked to the windows of the further room, pulled aside the curtains and pushed the glass up, letting in the air. The bare trees were visible in the gray gloom outside. Guildea leaned out for a minute drawing the night air into his lungs. Presently he turned round to the Father, and exclaimed abruptly, "Pestilent! Isn't it?"

"Yes—most pestilent."

"Ever hear anything like it?"

"Not exactly."

"Nor I. It gives me nausea, Murchison, absolute physical nausea."

He closed the window and walked uneasily about the room.

"What d'you make of it?" he asked, over his shoulder.

"How d'you mean exactly?"

"Is it man's, woman's, or child's voice?"

"I can't tell, I can't make up my mind."

"Nor I."

"Have you heard it often?"

"Yes, since I returned from Westgate. There are never any words that I can distinguish. What a voice!"

He spat into the fire.

"Forgive me," he said, throwing himself down in a chair. "It turns my stomach—literally."

"And mine," said the Father truly.

"The worst of it is," continued Guildea, with a high, nervous accent, "that there's no brain with it, none at all—only the cunning of idiocy."

The Father started at this exact expression of his own conviction by another.

"Why d'you start like that?" said Guildea, with a quick suspicion which showed the unnatural condition of his nerves.

"Well, the very same idea had occurred to me."

"What?"

"That I was listening to the voice of something idiotic."

"Ah! That's the devil of it, you know, to a man like me. I could fight against brain—but this!"

He sprang up again, poked the fire violently, then stood on the hearth rug with his back to it, and his hands thrust into the high pockets of his trousers.

"That's the voice of the thing that's got into my house," he said. "Pleasant, isn't it?"

And now there was really horror in his eyes, and his voice.

"I must get it out," he exclaimed. "I must get it out. But how?"

He tugged at his short black beard with a quivering hand.

"How?" he continued. "For what is it? Where is it?"

"You feel it's here—now?"

"Undoubtedly. But I couldn't tell you in what part of the room."

He stared about, glancing rapidly at everything.

"Then you consider yourself haunted?" said Father Murchison.

He, too, was much moved and disturbed, although he was not conscious of the presence of anything near them in the room.

"I have never believed in any nonsense of that kind, as you know," Guildea answered. "I simply state a fact, which I cannot understand, and which is beginning to be very painful to me. There is something here. But whereas most so-called hauntings have been described to me as inimical, what I am conscious of is that I am admired, loved, desired. This is distinctly horrible to me, Murchison, distinctly horrible."

Father Murchison suddenly remembered the first evening he had spent with Guildea, and the latter's expression almost of disgust, at the idea of receiving warm affection from anyone. In the light of that long-ago conversation, the present event seemed supremely strange, and almost like a punishment for an offense committed by the Professor against humanity. But, looking up at his friend's twitching face, the Father resolved not to be caught in the net of his hideous belief.

"There can be nothing here," he said. "It's impossible."

"What does that bird imitate, then?"

"The voice of someone who has been here."

"Within the last week then. For it never spoke like that before, and mind, I noticed that it was watching and striving to imitate something before I went away, since the night that I went into the Park, only since then."

"Somebody with a voice like that must have been here while you were away," Father Murchison repeated, with a gentle obstinacy.

"I'll soon find out."

Guildea pressed the bell. Pitting stole in almost immediately.

"Pitting," said the Professor, speaking in a high, sharp voice, "did anyone come into this room during my absence at the sea?"

"Certainly not, sir, except the maids—and me, sir."

"Not a soul? You are certain?"

"Perfectly certain, sir."

The cold voice of the butler sounded surprised, almost resentful. The Professor flung out his hand toward the cage.

"Has the bird been here the whole time?"

"Yes, sir."

"He was not moved, taken elsewhere, even for a moment?"

Pitting's pale face began to look almost expressive, and his lips were pursed.

"Certainly not, sir."

"Thank you. That will do."

The butler retired, moving with a sort of ostentatious rectitude. When he had reached the door, and was just going out, his master called, "Wait a minute, Pitting."

The butler paused. Guildea bit his lips, tugged at his beard uneasily two or three times, and then said, "Have you noticed—er—the parrot talking lately in a—a very peculiar, very disagreeable voice?"

"Yes, sir—a soft voice like, sir."

"Ha! Since when?"

"Since you went away, sir. He's always at it."

"Exactly. Well, and what did you think of it?"

"Beg pardon, sir?"

"What do you think about his talking in this voice?"

"Oh, that it's only his play, sir."

"I see. That's all, Pitting."

The butler disappeared and closed the door noiselessly behind him.

Guildea turned his eyes on his friend.

"There, you see!" he ejaculated.

"It's certainly very odd," said the Father. "Very odd indeed. You are certain you have no maid who talks at all like that?"

"My dear Murchison! Would you keep a servant with such a voice about you for two days?"

"No."

"My housemaid has been with me for five years, my cook for seven. You've heard Pitting speak. The three of them make up my entire household. A parrot never speaks in a voice it has not heard. Where has it heard that voice?"

"But we hear nothing?"

"No. Nor do we see anything. But it does. It feels something too. Didn't you observe it presenting its head to be scratched?"

"Certainly it seemed to be doing so."

"It was doing so."

Father Murchison said nothing. He was full of increasing discomfort that almost amounted to apprehension.

"Are you convinced?" said Guildea, rather irritably.

"No. The whole matter is very strange. But till I hear, see or feel—as you do—the presence of something, I cannot believe."

"You mean that you will not?"

"Perhaps. Well, it is time I went."

Guildea did not try to detain him, but said, as he let him out, "Do me a favor, come again tomorrow night."

The Father had an engagement. He hesitated, looked into the Professor's face and said, "I will. At nine I'll be with you. Good night."

When he was on the pavement he felt relieved. He turned round, saw Guildea stepping into his passage, and shivered.

v

Father Murchison walked all the way home to Bird Street that night. He required exercise after the strange and disagreeable evening he had spent, an evening upon which he looked back already as a man looks back upon a nightmare. In his ears, as he walked, sounded the gentle and intolerable voice. Even the memory of it caused him physical discomfort. He tried to put it from him, and to consider the whole matter calmly. The Professor had offered his proof that there was some strange presence in his house. Could any reasonable man accept such proof? Father Murchison told himself that no reasonable man could accept it. The parrot's proceedings were, no doubt, extraordinary. The bird had succeeded in producing an extraordinary illusion of an invisible presence in the room. But that there really was such a presence the Father insisted on denying to himself. The devoutly religious, those who believe implicitly in the miracles recorded in the Bible, and who regulate their lives by the messages they suppose themselves to receive directly from the Great Ruler of a hidden World, are seldom inclined to accept any notion of supernatural intrusion into the affairs of daily life. They put it from them with anxious determination. They regard it fixedly as hocus-pocus, childish if not wicked.

Father Murchison inclined to the normal view of the devoted churchman. He was determined to incline to it. He could not—so he now told himself—accept the idea that his friend was being supernaturally punished for his lack of humanity, his deficiency in affection, by being obliged to endure the love of some horrible thing, which could not be seen, heard, or handled. Nevertheless, retribution did certainly seem to wait upon Guildea's condition. That which he had unnaturally dreaded and shrunk from in his thought he seemed to be now forced unnaturally to suffer. The Father prayed for his friend that night before the little, humble altar in the barely furnished, cell-like chamber where he slept.

On the following evening, when he called in Hyde Park Place, the door was opened by the housemaid, and Father Murchison mounted the stairs, wondering what had become of Pitting. He was met at the library door by Guildea and was painfully struck by the alteration in his appearance. His face was ashen in hue, and there were lines beneath his eyes. The eyes themselves looked excited and horribly forlorn. His hair and dress were disordered and his lips twitched continually, as if he were shaken by some acute nervous apprehension.

"What has become of Pitting?" asked the Father, grasping Guildea's hot and feverish hand.

"He has left my service."

"Left your service!" exclaimed the Father in utter amazement.

"Yes, this afternoon."

"May I ask why?"

"I'm going to tell you. It's all part and parcel of this —this most odious business. You remember once discussing the relations men ought to have with their servants?"

"Ah!" cried the Father, with a flash of inspiration. "The crisis has occurred?"

"Exactly," said the Professor, with a bitter smile. "The crisis has occurred. I called upon Pitting to be a man and a brother. He responded by declining the invitation. I upbraided him. He gave me warning. I paid him his wages and told him he could go at once. And he has gone. What are you looking at me like that for?"

"I didn't know," said Father Murchison, hastily dropping his eyes, and looking away. "Why," he added, "Napoleon is gone too."

"I sold him today to one of those shops in Shaftesbury Avenue."

"Why?"

"He sickened me with his abominable imitation of— his intercourse with—well, you know what he was at last night. Besides, I have no further need of his proof to tell me I am not dreaming. And, being convinced as I now am, that all I have thought to have happened has actually happened, I care very little about convincing others. Forgive me for saying so, Murchison, but I am now certain that my anxiety to make you believe in the presence of something here really arose from some faint doubt on that subject—within myself. All doubt has now vanished."

"Tell me why."

"I will."

Both men were standing by the fire. They continued to stand while Guildea went on.

"Last night I felt it."

"What?" cried the Father.

"I say that last night, as I was going upstairs to bed, I felt something accompanying me and nestling up against me."

"How horrible!" exclaimed the Father, involuntarily.

Guildea smiled drearily.

"I will not deny the horror of it. I cannot, since I was compelled to call on Pitting for assistance."

"But—tell me—what was it, at least what did it seem to be?"

"It seemed to be a human being. It seemed, I say; and what I mean exactly is that the effect upon me was rather that of human contact than of anything else. But I could see nothing, hear nothing. Only, three times, I felt this gentle, but determined, push against me, as if to coax me and to attract my attention. The first time it happened I was on the landing outside this room, with my foot on the first stair. I will confess to you, Murchison, that I bounded upstairs like one pursued. That is the shameful truth. Just as I was about to enter my bedroom, however, I felt the thing entering with me, and, as I have said, squeezing, with loathsome, sickening tenderness, against my side. Then—"

He paused, turned toward the fire and leaned his head on his arm. The Father was greatly moved by the strange helplessness and despair of the attitude. He laid his hand affectionately on Guildea's shoulder.

"Then?"

Guildea lifted his head. He looked painfully abashed.

"Then, Murchison, I am ashamed to say, I broke down, suddenly, unaccountably, in a way I should have thought wholly impossible to me. I struck out with my hands to thrust the thing away. It pressed more closely to me. The pressure, the contact became unbearable to me. I shouted out for Pitting. I—I believe I must have cried—'Help.' "

"He came, of course?"

"Yes, with his usual soft, unemotional quiet. His calm—its opposition to my excitement of disgust and horror—must, I suppose, have irritated me. I was not myself, no, no!"

He stopped abruptly. Then—

"But I need hardly tell you that," he added, with most piteous irony.

"And what did you say to Pitting?"

"I said that he should have been quicker. He begged my pardon. His cold voice really maddened me, and I burst out into some foolish, contemptible diatribe, called him a machine, taunted him, then—as I felt that loathsome thing nestling once more to me—begged him to assist me, to stay with me, not to leave me alone—I meant in the company of my tormentor. Whether he was frightened, or whether he was angry at my unjust and violent manner and speech a moment before, I don't know. In any case he answered that he was engaged as a butler, and not to sit up all night with people. I suspect he thought I had taken too much to drink. No doubt that was it. I believe I swore at him as a coward—I! This morning he said he wished to leave my service. I gave him a month's wages, a good character as a butler, and sent him off at once."

"But the night? How did you pass it?"

"I sat up all night."

"Where? In your bedroom?"

"Yes—with the door open—to let it go."

"You felt that it stayed?"

"It never left me for a moment, but it did not touch me again. When it was light I took a bath, lay down for a little while, but did not close my eyes. After breakfast I had the explanation with Pitting and paid him. Then I came up here. My nerves were in a very shattered condition. Well, I sat down, tried to write, to think. But the silence was broken in the most abominable manner."

"How?"

"By the murmur of that appalling voice, that voice of a lovesick idiot, sickly but determined. Ugh!"

He shuddered in every limb. Then he pulled himself together, assumed, with a self-conscious effort, his most determined, most aggressive, manner, and added, "I couldn't stand that. I had come to the end of my tether; so I sprang up, ordered a cab to be called, seized the cage and drove with it to a bird shop in Shaftesbury Avenue. There I sold the parrot for a trifle. I think, Murchison, that I must have been nearly mad then, for, as I came out of the wretched shop, and stood for an instant on the pavement among the cages of rabbits, guinea pigs, and puppy dogs, I laughed aloud. I felt as if a load was lifted from my shoulders, as if in selling that voice I had sold the cursed thing that torments me. But when I got back to the house it was here. It's here now. I suppose it will always be here."

He shuffled his feet on the rug in front of the fire.

"What on earth am I to do?" he said. "I'm ashamed of myself, Murchison, but—but I suppose there are things in the world that certain men simply can't endure. Well, I can't endure this, and there's an end of the matter."

He ceased. The Father was silent. In the presence of this extraordinary distress he did not know what to say. He recognized the uselessness of attempting to comfort Guildea, and he sat with his eyes turned, almost moodily, to the ground. And while he sat there he tried to give himself to the influences within the room, to feel all that was within it. He even, half unconsciously, tried to force his imagination to play tricks with him. But he remained totally unaware of any third person with them. At length he said, "Guildea, I cannot pretend to doubt the reality of your misery here. You must go away, and at once. When is your Paris lecture?"

"Next week. In nine days from now."

"Go to Paris tomorrow then; you say you have never had any consciousness that this—this thing pursued you beyond your own front door?"

"Never—hitherto."

"Go tomorrow morning. Stay away till after your lecture. And then let us see if the affair is at an end. Hope, my dear friend, hope."

He had stood up. Now he clasped the Professor's hand.

"See all your friends in Paris. Seek distractions. I would ask you also to seek—other help."

He said the last words with a gentle, earnest gravity and simplicity that touched Guildea, who returned his handclasp almost warmly.

"I'll go," he said. "I'll catch the ten o'clock train, and tonight I'll sleep at a hotel, at the Grosvenor—that's close to the station. It will be more convenient for the train."

As Father Murchison went home that night he kept thinking of that sentence: "It will be more convenient for the train." The weakness in Guildea that had prompted its utterance appalled him.

VI

No letter came to Father Murchison from the Professor during the next few days, and this silence reassured him, for it seemed to betoken that all was well. The day of the lecture dawned, and passed. On the following morning, the Father eagerly opened the *Times*, and scanned its pages to see if there were any report of the great meeting of scientific men which Guildea had addressed. He glanced up and down the columns with anxious eyes, then suddenly his hands stiffened as they held the sheets. He had come upon the following paragraph:

We regret to announce that Professor Frederic Guildea was suddenly seized with severe illness yesterday evening while addressing a scientific meeting in Paris. It was observed that he looked very pale and nervous when he rose to his feet. Nevertheless, he spoke in French fluently for about a quarter of an hour. Then he appeared to become uneasy. He faltered and glanced about like a man apprehensive, or in severe distress. He even stopped once or twice, and seemed unable to go on, to remember what he wished to say. But, pulling himself together with an obvious effort, he continued to address the audience. Suddenly, however, he paused again, edged furtively along the platform, as if pursued by something which he feared, struck out with his hands, uttered a loud, harsh cry and fainted. The sensation in the hall was indescribable. People rose from their seats. Women screamed, and, for a moment, there was a veritable panic. It is feared that the Professor's mind must have temporarily given way owing to overwork. We understand that he will return to England as soon as possible, and we sincerely hope that necessary rest and quiet will soon have the desired effect, and that he will be completely restored to health and enabled to prosecute further the investigations which have already so benefited the world.

The Father dropped the paper, hurried out into Bird Street, sent a wire of inquiry to Paris, and received the same day the following reply: "RETURNING TOMORROW. PLEASE CALL EVENING. GUILDEA." On that evening the Father called in Hyde Park Place, was at once admitted, and found Guildea sitting by the fire in the library, ghastly pale, with a heavy rug over his knees. He looked like a man emaciated by a long and severe illness, and in his wide-open eyes there was an expression of fixed horror. The Father started at the sight of him, and could scarcely refrain from crying out. He was beginning to express his sympathy when Guildea stopped him with a trembling gesture.

"I know all that," Guildea said, "I know. This Paris affair—" He faltered and stopped.

"You ought never to have gone," said the Father. "I was wrong. I ought not to have advised your going. You were not fit."

"I was perfectly fit," he answered, with the irritability of sickness. "But I was—I was accompanied by that abominable thing."

He glanced hastily round him, shifted his chair and pulled the rug higher over his knees. The Father wondered why he was thus wrapped up. For the fire was bright and red and the night was not very cold.

"I was accompanied to Paris," he continued, pressing his upper teeth upon his lower lip.

He paused again, obviously striving to control himself. But the effort was vain. There was no resistance in the man. He writhed in his chair and suddenly burst forth in a tone of hopeless lamentation.

"Murchison, this being, thing—whatever it is—no longer leaves me even for a moment. It will not stay here unless I am here, for it loves me, persistently, idiotically. It accompanied me to Paris, stayed with me there, pursued me to the lecture hall, pressed against me, caressed me while I was speaking. It has returned with me here. It is here now—" he uttered a sharp cry—"now, as I sit here with you. It is nestling up to me, fawning upon me, touching my hands. Man, man, can't you feel that it is here?"

"No," the Father answered truly.

"I try to protect myself from its loathsome contact," Guildea continued, with fierce excitement, clutching the thick rug with both hands. "But nothing is of any avail against it. Nothing. What is it? What can it be? Why should it have come to me that night?"

"Perhaps as a punishment," said the Father, with a quick softness.

"For what?"

"You hated affection. You put human feeling aside with contempt. You had, you desired to have, no love for anyone. Nor did you desire to receive any love from anything. Perhaps this is a punishment."

Guildea stared into his face.

"D'you believe that?" he cried.

"I don't know," said the Father. "But it may be so. Try to endure it, even to welcome it. Possibly then the persecution will cease."

"I know it means me no harm," Guildea exclaimed, "it seeks me out of affection. It was led to me by some amazing attraction which I exercise over it ignorantly. I know that. But to a man of my nature that is the ghastly part of the matter. If it would hate me, I could bear it. If it would attack me, if it would try to do me some dreadful harm, I should become a man again. I should be braced to fight against it. But this gentleness, this abominable solicitude, this brainless worship of an idiot, persistent, sickly, horribly physical, I cannot endure. What does it want of me? What would it demand of me? It nestles to me. It leans against me. I feel its touch, like the touch of a feather, trembling about my heart, as if it sought to number my pulsations, to find out the inmost secrets of my impulses and desires. No privacy is left to me." He sprang up excitedly. "I cannot withdraw," he cried, "I cannot be alone, untouched, unworshiped, unwatched for even one-half second. Murchison, I am dying of this, I am dying."

He sank down again in his chair, staring apprehensively on all sides, with the passion of some blind man, deluded in the belief that by his furious and continued effort he will attain sight. The Father knew well that he sought to pierce the veil of the invisible, and have knowledge of the thing that loved him.

"Guildea," the Father said, with insistent earnestness, "try to endure this—do more—try to give this thing what it seeks."

"But it seeks my love."

"Learn to give it your love and it may go, having received what it came for."

"T'sh! You talk like a priest. Suffer your persecutors. Do good to them that despitefully use you. You talk as a priest."

"As a friend I spoke naturally, indeed, right out of my heart. The idea suddenly came to me that all this —truth or seeming, it doesn't matter which—may be some strange form of lesson. I have had lessons—painful ones. I shall have many more. If you could welcome—"

"I can't! I can't!" Guildea cried fiercely. "Hatred! I can give it that—always that, nothing but that—hatred, hatred."

He raised his voice, glared into the emptiness of the room, and repeated, "Hatred!"

As he spoke the waxen pallor of his cheeks increased, until he looked like a corpse with living eyes. The Father feared that he was going to collapse and faint, but suddenly he raised himself upon his chair and said, in a high and keen voice, full of suppressed excitement, "Murchison, Murchison!"

"Yes. What is it?"

An amazing ecstasy shone in Guildea's eyes.

"It wants to leave me," he cried. "It wants to go! Don't lose a moment! Let it out! The window—the window!"

The Father, wondering, went to the near window, drew aside the curtains and pushed it open. The branches of the trees in the garden creaked dryly in the light wind. Guildea leaned forward on the arms of his chair. There was silence for a moment. Then Guildea, speaking in a rapid whisper, said, "No, no. Open this door—open the hall door. I feel—I feel that it will return the way it came. Make haste—ah, go!"

The Father obeyed—to soothe him, hurried to the door and opened it wide. Then he glanced back to Guildea. He was standing up, bent forward. His eyes were glaring with eager expectation, and, as the Father turned, he made a furious gesture toward the passage with his thin hands.

The Father hastened out and down the stairs. As he descended in the twilight he fancied he heard a slight cry from the room behind him, but he did not pause. He flung the hall door open, standing back against the wall. After waiting a moment—to satisfy Guildea, he was about to close the door again, and had his hand on it, when he was attracted irresistibly to look forth toward the park. The night was lit by a young moon, and, gazing through the railings, his eyes fell upon a bench beyond them.

Upon the bench something was sitting, huddled together very strangely.

The Father remembered instantly Guildea's description of that former night, that night of Advent, and a sensation of horror-stricken curiosity stole through him.

Was there then really something that had indeed come to the Professor? And had it finished its work, fulfilled its desire and gone back to its former existence?

The Father hesitated a moment in the doorway. Then he stepped out resolutely and crossed the road, keeping his eyes fixed upon this black or dark object that leaned so strangely upon the bench. He could not tell yet what it was like, but he fancied it was unlike anything with which his eyes were acquainted. He reached the opposite path, and was about to pass through the gate in the railings, when his arm was brusquely grasped. He started, turned round, and saw a policeman eyeing him suspiciously.

"What are you up to?" said the policeman.

The Father was suddenly aware that he had no hat upon his head, and that his appearance, as he stole forward in his cassock, with his eyes intently fixed upon the bench in the Park, was probably unusual enough to excite suspicion.

"It's all right, policeman," he answered quickly, thrusting some money into the constable's hand.

Then, breaking from him, the Father hurried toward

the bench, bitterly vexed at the interruption. When he reached it, nothing was there. Guildea's experience had been almost exactly repeated and, filled with unreasonable disappointment, the Father returned to the house, entered it, shut the door and hastened up the narrow stairway into the library.

On the hearth rug, close to the fire, he found Guildea lying with his head lolled against the armchair from which he had recently risen. There was a shocking expression of terror on his convulsed face. On examining him the Father found that he was dead.

The doctor, who was called in, said that the cause of death was failure of the heart.

When Father Murchison was told this, he murmured, "Failure of the heart! It was that then!"

He turned to the doctor and said, "Could it have been prevented?"

The doctor drew on his gloves and answered, "Possibly, if it had been taken in time. Weakness of the heart requires a great deal of care. The Professor was too much absorbed in his work. He should have lived very differently."

The Father nodded.

"Yes, yes," he said, sadly.